The Tangled Web

Cheryl J. Corriveau

Copyright © 2022 Cheryl J. Corriveau

All rights reserved. No part of this book may be reproduced or transmitted in any form or by any means, electronic or mechanical, including photocopying, recording or by any information storage and retrieval system without permission in writing from the publisher.

Endless Endeavors Publishing—Miramar Beach, FL
Paperback ISBN: 979-8-9872331-0-8
eBook ISBN: 979-8-9872331-1-5
Library of Congress Control Number: 2022921055
Title: *The Tangled Web*
Author: Cheryl J. Corriveau
Digital distribution | 2022
Paperback | 2022

This is a work of fiction. The characters, names, incidents, places, and dialogue are products of the author's imagination, and are not to be construed as real.

Chapter 1

This cold Jacksonville, Florida January day will be etched in my mind forever. I stood on the front porch looking through the canopy of treetops watching the trail of black smoke streaming from a Cessna airplane. The sputtering engine made my skin crawl then the loud boom jarred the house windows making my heart skip a beat. Midafternoon Robert's boss rang our doorbell. The flow of tears came automatically when I saw his solemn facial expression.

He reached for my hand. "Ms. Stone, I have no words. The mechanic finished the annual check yesterday and everything was in order. The plane nose-dived into an empty mall parking lot three blocks away. No one was hurt on the ground, but the plane had no survivors."

"Mr. Branson, you can call me Julia. Thank you for coming."

"Julia, if you need anything and I mean anything at all let me know."

For the rest of the day, I stayed on the front porch rocking numb with emotions running high and low trying to put my life in order.

Lydia, my next-door neighbor ran down the sidewalk chasing her Cocker Spaniel. It appeared that the dog had escaped before she could get his leash attached. She didn't look too concerned, waved, and kept her pace.

At 7:00 p.m. my kitchen was filled with food and comforting thoughts from my neighbors. Lydia gently pushed my auburn hair away from my blue eyes. She put her arm around my waist and guided me to the sofa. "You need to talk. Tell me about Robert and how you met and why you left Charleston."

I clutched the wet linen handkerchief tighter. "Three months after our wedding in Charleston, Robert decided to retire as a Naval Captain and not move up to Rear Admiral. A small technology company in Jacksonville had offered him a CEO position. My boss offered to transfer me to the FBI office there, but I didn't want to start over in a new place in the criminal justice field. Our antebellum home overlooked Charleston Harbor on The Battery. I didn't want to leave, but Robert was much older than me and I wanted him to be happy."

Lydia stood up, smiled, and walked away. She returned with a cold glass of water. After taking a sip my tears returned.

Lydia gestured with a wave of her hand. "I know there's more. Continue."

The large lump that was in my throat was still there. "My first marriage was a long two years that ended with my husband leaving me for another woman. We married the month after college graduation, and before we started our careers. We were young and didn't know what life was about. In comparison to that, Robert and I had five short years. This was Robert's first trip out of town with his new company. Who knew it was going to be his last."

The tears started to flow again and emptiness ran through my being. The love of my life had been whisked away without any warning. The feeling of old before my time drifted over me.

Lydia gave me a quick hug and left with the neighbors.

The next morning, I decided to return to South Carolina to visit my close friends and look for a house to buy. Robert was buried in his family's plot in Virginia leaving me with no ties to Jacksonville.

A month after Robert's funeral, I received his life insurance benefits, his company's death policy, and money from his family's estate. I sat frozen looking at the checks made out to Julia Stone.

Six months later after my Charleston trip, the house on Rainbow Row that was on the for sale had been sold. I bought a turn-of-the-century two-bedroom, two-bath house on The Battery that overlooked the Atlantic with the backyard adjacent to White Point Gardens. I was comfortable going home with nothing but sentimental feelings.

Thursday morning, Allied Movers called reminding me they would be at my house in the morning at seven-thirty. My personal belongings were packed, all I needed to do was load them into the car for my trip to Charleston.

Lydia stopped by on her return run with her Cocker Spaniel to say her final goodbye. "I'm going to miss you."

Giving her a slight smile, I replied. "I'll miss you too. I told Robert we should rent our house rather than sell it, but he said we wouldn't be back in Charleston. I never expected, or even gave a thought about returning after that conversation." Shaking my head, I responded with. "Hindsight is always twenty-twenty.

The late-night movie last night reminded me of Adam. I hadn't thought about him since I married Robert. The bedroom nightstand was full of papers. I know the paper was folded into a duck's beak and Adam used a bright blue ink pen to write his address and phone number. The sales receipt he used should be jumping out at me. I had almost given up when it appeared pressed against the front of the drawer. Snatching it up as if someone were going to take it from me, even though I was alone in my bedroom with the draperies closed, I held it close to my chest.

Grabbing a cup of coffee and Adam's piece of paper, I retreated to my front porch rocker. With the humidity gone, the November air felt crisp against my skin, I pulled my cardigan sweater tighter to make my body feel warmer. My thoughts returned to Adam.

I stared at the blue ink. It said, 'Remember me. You never know when you might want one of my paintings.' I touched my face with my left fingertips and smiled remembering Adam's gentle kiss on my lips. He flipped his green and yellow striped tie over his shoulder and gave me a big smile before he turned to walk away. Meeting Adam at the art show had been an education and a surprising, delightful day.

The movers arrived early the next morning and by noon they were on their way to Charleston, despite me following them around like a puppy making sure that nothing was left behind. After the two hundred-plus mile drive north to Charleston, I checked into the Two Meeting Street Inn, a bed and breakfast. Tomorrow the movers would place my belongings in what would be my new home.

Saturday afternoon, I had no emotions unpacking the boxes while the movers shuffled my furniture in place. The box marked kitchen, to be opened first, was placed next to the refrigerator. I glanced out the great room window seeing the Atlantic waters splash over The Battery wall. The fall winds made the waves stronger with each one trying to batter the seawall harder than the one before it. The look of this scene will never grow old to me. This was home.

The house, half the size of my former one, was easy to settle into. The open layout gave both my great room and kitchen a harbor view. With so many bare walls and unpacked boxes, it gave me the sensation of rattling around alone in a hollow space. I took in a deep breath and let out a long sigh knowing the days ahead would prove this house, nestled on a quiet street was mine.

The next morning thoughts of how different my life was going to be, ran through my head, I squatted next to a box in the kitchen and pulled off the tape. The box had been labeled incorrectly. Photos and memories stared back at me. Robert in his dress uniform and on the other side in the split frame was Robert in a dark blue suit the first day he went to work as a civilian. My chest moved in and out as if I had run a marathon. At the bottom of the box was a Polaroid picture of Adam and me. I remember teasing him about his antique camera and him saying he kept it so he could lay several pictures next to one another to get a full view of the scene he might want to paint. I took several deep breaths and with my eyes closed, remembered Adam—tall, muscular, broad shoulders, blond hair, blue eyes, and handsome.

A wave of calmness assured me that everything was going to be fine.

Chapter 2

Monday morning, the pair of red capris and white tank top fit well for my morning jog. I bent over and reached for my running shoes and saw the folded paper with blue ink lying on the floor between my nightstand and the bed. Shuffling to my favorite chair on the front porch and rocking slowly, my finger traced each letter and number. They were slanted and written to perfection. It was ridiculous for me to think two men that I met on the same day, Robert and Adam, that Adam would still remember me after seven years, or that he had ever given me another thought. On impulse, I dialed the number.

My hand shook and my heart pounded waiting for him to answer. My hand was perspiring so much that the phone almost dropped into my lap. On the sixth ring, a woman said, "Hello." Her voice was soft and pleasant.

To me, it seemed like several minutes had passed before I could say a word. "Hi, is this Adam Robinson's number?" The thought that he had married flashed through my mind like lightning.

She replied, "I'm sorry, I've had this number for a year but I still get calls for him."

My voice was soft and in a whisper. "I'm sorry I disturbed you."

"You didn't. Maybe you'll find him." Then the phone clicked silent.

What possessed me to make this call? I went to the computer, took in a long sigh, and googled *Adam Robinson, artist,* then waited as if time passed in slow motion wondering what was going to pop up on the screen. After what seemed like five minutes the results showed no artist by that name.

At sunset, the sound of my doorbell made me spring from my big comfy chair. Whoever was at the front door had their finger frozen on the ringer.

"Kevin, what are you doing here? Why didn't you call?"

"Sis, you know I've always loved surprising you. Thought maybe you might need help unpacking." He gave a quick survey around the room. "As usual though, you have everything under control."

Releasing my brother from a bear hug, I said, "This is a warm and cozy homecoming. How long can you stay?"

His eyes narrowed. "Long enough to make sure you're going to be all right coming back here."

"What about your clients?"

He smiled. "I have a colleague taking care of them. He owed me a favor."

You know I hated leaving Charleston." I took two glasses from the cupboard. "Which wine would you like?"

"You choose." He waved his hand towards the wine rack and wrinkled his nose. "It's about time you chose. You've always put others first. You catered to your first husband's every whim, and he left you. Robert put you first, but you worked harder to make him the priority. Now it's your time. Everything from now on should be all about you."

After pouring a glass of Pacific Rim Riesling, I turned toward the window, smiled, and pointed to the ocean. "It is about me. Look at the harbor and the gardens. It doesn't get any better than this."

Kevin clasped his hand on my elbow and guided me to the sofa. "You don't need to sit here every day by yourself. Have you thought about traveling to places you've always wanted to go, but didn't?" He kicked off his shoes and nudged my toes.

"I've wanted to return to Paris. The last time there my time was limited. I've never visited the Palace of Versailles. We drove by it a couple of times. The intriguing factor to me is that Louis XIII built a small hunting lodge in 1623 and over ninety-two years it was added on to become a chateau and then became the palace." I leaned my head back against the sofa as if in thought. "I want to find the people that I'd crossed paths with over the years. Where are they now and what are they doing?" A crooked smile crossed my lips. "I met someone the same day I met Robert."

Kevin's wine almost dribbled from the corner of his mouth. "You never said anything about meeting anyone."

I stared into my glass and swirled the wine. Then smiled. "There was nothing to tell. He was an impressionist artist from Greenville, South Carolina. He was at the art show here in the park with his paintings. I met Robert that night at the Citadel Cadet Ball. Carla, one of my best friends' late husband was being honored that night for being the longest-tenured faculty member on record. She asked me to accompany her. Robert was a naval officer. Adam was an artist and traveled from show to show. I didn't give Adam another thought."

I took the bright blue ink paper from the coffee table drawer and handed it to him. "I called his number this morning but after seven years someone else answered. I have googled him but there was no one with his name who was an artist."

My brother's surprised look was followed by, "I'm impressed you called the number. Maybe you are going to put yourself first. What else do you know about him?"

"Nothing really. He grew up in Greenville. He walked me around the show explaining the artists' paintings and why they chose the paints and colors. We had a hotdog and a soft drink for lunch from a vendor's stand. Then we sat on a park bench ate and talked about his paintings. He went to Folly Beach after the show to paint. I saw him a few times that week when he came back here to the art galleries."

Kevin sauntered over to the window, flexed his chest muscles, then yelled! "There! That's your starting place." After watching the waves for a minute, he shouted! "Road trip! Go see if you can find him."

Still watching the waves hit The Battery wall and in a loud voice responded. "I can't do that!"

"When has the word "can't" ever stopped you? You know he's an artist and he's from Greenville. Someone in the town must know him. There's not a better way to start an adventure."

Kevin knew he had pushed my buttons. He raised his glass in a toast. "To the next chapter in your life. It will be all about you this time."

He clinked his glass against mine and smiled. I rolled my eyes. "I'm going to bed."

Tossing and turning, the thought of letting Robert go to find Adam preyed on my mind. Did I really want to push forward to find Adam?

The next morning, three of my senses woke me. Kevin was in the kitchen making coffee. Taking a deep breath and not ready for my other four senses to awaken, I slowly moved my eyes around the bedroom then swung my legs over the side of the bed seeing both hands of the clock resting on the eight. Across the room leaning against the wall were a stack of paintings that needed to be hung. Kevin was opening and closing cabinet doors as if he was angry.

Entering the kitchen, Kevin's blond hair was a mess but his big blue eyes were smiling. "Good morning."

"Good morning to you." I pointed to the fridge. "There's nothing for breakfast."

"I noticed. I'm glad I drink my coffee black." Smiling, he poured me a cup.

"I'll go to the grocery store later this morning. Panera Bread is two blocks away. You can get us coffee cake slices or muffins. Go south to the corner then turn right, it's on the next block."

After our muffins and coffee, "Kevin, let me show you where to hang the pictures while I go grocery shopping."

When I returned, Kevin was rocking on the front porch, using every inch of the rockers from the front to the back.

He stood, gave me a hug, and patted the top of my head. "You're all settled. There's nothing else I can do. I'll call you when I get back to Hilton Head. You have a trip to plan. Don't chicken out."

"I won't. I needed your push. I'll send you texts along the way."

The next morning, I thought three days would give me enough time to find Adam or someone who might know where he lived. It was nine when I merged onto Interstate 26. I was two hundred and fifteen miles from Greenville. The knot in my stomach confirmed that this might be a misguided adventure. It's a road trip nothing else, but deep down I knew that wasn't true.

Close to noon and thirty miles outside Greenville on I-385, I pulled into a rest stop to stretch my legs and buy a diet Dr. Pepper from the vending machine. Doubts were rattling around in my mind as to why I had let Kevin talk me into this trip. There were picnic tables where families were eating lunch, and children were tossing balls to one another, a pet walk path and at the back of the parking lot a woman was walking her horse. He came to a standstill to nibble grass. She pulled on his lead to keep him moving. He balked a bit when she tried to lead him up the ramp back into the trailer. I found myself at the back of the rest stop, where the big green mountain tops were surrounded by the cloudless blue sky and sparrows, ravens, and woodpeckers darted from tree to tree, calling for their mates. With their talons extended, two large hawks sparred at one another in midair.

A voice behind me made me jump, I turned to see an elderly man with binoculars. He looked distinguished with his white hair shimmering in the sun. "We have lots of hawks around the mountains. Those two look like they're hunting." As he said that, one of the hawks took a dive and captured a sparrow in its talons then soared high once more towards the tree line.

I gasped. "He swooped down and caught that bird in midair."

The man smiled. "Yep, that's what they do. Birds can see things we can't."

We stood in silence for a few more minutes. I looked back up at the sky to see more hawks flying over us. Then a falcon swooped down and made a perfect graceful landing about twenty-five feet from me. "Did you see that?" When I turned around the man was gone.

At two the Downtown Greenville sign came into view. I drove past the post office and several churches, then turned onto a side street looking for the bed and breakfast where my reservations were booked. It was in an old section of town with restored Victorian homes. Behind the inn, the loose gravel stones in the parking lot crumpled under my tires, I strolled around the concrete and brick path to the front steps. Dark brown wicker furniture sat on the white-painted porch. Large pots of red geraniums were placed around the front and side of the porch at the base of the banisters. Every time my foot stepped on a step, it creaked. When the front door opened; it moaned like a haunted mansion and the foyer was dimly lit. It took a few minutes for my eyes to adjust from the bright sunlight. The air smelled stale and stuffy. A heavy-set woman was standing behind the front desk typing on a computer. "Welcome, I'm Sadie, the owner. You must be Julia Stone."

I nodded, then shook her outreached hand. While she checked me in, I glanced around the lobby taking in the sitting room with the small grouping of Victorian furniture. All the pieces were dark wood and covered with fabric had huge flowers in dull red and pink hues.

Sadie asked. "May I see your ID and what is your car tag number and don't forget to sign the guest book."

She handed me my driver's license along with a metal key. I grabbed my suitcase and turned to walk away then turned back around and asked. "By any chance, would you know an artist by the name of Adam Robinson?"

"No." She pointed to the East. "But there are several art galleries within walking distance from here. Somebody might know him."

I unpacked my toothbrush and other toiletries then picked up a Hall's Chop House menu that lay on the small table. From the map on the back cover, it looked like the restaurant was less than a mile away and a steak sounded good.

Around four-thirty, I entered the chop house. The hostess smiled. "There's a twenty-minute wait." She pointed to the left. "You can wait in the lounge."

I sat in a high-back wooden bar chair in front of the bartender. He pulled out a small cutting board, a knife, and several limes from under the counter. "We have our rum drinks on special tonight. Your choice?"

"Thanks, but I would like an Old Fashioned."

He was chatty. He talked about the weather, then how he made his way from Dallas to Greenville. He stopped slicing the limes and looked at me. "Where are you from? Are you passing through or moving here?"

"I drove in from Charleston earlier today." In a loud voice, I blurted out. "I'm looking for someone."

He grinned. "I knew it. You didn't look like you were here for a work-related job."

"What's his name?"

"How did you know it's a him?"

He laughed. "Didn't you know, we bartenders are psychics. This is what we do as a second job."

I smiled, then took a sip. "We met a long time ago then lost touch. His name is Adam Robinson. He's an artist. Have you heard his name?"

He shook his head. "Can't say that I have. He hasn't been in here or I would know the name. Ask over at Stephanie's Coffee Shop in the morning. She was born here. She knows everyone."

After dinner, I walked by the coffee shop. It was small and looked like a place where the locals would gather. Maybe Kevin was right. I did need the road trip to start moving forward with my life.

Chapter 3

The sun cast a bright beam across my bed waking me. I brushed my teeth then rinsed my mouth with Listerine, applied my makeup, put my hair into a ponytail, and pulled on my jeans and a flowered tee shirt. Downstairs the sitting room was empty. There was one dry-looking muffin left on the breakfast tray. I headed down to Stephanie's Coffee Shop.

The café was small and screeched the 1920s with the distressed wood tables and chairs, and the walls covered in small, flowered wallpaper. The aroma of cinnamon and coffee filled the room. Stretching my neck, I couldn't see a vacant table. Several people were reading newspapers at their tables, two young men and a woman were working on their computers at a table in one corner, and others were texting or talking on their phones in their booths. After a few minutes, a middle-aged woman with black and blond hair and long braids greeted me.

"Hi, I'm Stephanie. I have a man by himself in the corner booth over there who wouldn't mind if you joined him if you want to."

I cast a glance his way. The white-haired man with pool blue eyes motioned me over. He had on a suit coat, and jeans and his feet were in sandals. To my surprise, this was the man from the rest stop yesterday.

Stephanie put her hand on his shoulder. "Jack, your order is on the way out. Do you want another cup of coffee now?"

He answered in a baritone voice. "Bring it with my pancakes."

She looked my way. "Would you like coffee?"

"Yes, please."

I smiled at the man. "Thank you for letting me share your table. This is a busy place." I stretched my hand across the table. "I'm Julia."

He returned the smile. "I'm Jack. This is a locals' place, but the tourists are discovering it. Did you see any more hawks yesterday?"

I nodded. "Yes, and lots more flew down from the mountains. I turned to talk to you, but you were gone."

"I go there every couple of weeks to get out of town. It's a short drive and the only place around with so many birds. They like to soar with the air currents through the mountains. My late wife would pack us a picnic lunch, and we would spend the whole afternoon there." His cheekbones were high which made his brown eyes look big and wide. His entire face screamed masculinity. He cleared his throat. "Are you here on business or vacationing?"

"Vacation, here for a couple of days."

"Are you traveling alone?" His eyes twinkled and his smile showed the creases on his face.

"Yes."

The waitress set a hungry man's plate of pancakes in front of him. "Jack, do you need anything else?"

"No, I'm good."

She placed her hand on her hip. "Madam, what would you like to order?"

"The pancakes look delicious, but a blueberry muffin and another cup of coffee will be fine."

We ate in silence. Doubts flooded my mind. I should go home and forget this ridiculous excursion and forget the past.

When I raised my eyes, he was staring at me. "Jack, tell me a little about this area of town."

He pushed his plate to the side. "After most of the professional businesses moved out to the Office Park Complex, the downtown area started to see several boutique shops open. We have Falls Park which has a suspension bridge over the Reedy River. Liberty Bridge connects downtown to the West End area."

Images jumped into my head of some of Adam's paintings of the river, the bridge, and the falls.

Jack raised his eyebrows. "What made you choose Greenville for a vacation?"

"I wanted to explore the area."

He pursed his lips. "You've piqued my curiosity." He winked. "There's more to your story than you're telling."

"Not really. I'm taking a short road trip."

He lightly shrugged his shoulders like he didn't believe me. "If you say so."

The noise in the coffee shop grew louder. I looked around and people were standing everywhere including a long line down the sidewalk.

Jack nodded. "We should let others have the table. Stephanie, the check, please?"

He handed some bills to Stephanie and gave her a slight hug. He reached for my hand to help me out of the booth. I picked up my bill. He took the receipt from my hand, crumpled it, and tossed it back on the table.

He smiled. "There was no charge."

"Thank you. You weren't supposed to pay for my breakfast."

"I enjoyed the company."

When we reached the sidewalk. I said, "Have a good day. I'm off to check out some art galleries."

He pointed down the street and smiled. "Christopher's Art Gallery is on the next block. Have fun."

I shook Jack's hand and thanked him again.

Walking towards Christopher's, I window shopped and thought that Adam probably wasn't in Greenville and if I did find him, he wouldn't remember me. This was all Kevin's fault for me being here. If no one knows Adam today, I'm going back to Charleston and figure out what I'm going to do with the rest of my life. After Stephanie's was so busy, and talking to Jack, I forgot to ask either one of them about Adam. Hopefully, I can find my answers at Christopher's.

Kevin's name appeared on my caller ID. I wasn't in the mood to answer all his questions now, so it went to voicemail. My phone buzzed with his text 'I know you're thinking about going back home but you are there. Keep asking around town. No harm will come from that.' I was surprised that he hadn't flooded the text with questions. He had always been good at reading my thoughts. Maybe, it's what big brothers do.

Christopher's Art Gallery encompassed several rooms. It wasn't until the third area that I noticed the art was organized by periods, watercolors, acrylics, and oils and realized my pace increased in each room searching for paintings that might look like something Adam would have painted. Either it had been too long, or I had forgotten his work, or this wasn't a gallery that was suited to him.

In the last room, a thin man with short, dyed black hair, dressed in a black suit, white shirt, and a red tie approached me. "Hello, I am the gallery director, Frank. How may I help you today?"

I smiled. "I'm browsing. The paintings are beautiful. Are they from local artists?"

"Some are, but I feature artists from all around the world. Is there a particular painting, or artist that you are looking for?"

I blinked and took one step back. "I'm looking for the artist, Adam Robinson."

"Are you looking for him personally, or his work?"

Because I had almost yelled his name my voice was now a whisper. "Both."

"I have some of his paintings in storage, but they are earmarked for someone. Adam is deceased."

All the blood seemed to drain from my head. I heard my voice scream! "Dead!"

"Yes, last year. Do you know his brother and sister?"

I shook my head no. "I've never met them."

"May I ask your name?"

"I'm Julia Stone. I didn't expect to hear the word *deceased*."

His eyes widened. "Come with me."

His walk was brisk, I was almost jogging to keep up with him. He pressed a button that opened a set of double steel doors. He flipped on the lights revealing a room that looked like a huge warehouse. I jogged again staying close behind him. He came to an abrupt stop in front of three long shelves that towered from floor to ceiling. My whole body tingled and my knees weaken seeing *Julia Stone* handwritten on the side of three crates on the middle shelf. A trance came over me.

"Ms. Stone, are you, all right?"

I muttered. "That's my name."

"Adam asked me to store these for you. After his death, his uncle asked me to keep them. Come with me to my office, please."

Following him back to his office was a much slower pace. "May I see a picture ID, please? Not that I don't trust you, but I do need to verify who you are."

I handed him my driver's license.

"This is a Florida license. Adam said you lived in Charleston."

"I did when I met Adam, but my husband took a job in Jacksonville. When he was killed in a plane crash and I moved back to Charleston. I haven't had time to get a South Carolina license yet."

"That explains why I couldn't find you." He handed me a business card. Jackson Price, Attorney at Law. "You need to call Adam's attorney. He has all of Adam's instructions."

I lowered my head and whispered. "Instructions? I'll give him a call. Thank you."

Frank extended his hand. "I'm looking forward to seeing you again, Ms. Stone."

My gait was uneven as I staggered outside and collapsed on an iron bench in front of the gallery. I stared at the card in my hand and then looked down the street in both directions. This was the first time I had noticed how beautiful the street looked lined with all the different color pansies. I stared back at the business card. I couldn't wrap my head around all that I'd learned. So many thoughts raced through my mind at one time. How did Adam die? Was he married? Why is my name on those crates? I sat on the bench for an hour before I pressed redial on my phone.

"Hey Sis, what's up? Did you find Adam?"

Out of nowhere came uncontrollable tears. The realization of Adam's death had sunk in.

"Julia, where are you? I can't understand what you're saying. Are you all right?"

"Yesss, yes. I am okay." My body tingled from my head to my toes. "Kevin, Adam is dead. He left some of his paintings to me. Let me call you back in ten minutes." Before I let him respond, I pushed the off button.

Back in my room, I sat on the edge of the bed. My visions of reconnecting with Adam had vanished. Maybe if I had had the courage seven years ago to choose Adam and not Robert my life would be different now. Robert had the stability. I should've given Adam more credibility. Now I am pushing forty years old and alone. I called Kevin back.

"Hi Sis, I was worried."

"I'm sorry. So much has happened in the last couple of hours. Bear with me, I think I can tell you without crying."

I explained what had happened at Christopher's.

"Julia, are you sure you're, okay? That's a lot to take in all at one time. I'll fly to Greenville in the morning. I'll text you my flight information. You go see the attorney today."

"Kevin don't book your flight yet. Let me talk to the attorney first. If I need you, I'll call."

I washed my face and reapplied my make-up. Sadie was behind the front desk. I showed her the business card. "I know Mr. Price. His office is within walking distance."

Once there, his secretary informed me that Mr. Price had gone home for the day. "My name is Julia Stone. The gallery director at Christopher's Art Gallery sent me here."

The surprised look on her face startled me.

She stuttered. "I'll call Mr. Price now."

She laid the receiver down gently and handed me a piece of paper with Mr. Price's home address and directions.

Chapter 4

The directions to Mr. Price's house sent me nine miles north of Greenville. Rain was lightly falling when my car started up the mountain. Halfway up Paris Mountain, a horrendous rain and hailstorm had moved across the sky. The mental image of me sliding off the steep grade mountain road made me keep my left foot on the brake and my right foot occasionally touching the gas pedal.

At the top of the last winding curve, a small light came into view on my left, along with the side of the mountain looking like a waterfall. There was so much water running downhill it was like driving in a riverbed. The noise of the hail pellets pounding on the car's roof made me grip the steering wheel even tighter. Hearing myself scream when the water pushed my car into the guard rail didn't help my nerves. My door was jammed against the rail, I reached for my umbrella on the back seat and gathered my purse from the floorboard. It wasn't easy climbing over the console and out the passenger door.

The moment my umbrella opened the wind took it from my hand. Soaked to the skin, I watched it dip and rise with the wind across the mountain getting smaller and smaller. The hail had stopped and the sky was lighter, but the torrential rain was still falling. This wasn't a normal rainstorm. It was a monsoon. The light in the distance was my map up the road. The more I climbed the more realization set in that it was the highest and steepest part of the mountain road. At the top of the hill, the light became brighter.

The brass door knocker made a thud sound, and Jack opened the door, still dressed as he was this morning at breakfast but minus his suit coat. He gently pulled my arm making my body follow him into the foyer. "Julia? His eyes were question marks, but his smile was warm. "I didn't know this morning that your last name was Stone."

My hair was dripping, my clothes were soaked, and my body was shivering.

"Wait here." Jack reappeared with a towel, sweatshirt, sweatpants, a pair of socks, and a large golden retriever. "Meet my best friend, Roxy." When Roxy heard her name, she wagged her tail and gave a soft woof. "I'm six-three, these are going to be too big for you, but they will keep you warm until Margaret, my housekeeper, can dry your clothes."

I cracked a half-smile. "This is one way to make a lasting impression. My car is against the guard rail."

"I'll call for a tow truck." Jack returned. "Two things. They are busy towing lots of wrecked cars and with the rain, the truck can't get up the mountain until morning. You'll have to spend the night."

A woman in a white starched apron, who looked to be in her late sixties, handed me a cup of hot tea. "Hello dear. I'm Margaret, this should help warm you."

Before Jack could say another word, I blurted out. "I came to Greenville looking for Adam."

Jack ignored my words. "Margaret will get you settled and your dinner. We'll talk in the morning."

I followed Margaret upstairs squishing all the way. "Ms. Stone, this is your bedroom and the bath is across the hall. I'll see you downstairs for dinner." After dinner, Margaret smiled. "If there's anything else you need let me know. I usually don't spend the night but with the storm, I'll be in the next room. Breakfast is at eight. "Good night." She smiled and closed the door behind her.

A large four-poster bed dominated the palatial room and on the other side was a large stone fireplace. After such a distressing day and a terrifying trek to get here, exhaustion sent me into a deep sleep.

I woke to the morning sun streaming through the gaps in the velveteen draperies. My clothes were folded and lying in a high-back rocker next to the dresser. I dressed and hurried downstairs.

I passed by the kitchen. "Good morning, Margaret." Her hands were covered in flour and a few biscuits had been placed on a baking sheet.

Jack called from nearby. "I'm here in my office. Down the hallway."

Jack scratched Roxy's head moving her to the side for me to enter. The dog lay next to his chair as if this was her permanent place when Jack was in his office.

I looked around the ceiling-to-floor windows that overlooked the front porch. Two other walls were lined from ceiling to floor with dark mahogany bookshelves. There wasn't one space available for one more volume to be placed on any of the shelves.

Margaret lightly knocked on the office doorjamb and entered. "Breakfast is ready."

Jack nodded. "We'll be in shortly."

I scooted forward in the large leather chair. "Did Adam ever say anything to you about me? I don't know why he left his paintings to me."

Jack smiled. "We'll get to that after breakfast."

I gave him a slight smiled. "The day I met my husband, I also met Adam at an art show in Charleston. We talked about his paintings and the other artists who were displaying their work at the show. We spent the entire day walking from booth to booth. He interpreted each painting, telling me how and why he thought that particular artist painted the picture, or why each artist might have chosen the paints they used. Adam's paintings were some of the bests at the show. I fell in love with several of them. The week he was there we had lunch and dinner every day. We laughed as if we had known one another for years. He told me he didn't start painting until he took an art class in college.

When we said our goodbyes, he wrote his name and phone number on a piece of paper and said if I ever needed anything to let him know. Fate or some strange phenomenon made me keep the small paper." Despite my watery eyes, I forced a smile. "I didn't know if I could locate him, or if I did, I expected him to be married and have children. Yesterday, when I arrived in town, I asked several people if they knew Adam, but no one said they knew him. I researched Greenville art galleries before I left Charleston and that is where I was headed when I met you in the coffee shop. When the curator handed me the Jackson Price business card, I didn't associate Jack with Jackson."

Fidgeting in my chair, crossing and uncrossing my legs, I stared out the window waiting for Jack to respond. His facial expression had changed from questionable to listening intently. In my mind, the silence lasted for more than five minutes.

Pots and pans rattled from the kitchen. Jack laughed. "We better go to breakfast."

After eating, Jack was pushing his plate away when a loud knock on the door made me jump.

Margaret announced. "The tow truck driver wants to see Ms. Stone."

My car was loaded on the tow truck which was parked in front of the two large black iron gates. The bright morning sun showed every detail of the large colonial house that screamed *plantation*. Last night in the rainstorm, I hadn't paid attention to the house or the yard. Beyond the manicured grass, the tall meadow grasses swayed in the light breeze. Twelve white high-back rocking chairs lined the front porch as if they were standing at attention. Baskets of pink begonias, in full bloom, were hung between each of the large white columns along the full length of the porch.

"Ms. Stone, you're one lucky lady. Your car has a long scratch down the driver's door. That's the only damage. You can pick it up this afternoon at my garage."

After the tow driver left, I followed Jack into his office. He cleared his throat. "Adam was my nephew. My sister and brother-in-law were killed in an auto accident. Adam was seventeen, his brother Eli was in dental school, and April, their sister was twelve. My wife and I never had any children. My wife, died of cancer when Adam was nineteen. We raised Adam, Eli, and April, as our own. Eli has his dental practice now. We supported Adam's dreams to be an artist, putting him through school and watching him blossom as an artist. April has become a free spirit. She will find her calling one day. After Adam came back from the art show in Charleston, he told me he had met someone but he had obligated himself to a year of art shows in France. When he returned to the States, he tried to find you. Adam never married. He buried himself in his work and in what spare time he had he painted. The paintings that are at Christopher's are ones he painted for you."

I sat still listening to every word, then said. "He gave me an education that week on impressionist artists from the nineteenth century."

Jack patted Roxy's head. "Adam never forgot you. For some reason, he always felt that you would come looking for him. I tried telling him he knew you for a week. He replenished his artwork and headed off to Paris. Julia, you're smart and beautiful, I understand why Adam never forgot you."

My face felt hot and flushed.

He turned to a side drawer and pulled out a manila folder. "Adam had me draw up specific instructions for you if he wasn't here. He was killed at my cabin in the mountains. He went there every season change to paint. On that last trip, Adam and Eli planned to stay for a month. I'm afraid that this will be shocking for you, but when Adam first got there and opened the front door, the cabin exploded. Adam was dead immediately. Eli was blown halfway down the mountain. Eli was lucky he walked away with a broken arm and several deep scratches on his legs. He had to have extensive skin grafts. The cause was a gas leak from the water heater. Somehow Adam had found out you had married and moved away, but he didn't change his instructions. Adam wrote your name on those crates himself. Christopher's agreed to keep them in storage until you claimed them."

I inhaled deeply and slowly, trying to dissolve the lump that had formed in my throat.

Margaret entered the office with cookies and lemonade. She set the tray on a side table next to the windows. Jack stood and Roxy followed him over to the table. She handed me a glass of lemonade on a white linen napkin.

He pulled a small leather chair from across the room and sat beside me. "You have some papers to sign before you take the paintings. Tomorrow, we'll meet you at the bank and I'll give you all the papers and items from the safe deposit box."

I frowned. "What items?"

Jack stood. "I'll take you to get your car now."

At the garage, I extended my hand to Jack. "Thank you for your hospitality."

"You're welcome." Jack smiled and shook my hand. "I'll see you tomorrow."

Chapter 5

Sitting in my car in the parking lot back at Sadie's, I tried to process what had happened yesterday, what Jack had said this morning, and why Adam painted all those pictures for me.

Kevin answered on the first ring. "I have an appointment with the attorney at the bank tomorrow morning at ten. Can you get a flight out today?"

"Julia, I'll try I for an afternoon flight and let you know."

I pressed the end button, and jumped when it rang back instantly.

"Julia, this is April, Adam's sister. Meet me in Falls Park by the downtown side of Liberty Bridge in an hour. I'm wearing a white shirt and flowered leggings." Before I could speak, she hung up.

I drove around Falls Park several times before parking the car. Doubts flooded my head as to why I was here. I wanted a quiet life, now everywhere I turned in this town I found myself surprised and in turmoil. Adam's sister was the last person I wanted to meet and why would she want to see me?

As I approached the girl at the bridge, she turned and reached for my hand. "Julia, hi, I'm April."

Her outstretched hand and sleeveless shirt showed that her right arm was tattooed from her shoulder to her wrist. She wore skintight leggings that matched her tattoos. Her black eyeliner framed her chocolate round eyes. She was young enough that she could have been Adam's daughter.

"You destroyed my brother." She ran her hand through her red-cropped hair. Then handed me a worn crinkled photo.

I clutched the picture of Adam and myself. "Where did you get this.?" The more I looked at the picture the more my hand shook.

"One of the artists at the art show in Charleston took it. He sent it to Adam the week after the show. Adam kept it in his wallet and looked at it every day."

I squinted. "I didn't know anyone had taken a picture of us."

My eyes were glued to the photo. I was mesmerized seeing Adam's short sun-bleached blond hair, and his sea-blue eyes. I traced my finger around the edge of the picture.

April touched my hand. "You look different there."

"I was younger then." I forced a half-smile and continued to stare at the picture, recalling that day in White Gardens Park. "It was a fun day."

April scuffed her feet. "Why did you come here now? You should've come a long time ago. If you had, I think Adam wouldn't have gone to the mountains that day." Her words were harsh and strong.

I gave April a slight smile. "You don't know that. I could've been with him and we both could be dead."

"You don't know that either." April kicked the boards on the side of the bridge portraying her anger. "Maybe he wouldn't have gone up to the cabin if you had been with him. He made the decision that day with his head, not with his heart."

I pondered what she said. "Why do you think he would still be alive if I had been with him?"

"Because he loved you. He talked about you all the time. He didn't paint as much after that show. He buried himself in his job. He wouldn't have gone to the cabin that day if you had been with him." April twisted the black snakehead ring on her middle finger.

I tried to ease her pain. "In time, the hurting will go away. But our loved ones will always be in our hearts."

I looked down at the photo and remembered his smile was one of the features that drew me to him. His teeth were perfect, straight, and bright white.

April stared out over the river. "I've heard rumblings that some people don't think it was an accident. They think the explosion was meant to happen."

April's words shocked me.

"Uncle Jack doesn't believe it was deliberate." She moved away from the rail of the bridge. I handed her the photo. "No, it belongs to you now. I've got to go."

I put my hand on her shoulder. "You don't think Adam committed suicide, do you?"

She looked across the bridge. "No! but people have been talking."

I reached for her hand. "I know what it is like to lose a loved one." Then without thinking, I hugged her small frame. She backed away, turned, and ran across the bridge.

On the way back to my room Kevin called. "I have a flight. Pick me up at eight in the morning."

"Good, see you tomorrow."

I closed the door to my room and sat in the rocking chair looking out over the garden until darkness covered the sky. I had an uneasy feeling about Adam's death. Is that why everyone was closed mouth? Silence wasn't going to bring him back.

Chapter 6

The sound of the alarm clock woke me at six a.m. I ran through the shower, dressed, then headed towards I-385 to the Greenville-Spartanburg Airport. At this time of the morning, the traffic was heavy but there was enough time for me to be at the airport by eight.

I gave Kevin a big hug. "I'm glad your flight was on time. You're cutting our meeting with Jack close. Have you had breakfast? We can stop at a fast-food drive-through."

"I grabbed a cup of coffee and a pastry at the Hilton Head Airport." Kevin placed his hand on top of mine. "With everything you told me that went on yesterday, and your conversation with Adam's sister you need me. I rented a room at your bed and breakfast. There sounds like some controversy over Adam's death."

"Yes, but I don't know why. Maybe there will be some answers in Adam's safety deposit box."

Ten steps led up to the entrance of the old red brick bank building. My hands were damp, but my eyes were dry. I grabbed Kevin's arm.

"Julia, you're going to be fine." He smiled and patted my hand.

"Kevin, there are so many unanswered questions running around in my head. The biggest one is why? Look there's Jack."

Jack was across the lobby talking to a young man with thick, black-rimmed glasses when he saw Kevin and me, he hurried toward us.

"Hi, Kevin. Nice meeting you. Good morning, Julia. Let's go this way."

We followed Jack down a short hallway. I was still clinging to Kevin's arm when we entered through a door that read Safety Deposit Room. The room was musty, and the smell of old money, paper, and dust reminded me of the age of the building.

A plump short woman with glasses perched on the top of her head entered behind us. "Jack, the air-conditioner isn't working in this room. Let's move next door." She set the deposit box on the table and turned to leave. At the door, she cocked her head to the side. "Is there anything else I can get for you?"

"No, Trudy, we're fine." He closed the door behind her.

Jack pulled a key from his pocket. He held it in the air and looked at me. "Julia, this inheritance is unusual, to say the least. Are you ready?"

I sucked in a breath and shrugged my shoulders. "As ready as I'll ever be."

Jack unlocked the box. My eyes widened when I saw the box full of papers and envelopes. Jack picked up the top envelope. "Julia, let's start with this letter first."

I sighed and held the envelope for a few seconds before opening it. Kevin placed his hand on my shoulder.

I looked at the date at the top. Seven years ago, almost to the day that I had met Adam. I hesitated and took a deep breath.

Dear Julia,
I'm writing from my hotel room in Charleston. The sun is setting over the harbor with all its orange and blue reflections from the water. I met "the girl" of my dreams. You're gone now, but as you learned today, I am an optimist, and I told you if you ever needed anything to let me know. I will wait until that day comes. I know you will say I am a romantic, but if you could see what I saw today, you would know there was a connection established. When you walked into my art booth the first thing, I saw was your big beautiful blue hydrangea color eyes. Your dark black hair with its streaks of sunlight told me you were an outdoors person. I watched your ponytail sway as you came toward me. We walked around the art booths and I saw your poise—like a princess. I'm writing to you to tell you that you're now my most favorite person in my world. My job is taking me to France, but I will have to live with my heartache for a year knowing I won't see you. Spending the day with you today was the best day of my life. Think of me whenever you see an impressionist painting. There are three things that matter in life: how much you love someone, how much you are loved in return, and how gracefully you can let go of things that are not meant for you. I pray I don't have to live with the last one.
Love,
Adam

After reading the letter, the memories of that first day in the park, and the feel of his embrace that last day, became vivid in my mind. My heart felt like it was twisted and hollow. Kevin pulled me to my feet and held me so tight that my air supply almost stopped. I tried to block my memory of the week we spent together. After regaining my composure, Kevin pulled me back into my chair.

Jack handed me the next paper. "This is the paper you have to sign for the paintings."

I wiped my eyes, took a deep breath, nodded to Jack, and signed the paper. Jack touched my arm with his fingertips. "You need to take this signed document to Christopher's. I'm going to give you a copy to keep. There is one more paper for you to read and sign. Adam made you his beneficiary."

Tears flooded my eyes again. "Why? His family should receive all the money from his paintings. I don't want his estate. Jack, no! He has a brother and a sister."

"Julia, it isn't your decision. This was Adam's request. The rest of the papers you can take with you and read them when you're ready."

We stood. Jack, shook Kevin's hand and gave me a long hug. "If you need advice or anything, call me."

I walked out of the bank with my body numb and clutching the envelope with the contents from the deposit box. Kevin put his arm around my waist and guided me out to the parking lot.

"Sis, this was a lot to take in. Do you want to wait before going to Christopher's?"

"I'll be all right, but I don't understand why Adam did this, and I may never find the answer." My sigh was long, slow, and deep.

"Before we go to the art gallery, do you feel like eating lunch? I'm starved."

"You've already had a busy day. Yes, and a glass of wine would be nice right now. The Chop House is across the street. The food's good."

I couldn't eat a bite something had shifted inside me, and my entire body was unsettled. Everything felt uncertain. My insides were doing flip-flops and my stomach growled, it was hard to swallow. I pushed the lettuce around on my salad plate. Kevin quietly chomped away on his hamburger and fries, giving me space to think.

After my second glass of Riesling, I stared at Kevin. "Why did I come here? When you said there was nothing to lose, I thought you were right. Now, my life is upside down again. Adam's brother and his sister are going to be upset for me being his beneficiary and giving me all his artwork."

"Julia, this is your new beginning. You'll probably never know why Adam gave you everything. Jack told you he would handle the brother and sister. Everything you read has told you he was in love with you. Romantic love makes people irrational. Adam loved you for the past seven years."

Kevin took out his credit card and smiled. "Are ready to go to Christopher's?"

Chapter 7

Frank, the gallery director, rushed to open the door when he saw us approach. "I've been waiting for you. Jack called several hours ago and said you were on your way."

I squeezed Kevin's hand so hard that he winched. "I'm fine. Let's see the paintings."

The pace back to the dealer's warehouse was more of a stroll than the jog yesterday. A man on a small forklift was taking down the last crate.

Frank handed me the envelope that was attached to one crate. "This is for you."

My stomach knotted as I unfolded the note.

Julia,
I want you to know why I chose these paintings for you. Monet was my favorite of all the Impressionists. I loved how he could make flowers and water flow together. I am giving you two paintings that I think were my best, and the closest thing I could do to Monet. I also painted several mountain scenes. I love staying at my uncle's cabin, and when there I can paint for days uninterrupted. To me, Claude Monet was the best artist at painting mountains. He used strong contrasts between light and dark. The way he painted dark foregrounds contrasted against high key colors always captured his mountains. I followed his path of our mountains here. I would have loved to have painted your portrait but felt I could not do you justice. Edgar Degas painted beautiful people. I was never good enough to capture people the way he could.
Love you,
Adam

Tears trickled down my cheeks. Kevin clutched my hand.

Frank stepped close to me. "You don't need to unpack them. They are packed in straw as you can see and are crated for travel. You can rent a U-Haul truck that'll be the best way to transport them back to Charleston."

"Frank, I'm still in shock that these are mine. I didn't think about moving them to Charleston. I don't have space to hang or store them. Can you sell them here?"

Kevin put his hands on my shoulders and turned me to meet him squarely. "I'll go rent a truck, come back, and load the paintings. You go back to the bed and breakfast and check us out. I'll meet you there, then follow you back to Charleston. We have enough time to be home before dark."

Frank smiled. "Ms. Stone, I know this is overwhelming. May I make a few suggestions?

"Sure. Any help will be appreciated."

"Most of the paintings are beach scenes. You should have the painting close to you. Let me give you some names of some gallery owners and directors in Charleston. They'll be glad to help you when you decide what you're going to do with them. You could display some of Adam's work there but my gallery scenes are more of the mountains than of the seashore. If you have questions or need my help, let me know."

I forced a slight smile. "Would you call one of them now to see if they would let me store them until a decision can be made?"

Frank was back after a few minutes. His eyes were almost as sparking as his smile was wide. "Atrium Art Gallery on Queen Street used to be Adam's dealer in Charleston. They'll be glad for you to bring the paintings there. Ask for Suzie."

Both of us thanked Frank and headed to the inn. Sadie greeted me at the front desk. "My brother and I are checking out."

"I didn't want to tell you Adam was dead. Why didn't you tell me you were Adam's girlfriend?"

"I'm not. We only knew one another for a week. We met at an art show in Charleston."

I hurried upstairs to collect my things and thought about how the word had spread like wildfire that I was Adam's girl. Was there anyone in the downtown area that didn't know me?

The next morning, I walked into my own kitchen at nine, which felt more like six. Kevin was sitting at the table finishing his second cup of coffee. "Why didn't you wake me?"

He stood and poured me a cup of coffee. "You were tired and needed the rest. Today is going to be another emotional day for you."

The sip of hot coffee along with a long sigh invigorated me. "The shock from yesterday doesn't seem as scary today. I need to call Suzie at Atrium's." Here's my laptop "You need to get your return flight ticket to Hilton Head."

Kevin parked the U-Haul in front of Atrium's. I took two steps from the sidewalk to the Atrium door. Suzie smiled and greeted me with open arms. Her bright red blouse with the black and white striped pencil skirt and her five-inch black heeled pumps gave her a stately appearance along with her long blond hair that she had pulled into a side ponytail. She took me by surprise when she hugged me. "Welcome, Julia."

My eyes took a quick wide sweep around her gallery. I didn't see any mountain or seascape paintings or anything that looked like what Adam might paint. "Thank you for seeing me so quickly. I don't know what Frank told you, but I inherited some of Adam Robinson's work. Frank suggested they stay crated so they could be transported."

Suzie's eyes widened. "You haven't seen the paintings?" I shook my head no. "This is going to be a treat for both of us. Tell your driver to pull around back."

Suzie's showroom was small, but her storage area was huge. The three of us unpacked the crates like it was Christmas morning. All of us oohed and aahed.

Suzie stood back and placed her hand on her chin. "My market is hot for all of these if you are interested in selling them. I have clients asking for his work all the time. His paintings sell quickly, especially from May to November because of his beach scenes and the mountain ones with the fall colors."

With a smile, I answered. Those are my favorite ones too, but I don't have room for them in my house. I'll keep two small ones. This one of the mountains and the one that looks like Folly Beach."

"Frank told me you're Adam's beneficiary. I have something for you." She reached in under the cash register drawer and handed me an envelope with a bright brass key. "The last time Adam was here, he left this. The address is in Folly Beach."

Instantly, a wave of uneasiness ran through my body. "I don't know anything about this. Nothing was said yesterday when Adam's estate was turned over to me."

Suzie smiled. "Adam bought a house there about four years ago. He would go and stay for weeks at a time painting. He asked me to open a second location there for him to display his beach scenes. He gave me this key in case something needed to be repaired at the house when he wasn't there. This belongs to you now."

My throat burned. I could barely say, "Thank you."

Suzie put a piece of paper in my hand. "Here's my cell number."

I followed Kevin to the U-Haul lot to return the truck, and then we headed to the airport for him to catch his flight.

"Sis, take care. I'll call you tonight." He held me tight. "Things are going to be good for you. Trust me."

His goodbye hug gave me strength.

Chapter 8

On the way home from the airport, an uneasy feeling of being followed and on someone's radar did bother me as much as the papers from the deposit box. Hurrying into the house and in a flurry, I scattered all the papers from the box on the kitchen table and looked out at the Atlantic waves pounding The Battery wall. My mind race through all the what-ifs. My hand shook when I reached for one of the envelopes.

Dear Julia,
It is never wrong to love someone even if the love is not returned. It was good for me to love you. Some of my best work came to me after the week we spent together. I wished for and wanted a lifetime with you. I know you must be married or I would have heard from you. This is crazy, but no one could love you more than I do. I still hope to hear from you one day.
Love forever,
Adam

I placed the letter back in the envelope and stared at the tattered photo that April had given me, and remembering his touches and kisses, I dried my eyes and backed out of the driveway to go find Adam's house at Folly Beach.

    I arrived at the beach in twenty-five minutes due to the light traffic. Turning down one street and then another how could the GPS be this wrong? Why were there so many dead-end streets, and why couldn't his address be on one of these houses? Five minutes later, the small cottage with sea oats swaying in front with the ocean breeze appeared in front of me. The exterior paint was peeling and the small porch level with the sand was missing some slats from the constant toll of the east winds.

    My fingers fumbled around in my purse for the key, thinking this shiny key wasn't going to work. Turning the lock slowly, it clicked without hesitation. A shiver ran down my spine as if an intruder. I took a deep breath before stepping inside, gently closing the door behind me and still feeling like a trespasser invading someone's private property.

A big open room greeted me. A worn fabric chair sat on the right side of a faded leather sofa in front of a large television screen that was attached to the wall. Another small armchair was placed next to the television. On the other side of the room was a large plate-glass window that overlooked the ocean. Adam's easel and paints were strewn over two small tables. It was as if he had walked away a few minutes ago. I stood in the kitchen and looked out over the Atlantic and then back at the white cabinets and the green and white granite countertops making the room look like it was an extension of the ocean.

Thoughts of Adam being here and the choice I made with Robert rattled around in my head. Adam and I could've been here for the past seven years, but instead, we had chosen another path.

Plates, saucers, and cups were neatly stacked in the kitchen cabinets. Towels were hung in the small bathroom to the shower. A bright blue blanket and decorative seashell pillows covered the queen bed and stunned to see the window open. The thin white organdy curtains swayed in the ocean breeze as the ocean calmly lapped the sand. On the dust-covered dresser was the same photo of me and Adam that April had given me. A few books on the ocean environment and artist renditions were stacked on the bedside table. The entire cottage gave me a feeling that someone was living here.

I opened a door off the bedroom that led to a small room where a small wooden writing desk fill half the room. A tiny lamp sat on the left corner. I sat down in the swivel chair and cautiously opened the center drawer, not knowing what to expect, but there were only paperclips, a stapler, and scotch tape. When a hand covered my nose and mouth.

In my groggy state, my eyes roamed around the room. The bed was soft, a blanket was covering me, and I was alone. When the shock wore off, I ran out of the bedroom, out the kitchen door, stumbling over the windblown sand that was piled against the door but catching myself before falling, and to the water's edge. I looked up and down the beach but saw no one.

My mind alerted me to call Jack. "This is Julia."

"It doesn't sound like you. Is there a problem?"

"I'm not sure. The owner of an art gallery here in Charleston and Folly Beach gave me a house key to a cottage. Did you know Adam owned property at the beach?"

"Yes, but I'd forgotten about it. You're the sole beneficiary of his estate which makes you the owner of the house. I'll do the necessary paperwork to put the title to the cottage in your name. Is there anything else you need?"

"I'm at the cottage now, it looks lived in. Adam's paints are everywhere as if he walked away to take a break. I was sitting at a desk in a small room with my back to the door when someone came up behind me and covered my face. I woke up on the bed."

"I don't know what to tell you, other than the house is yours. You can call the local police."

"And what would I tell them? There wasn't anyone in the house when I left and there are no descriptions to give."

"Julia, I'm sorry."

He couldn't do anything in Greenville, I thanked him and hung up. I walked along the water's edge taking in the strong salt air, feeling the grief of Adam. With each step, the tide washed away my footprints, I stopped and stared at the water ebb and flow against the sand thinking tides come and go and memories fade over time until forgotten like footprints that were once left in the sand.

I left Folly Beach mid-afternoon and was home by three-thirty. My comfy chair was the place that gave me comfort and warmth. The glass of Pacific Rim Riesling helped to make the event of the day easier. All the men in my life were gone. For the first time, I felt completely alone, starved for affection and friendship.

The next morning, at nine, I pushed through the door of the Atrium Gallery. "Suzie, do you know who's living in Adam's cottage?"

"No one, that I know of, but I haven't been there since Adam's death. When Adam painted there, he would let me swing by his house and pick up some beach scenes for my clients or if I needed to fill some space in the gallery. All his paintings are sold now but with him gone, there was no reason to go to the cottage. The next time I go out maybe you would like to go with me."

"Thank you, that would be great. We could have lunch on the beach." I heard the relief in my voice.

Three days later, Suzie called. "Julia, the gallery is slow this morning, how would like to go out to Folly Beach today? I'll pick you up in an hour."

The drive to the beach allowed for a get-to-know-you conversation between the two of us. Suzie was a native Charlestonian like me. The art teacher at Charleston High School, where we graduated, asked Suzie to give some introductory art history classes to her students. All this gave us an automatic bond. A strong sense of belonging washed over me. Everything felt right for the first time since Robert's death. Moving forward was going to be the start of my new life in a town that I loved and one that was filled with happy memories.

When we parked in front of the cottage. I gasped. "Suzie, look. The windows are all open. Someone is here." I didn't tell her about my last adventure.

Suzie stood next to me. We both held our breaths when the lock clicked. The two of us charged in. "Everything looks the same except Adam's paints have been put in a box under the easel. Who's living here?"

Suzie wandered through the house. "Julia look. The kitchen counters and floor are covered with moving boxes."

"Suzie, someone must have a key. The door was locked."

Suzie ran her hand across the kitchen counter. "Looks like whoever was here or is still here won't be here for long." Suzie walked to the back door and looked out over the Atlantic. "You should change the locks."

"I'm not sure I want to do that yet. Whoever is here, is leaving. I'll give them to next week, then come back and stay for a few days. I'll change the locks then."

Feeling a little uneasy, it was time to change the subject. "Let's go eat and you name the place."

Suzie pointed to the east. "Blu Beach has great seafood and they have patio seating overlooking the ocean."

After lunch, we went to the Atrium Gallery. Suzie took a quick inventory check, put her index finger to her lips, and smiled. "Adam's beach paintings here will look great here."

Our conversation on the way back to Charleston was sparse. It was as if we both were involved in our future thoughts.

Early evening Kevin called. I filled him in on all the updates.

"Julia, I don't think it's a good idea for you to be at the cottage by yourself. Let me come and stay with you for a few days."

"Kevin, that's not necessary. You running back and forth from Hilton Head to Charleston isn't going to solve my problem. Besides, it's a one-bedroom and you're not going to sleep on the sofa."

Before I went to bed, everything was packed for what was needed for a week at the beach.

Chapter 9

The next morning, I stopped for a deadbolt lock, cleaning supplies, paintbrushes, and two gallons of neutral color with a hint of light green paint. It was what Sherwin-Williams had named "Fog." After the Home Depot stop, the grocery store was next for microwavable ready-to-zap dinners, milk, and cereal.

Looking at the house from the outside, I didn't know what to expect inside. To my surprise, all the boxes had been removed, and the easel and paints were also gone. All the drawers in the bedroom had been emptied. Everything else looked the same. After the groceries were put away, I gave the kitchen a thorough cleaning and after lunch, there was one coat of paint on the living room walls.

I poured a glass of Riesling, strolled out on the small porch that overlooked the ocean to watch the sunset. Couples were walking arm in arm on the beach, and kids were splashing one another at the water's edge. In the opposite direction, a big red dog was running at full speed towards me with a stick in his mouth.

The Irish setter came to a halt dropping the stick at my feet. "Well, where did you come from?" I rubbed his head and looked at his tags. "Dexter, that's a great name." The second tag had a number, 5027893. He wagged his tail looking up at me with his large brown eyes as if to say I've been waiting for you all day. "Would you for like me to throw the stick?" His tail wagged faster. I grabbed the stick and was prepared to toss it when I saw a man standing in the distance staring at me. He was dressed in jeans, a white tee shirt, and running shoes. His long blond hair swirled in the wind. I assumed the dog was his and threw the stick toward him. The dog took off in a sprint, picked up his prize, and laid it at the man's feet. The man stood still for several minutes before picking it up. He turned and threw the stick in the opposite direction from me. I retreated into the cottage.

My night's sleep was spent tossing and turning, and when the sun's rosy glow covered the morning sky and my bed my body was still in a restless state. Today was a new day, in my new place, but a chill ran down my spine thinking about the person that had entered my house and the man and his dog on the beach.

The local tabloid lying on the table had good recommendations for restaurants. The Lost Dog Café breakfast menu moistened my taste buds. The hostess seated me on the veranda across from a long concrete wall with a painted mural of the ocean. The waves looked like they were going to come crashing over me. White puffy clouds were painted in between large multicolored kites that covered the blue sky. A silhouette of a woman with dark brown hair pulled into a ponytail was painted a quarter of the way down the mural. Could this be something that Adam had painted? And was this supposed to be me or was I imagining the similarity? When the waitress brought the check, I pointed to the wall. "Do you know who painted that mural?"

The young girl shrugged her shoulders and shook her head no.

I ran my hand along the wall searching it from one end to the other looking for a signature or a date but found nothing. My stomach tightened and deep inside me, I knew this had to be Adam's work.

At the electric company, the clerk said. "Next."

Smiling, I pushed an old electric bill in front of her. "This address needs to be put in my name."

She grinned. "This property's bill has been paid in advance for a year. You need to show proof that you own the property or leave the bill as is."

In a surprised voice, I asked. "Who paid the bill?"

She replied. "Eli Robinson."

The water and cable companies gave me the same information as the power company.

All afternoon the eerie feeling of being watched hung over me. Trying to stay busy and shake my uneasiness, I added the second coat of paint to the living room wall. A little before five, I decided to call Jack.

"Julia, how are you?" His voice was upbeat.

"I'm fine. Thank you. The utility companies today said all the cottage bills had been paid for a year by Eli" My voice was strained. "Where is Eli now?"

Jack cleared his throat. "No one knows. He disappeared after Adam's funeral. Is there something else you need?"

"No. Thank you."

Holding the phone close to my chest, I slowly made my way to the sofa thinking Eli was the person living in the cottage.

My cell rang bringing me back to the present. "Julia, this is Suzie. My manager quit this afternoon at the beach location. I know this is sudden, but since you're out there already, would you manage the Atrium? It would be for a couple of weeks, at the most, until I find a permanent manager. You wouldn't have to be in the gallery all day."

"Suzie, I don't know anything about art."

"You don't have to have any knowledge of art or the artist. If you had to answer questions, one of the two part-time salespeople could help you. I need someone trustworthy to make sure the shop opens on time and is locked at closing, and the deposits are made. The same people do not work every day. I'm sure this will be for a week or two at the most."

After thinking for a few seconds, my answer was yes. "I'll do it for you, Suzie, but this will be short-term."

At 4:30 p.m. I went to the gallery to see if a deposit was needed to be made, and to lock up for the night. When I approached the gallery door, a man brushed past me on the sidewalk wearing a faded dark blue bucket hat. He kept his head down as he continued east. I stood at the door watching his lean frame disappear around the corner of the building.

The sales clerk smiled. "Have a good evening. I'll see you tomorrow."

I couldn't shake the feeling or explain what made me think that the man that passed me at the gallery was the same man that I had seen on the beach with Dexter. He had been too far away for me to get a good look at him. The idea of seeing where he lived and untangling the unrelated thread of who he was fascinated me. If the dog showed up at the cottage again maybe I could get him to lead me to his house.

My thoughts were interrupted when two clients walked in. The woman smiled. "Suzie sent us here. I know it's closing time, but she said you had some beach paintings by a local artist."

My face felt warm. Maybe I was blushing at the idea that they wanted to buy one of Adam's paintings. "Yes, I have several sizes and scenes by him."

The woman walked around the paintings and looked at them from all angles. "These are what we were hoping to find." She turned to her husband and then back to me. "We'll buy all of them."

My shoulders dropped. Part of my connection to Adam was going to disappear. I wanted to scream they aren't for sale. The woman touched the back of my hand. "Are you all right, dear."

I forced a smile. "Yes. The work is one of a kind. I'm going to miss them." I cleared my throat. "You can pick them up tomorrow afternoon. They'll be crated in the morning for afternoon delivery."

I made out the deposit slip and locked the door behind me. Guilt burned in the pit of my stomach, I felt I had betrayed Adam. A honk of a car horn stopped me with one foot dangling over the curb. Losing my balance, I went down on my left knee on the pavement. I stayed in freeze-frame mode until I evaluated, I wasn't hurt. I stumbled back to the sidewalk. I was so occupied thinking about Adam, and the man with the dog, that I had almost gotten myself run over.

I walked back to the cottage from the gallery with the sensation that I was still being watched.

Upon returning to the cottage, the Irish setter was lying on the front stoop.

"Dexter, do you live close by?" I stooped down patted his head and looked at the number on his tag again, 5027893. He wagged his tail and barked one time. "Can you tell me what this number means?" I laughed, stepped over the dog, and entered the house. On the way to the bathroom to shower, I looked out the glass front door. Across the street, next to a tree, stood a man. I blinked and blinked again, trying to make my eyes to focus on his face from so far away. After the last blink, the white tee shirt and blue jeans disappeared.

I dropped my clothes on the bathroom floor and took some deep breaths before stepping into the shower. The warm water flowed over my head and gently down my body. The scent of soap and shampoo calmed my anxiety.

Chapter 10

My everyday ritual was walking down the beach close to the water's edge and letting the incoming tide rush over my feet as the sunrise followed me down the beach. The sunsets were beautiful and sitting on the weathered wooden bench had become my evening peaceful place, watching the dark pink, blue and green colors splash across the sky giving a magnificent cotton candy sunset. I had started a shell collection, but it was hard to find unbroken ones, every now and then a whole one surface. My thoughts of Adam weren't so hard to deal with now and I was getting used to my new life at the beach, but I wasn't willing to live here full-time.

Late the next afternoon when I was sitting on my bench watching the waves and enjoying my wine, a nudge at my feet made me jump. "Dexter!" My eyes roved up and down the beach without finding anyone who looked like his owner or the mysterious man. The thought entered my mind that maybe Dexter lived here at one time. Had the man I kept seeing lived here too? Suddenly, a shadow appeared between me and the sunset. With the sun on his back, his face was hidden. I stood not moving closer to him but shifted towards his right side. My body stiffened and for a few seconds, I held my breath and stood frozen, not moving a muscle. The six-foot man or taller took three steps toward me.

I yelled. "Don't come any closer! Stay where you are!"

"Julia, I'm Eli Robinson. I never meant to frighten you."

I slowly backed against the bench and sat in silence for a moment before asking him to sit.

Eli let out a long sigh before he spoke. "When Dexter ran up the beach a couple of weeks ago, I couldn't bring myself to meet you then when you left, I didn't think you would come back. When you returned, you startled me. I knew I couldn't stay here, but Dexter wouldn't stay away from the cottage or you."

I stared at the water as if searching for words. "I thought you were stalking me. You always stood too far away or stayed in the shadows."

He gazed deep into my eyes as if he knew me. "I was cleaning out my things when you resurfaced. You caught me by surprise. I put my hand over your mouth so you wouldn't scream. I didn't mean to cover your nose too. But when you lost consciousness that freaked me. I moved you to the bed and waited outside watching you through the window until you stirred. I'm sorry, it was an accident. Uncle Jack called me and said you had asked about the utilities. I knew then you were going to stay."

"Jack told me Adam had a brother and a sister, but he said you disappeared after his death."

Eli shuffled his shoes across the weathered beaten porch slats. "The thought of Adam not being here was difficult. For the longest time, I couldn't function. A dentist across town bought my practice. I was floundering so I came here."

"Can you talk about it or is it too painful?"

Eli paced back and forth again kicking the sand with the toe of his tennis shoe. He wrinkled his brow and his body started to shake as if he had been shocked by a bad electrical socket. "I haven't been able to talk to anyone, but you need to know that Adam loved you. He talked about you constantly. He kept his heart closed to anyone thinking you would come to him one day." Eli's cheeks were tear streaked. "Adam called me to go with him to the cabin that day. He said illegal things were happening at work and he thought he was being watched. I told him to be silent and keep his eyes and ears open. If he felt he was in danger, he needed to resign. When we reached the front door of the cabin Adam thought he heard a noise inside. He told me to go around back. Adam opened the door then a loud boom sounded. When I gained consciousness, I had been blown two hundred yards down the mountainside. All I remember is hearing a loud boom." Eli's face was drawn and pale.

I brushed my wind-blown hair away from my face. "Illegal things at work. What does that mean? Adam was an artist, he worked for himself."

Eli closed his eyes. "He was a CIA officer. His art was his escape from reality."

"CIA!" I screamed.

He gently tugged on Dexter's left ear and sat down again. Dexter yawned then laid between our feet and closed his eyes. "Yes, Adam went to work for the CIA after college graduation." My brain was trying to comprehend what Eli had said. I dug my toes in the sand and kept staring at the Atlantic. Eli continued. "After the explosion, the cabin looked like a bomb had gone off. Adam was charred. What walls that were left were still burning. The authorities ruled it an accidental explosion caused by a faulty water heater." He cocked his head to the side, then rubbed the wetness from his cheeks with his tee-shirt sleeve. "I needed to get out of Greenville. I had been here many times with Adam over the years so I moved here. Then when you came, I was unsure what to do."

I placed my hand on his knee and then quickly removed it. "Where are you staying now?"

He pointed to the east. "About a block up the street. I rented a cottage."

"Eli, this is your house. You can stay. My home is in Charleston. I understand why you came here. I've had many surprises—the meeting with Jack, the paintings at the gallery with my name on them, the cottage, and then seeing Adam's paints spread out here as if he were still painting."

He stood up and started pacing again. "Adam taught me a little about painting."

The sun lowered into the water and darkness covered the ocean. All I could hear was the lapping waves. "Eli, would you like something to drink?"

He smiled. "Sure, if you don't mind." He followed me into the kitchen with Dexter on his heels.

I pointed to the two bar stools at the counter. "Please, take a seat. What would you like to drink? Your beer is still in the refrigerator."

"What are you going to have a drink?"

"Wine."

"Okay, I'll have a beer."

I told Eli about Robert and finding Adam's telephone number when moving from Jacksonville back to Charleston, the number belonging to someone else, and how my brother had insisted on me taking a road trip to Greenville. "All this was a big surprise and hard to comprehend, from meeting Jack to Adam leaving his estate to me. You can have whatever you want." I refilled my wine glass and handed Eli another beer.

"Julia, he told me about the week he spent with you. He said when I met you, I would understand why it only took a week to fall in love with you. I told him for years he was crazy. He couldn't love someone that much in a week. He stopped talking to me about you, but I know he never gave up hoping that one day he would find you again. This was Adam's wish. I want nothing."

Tears clouded my vision and sipping the wine helped me to stay in control. "I met Robert the same day I met Adam. He was going to France for a year and Robert was in Charleston." Eli wiped my eyes. "If we knew the future, maybe there would've been a different decision."

He swirled his beer. "That's true of anything and everything we do."

Eli peered down at Dexter sprawled out on the floor with all four paws stretched as far as they could reach. He pulled at the beer bottle label. "Adam's work sent him to France, he thought since he was going to be there, he would exhibit some of his paintings. He did sign a year's contract with a gallery, but it was only because he was going to be there for that length of time." He sat quietly and played with the bottle label until it fell off. "I've always had a sense that the cabin explosion wasn't an accident."

"Eli, what do you mean?"

He ran his hands through his long blond hair and paced back and forth. "Adam said he needed to talk to me where no one could hear our conversation. That is why he chose the cabin." Eli walked to the door, then turned around. His eyes were bright. "Thank you for listening. I never thought I would have ever talked to Adam's love about this."

My wine glass was almost empty again. "There have been several times in the past few months that I wondered where he was. It was like I was in a cloud chasing a dream."

"Julia, it wasn't a dream. Adam loved you and he wanted you to have everything he had." He turned the doorknob and called Dexter. "Can I see you tomorrow?"

I took my last swallow of wine. "Sure."

He closed the door behind him. My stomach did a somersault.

Chapter 11

I woke at 7:30 a.m. to the sound of Eli knocking on the cottage door. Smiling he asked. "Do you have coffee ready?"

I laughed. "It will be in a few minutes." I held the door open for him to enter. "What are you doing here so early?"

He pointed to the ocean. "It's a great sunny August day to play on the beach."

After we finished our second cup. Eli and I ran down the beach, side by side. I jumped in and out of the waves like a teenager. Dexter thought it was a game and he ran in and out of the waves in front of me and behind. Eli bought two kites from a beach vendor. We let the kites fly as high as we could against the blue sky. They were like large birds dipping and climbing with the wind currents. I was laughing so hard and running in and out of the waves that I was swallowed up by the surf. Eli rescued me from the water, then pulled me down onto the warm, soft sand next to him. He propped his elbows upon the sand. The kite strings were still entwined between our fingers.

Eli brushed my hair away from my face. "Now I know why you had such an impact on Adam and why he fell in love with you in a week. Not only are you beautiful, but you're also fun."

The sun's rays bounced off the water and the white sea foam ebbed and flowed with the waves. A few seagulls were bobbing up and down like they were surfing. "Thank you. I have no regrets about my marriage. I'm surprised that Adam never married."

Eli glanced at the sky. "Adam always said there was no room for romance because of his work. I think he changed his mind after he met you."

The wind had picked up and white caps covered most of the waves. "The whole week we were together he never said anything about his paintings being a hobby or that he worked for a company, let alone the CIA."

Eli didn't respond. I could see the pain and sadness in his eyes. His blond hair hung in disarray. I touched his soft strands, pushing his hair back away from his face. He twisted the towel he was holding around his hands. I felt his loss of losing Adam. I wanted to hold him and tell him he was going to be fine like everyone told me I was going to be after Robert's death.

Eli spoke in a soft tone. "I see why Adam never forgot you."

I stood, stared at him, and pulled him to his feet. "We should go."

He moved away from me a few inches, smiled, and said, "Yes, we should."

Dexter ran ahead of us occasionally he would double back and weave in and out our legs.

Eli had a lot of the same mannerisms as Adam. I was trying hard to keep space between us.

At 2:00 a.m., my phone woke me, Eli was yelling and talking so fast I could barely understand his words. "Calm down, Eli."

He lowered his voice. "Julia, have you heard the weather report?"

"No, I was asleep."

"The storm that was in the Bahamas is now a Category 2 hurricane. They don't know where it's going to hit land next, but they are predicting it will come up the east coast of Florida."

"Eli, it's hundreds of miles away. You have been through hurricanes before, haven't you?"

He screamed. "No! We don't have hurricanes in Greenville. We have ice and snowstorms."

I laughed. "I've been through many hurricanes. It's too far away to know where it will come ashore. Storms have minds of their own. There's a good chance it will fall apart before it reaches land. Go back to sleep. Come for breakfast. We'll see where the storm is then."

I had slept a couple of hours and had enough sleep that I couldn't get comfortable again, let alone go back into a sound sleep. At 3:00 a.m. I turned on the television. The storm formed off the coast of Cape Verde and crossed over the northern part of the Bahamas. Her increasing speed and winds were headed to the southeastern part of the US. The forecasters were predicting Hurricane Sharon to hit Florida around the Daytona Beach area.

Between my sips of coffee, I watched the sunrise. The palm tree's fronds were barely moving. Folly Beach was showing no signs of a storm coming. The Weather Channel was now announcing there was another storm behind Sharon in the Atlantic. Sharon's wind speed was being recorded at 65 mph and headed to Jacksonville. Eli pounded on my door at seven.

"You didn't say what time to be here for breakfast." He smiled. "I couldn't sleep."

"Come on in." I laughed. "I can tell this is going to be a long day watching Hurricane Sharon. I'm going to Charleston tomorrow. The cottage isn't the place to be in a storm."

"I was going to go to Greenville today. That's why I came by early, but I don't want to leave you by yourself."

"I'll be fine. You should leave for Greenville after breakfast."

Late that afternoon, All the other channels were reporting wars, politics, tornados, and earthquakes around the world. Eli was still glued to The Weather Channel. Hurricane Sharon had been upgraded to a Cat 3 with winds of 120 miles per hour. They were predicting she was going to hit land close to St. Simon's Island.

Eli was in a panic. "Julia, do you think it'll hit Folly Beach? They keep changing where the eye is going to come ashore."

"Storms are hard to forecast. It's still hundreds of miles away. In the morning, I'm going to Charleston, you need to go to Greenville. The mayor here is encouraging everyone to leave, but the governor hasn't issued a mandatory evacuation order yet for Folly Beach."

"I can't go to Greenville. Adam wouldn't want me to leave you."

The next morning, we stuffed both cars with as many items as we could. Eli and Dexter followed me up Highway 171. Thirty minutes outside Folly's city limits, Eli called. "Julia, the cars are inching along at a snail's pace it's going to take hours to get to Charleston."

"I know. Lots of people are evacuating and now we have hit the St. James Island traffic. DOT closes the bridges when the wind reaches 45 mph. It'll be like this all day, but tomorrow will be worse."

We came across the Ashley River Bridge into Charleston as the sky turned to gold, violet, and tangerine. A beautiful sunset before the storm. The wind was calm and there were no signs of an August hurricane.

At midnight, I was still awake in my bed listening to The Weather Channel blasting away in the other room. There was no way I was going to sleep with Eli rummaging around in the kitchen. He made coffee several times, and I kept hearing the squeaky pantry door open and close, along with the refrigerator door. It was like he was trying to see how many times he could open both doors in an hour.

It was now dawn and the sun and the clouds were playing peek-a-boo. I watched a purple rain cloud move over the sun. The Spanish moss that once dangled in the big oaks was blowing across everyone's lawns like tumbleweeds. I started breakfast and the Keurig was finishing its cycle when Eli shuffled into the kitchen. He stood by the coffeemaker waiting for it to make its last swoosh. He watched the Atlantic from the bay window. "The ocean is angry. Will the seawall hold?"

I smiled. "The turbulent waves will be angry for several days after the storm. The Battery wall will take a beating but it will hold. It has withstood many storms over the years."

Eli walked over to the kitchen. "What can I do?"

With a smile, I handed him two plates. "Put the bacon and eggs on our plates, then pour yourself a cup of coffee. The mugs are in the cabinet above the Keurig." I laughed. "But you already knew that."

He ran his hand through his bird's nest hair and returned to the bay window. "I didn't expect to see the sun today."

I poured my coffee and stood beside him. "The sun will dart in and out of the clouds all day."

Eli picked at his plate and stirred his food around.

A knock at the front door interrupted our breakfast. I peeked through the glass and saw my neighbor. "Hi, Keith. How are you? Do you need something?"

"I'm fine. I came to board up the house next door. You know they're out of town. Do you need anything boarded up?"

"I hadn't thought about securing anything. You can look around. If something needs to be done, please go ahead and do it. Thank you for checking on me."

When I returned to the kitchen all the cabinet doors were open. "Eli, what are you looking for?"

"Liquor! Beer! Wine! Anything that has alcohol in it."

Laughing, I pointed to the pantry. "It's too early to start drinking. We need to go to the grocery store. The pantry needs to be stocked with canned goods and batteries and we can stop by the liquor store. I don't know if we are going to lose power or not. I'm going to plan for a week without it."

Eli's smile turned to a frown. "Really? That long."

"Depends on the strength of the wind and the damage."

At seven-thirty that night, soft raindrops patted the roof. Hurricane Sharon's eye was predicted to be over Charleston around midnight with 125 miles per hour winds.

Eli paced back and forth. "Will you go to bed tonight?"

I laughed. "No, I'll stay up and keep you and Dexter company. Dexter knows the weather is changing, he keeps going from room to room. I'm going to give you a heads-up, the wind is going to howl and you will hear strange sounds. I've put several flashlights throughout the house, the bathtub is filled with water, the porch furniture is inside, and Keith boarded the windows on the ocean side. We've done all we can do."

At 2:00 a.m. the wind howled, and the trees cracked. The rain now was relentlessly pounding the roof and windows. Eli went from window to window looking for downed trees with Dexter following his every step. "Look, the street looks like a river." He let out a yell when a tree crashed in the driveway.

The wind became still around 3:00 a.m. There was no wi-fi and no air-conditioning. Charleston was in the eye of Hurricane Sharon. At daybreak, I opened the front door. The August air was hot and still. The entire neighborhood was quiet. At five, a few sun rays were forcing themselves through the dark clouds in the distance. Roof shingles were lying in the street and over everyone's yards. A few large oak limbs were dangling but were still attached to their trees. I could hear generators running and sirens squealing down towards the Cooper River Marina.

At 7:30 a.m., Eli wanted to go to Starbucks. I looked at him and laughed.

At 8:00 a.m., I called Kevin. "I'm fine. I don't think I have a lot of damage. Eli stayed with me last night."

"Sis, this is the first time that I could get through to you. I was worried. The news is showing that North Charleston had severe damage."

"I'm without power, but I can see the power trucks in the next block. My power should be on shortly. I'll call you back tonight."

I rechecked all the windows and then stopped in the kitchen. "Eli, I didn't buy milk yesterday in case the power went out but there is enough for cereal. Then we can walk down to The Battery and that will give us a good view of how much damage there is."

Outside there were a few shingles missing, and on two sides of the house, the gutters were down and twisted. Eli gasped at all the destruction of the downed trees and power lines and the twisted limbs. People were out and about piling what debris they could to the curb. The Atlantic waves were still splashing over The Battery wall. The wall showed no signs of damage. Considering this was a Category 3 hurricane, the town seemed to have weathered it well. Nothing like the devastation that Hugo had bestowed on Charleston in 1989 when boats had been tossed from the marinas and hurled into the middle of downtown.

At 3:00 p.m. my lights flickered, went off, then flickered again. After the last flicker, the electricity was restored. Eli smiled and gave me a quick hug. Relief covered his face.

At 5:00 p.m. Keith came by to remove the plywood from the boarded windows.

Chapter 12

Tuesday morning, I met with the insurance adjuster. He informed me that my house was one of the ones that had survived on my block and the downed large oak trees were the major cause of the damage. After the adjuster left, Eli asked. "Do you think we need to go to the cottage and see what damage has been done there?"

I shook my head. "I don't know the road conditions. The Ashley and Cooper River bridges are only open to emergency and cleanup crews. Let's go tomorrow."

Eli and I spent the rest of the day clearing limbs, shingles, and other debris from the yard. Several whirlwinds swept leaves across the porch as fast as I could sweep them away. A neighbor stopped to inform us that a few grocery stores, a couple of gas stations, and some restaurants were open.

I turned to Eli. "See, the town is coming back to life."

The next morning, I pushed my legs to the side of the bed, slowly placing my feet on the floor. The rest of my body followed but my stiffness made moving difficult. The message was strong that I should've hired someone to clean up the yard. I lumbered into the kitchen.

"Good morning, sunshine." Eli smiled. "I'm on my second cup of coffee."

"My body is inflicting revenge on me for yesterday's work. When I move everything hurts."

He smiled. "I'll give you a body rub if you think it'll help."

I smiled and answered. "No, but thanks."

Eli looked at Dexter. "How about us going to the beach?" Dexter wagged his tail.

I watched the Atlantic's angry waves from my bay window but I knew tomorrow there would be no sign of a storm. "Eli, I have given a lot of thought about Folly Beach. You go. The cottage is yours. I'm not going back there."

"Julia, the house belongs to you. It was Adam's wish. My final word is I'm not taking it."

"You will. I'm putting the deed in your name. The discussion is closed. I've checked and all the bridges are open. You go to Folly. I'll go grocery shopping. You can call me with a damage report. If the cottage is not habitable, you can come back here and spend the night. Leave Dexter with me."

After Eli left, I found myself relying on him more and more. Space and time apart would break the attachment between us, if he thought there might be one. My actions need to be guarded to make sure there weren't going to be any emotional ties.

Mid-morning, Eli's voice rang loudly in my ear. "Julia, I'm stunned. Folly Beach is in shambles. You wouldn't believe all the devastation. The local people that stayed are wandering around in a daze. There are no tourists and from the looks of things, it's going to be months before they'll return. One grocery store is open. There's a line down the street. It looks like the owners are only letting a few people in at a time. People are tossing debris into the city dumpsters even though they are full. FEMA is setting up trailers and tents. Compared to last week, the beach looks like a war zone and a ghost town. The storm has completely disrupted the beach's way of life. I think it may be a couple of years before everything returns to normal. I'm pulling up to what's left of the cottage. The roof is lying in the street and the entire structure is gone. A few studs are standing here and there where the walls used to be. Julia, I'm sorry, the only thing you own is a vacant lot. I'll be back in Charleston this afternoon."

At noon, Suzie's number appeared on my phone. "Hi, how are you? Did you have much damage? My gallery in Charleston is fine. The gallery here in Folly Beach is standing but most of the roof is gone, fortunately, we had put all the paintings in my storage building in Charleston. They're fine. I'll reopen the gallery but it'll take a few months. I haven't been by your cottage yet."

"I'm fine. I'm in Charleston. Eli is at the beach now. He said there was nothing left. I'm not going to rebuild. I don't need two places to worry about. The storm has made it evident, that I need to stay in Charleston. When things settle down again, we'll have lunch. Suzie, thanks for calling."

I was at peace about the couple who had bought Adam's paintings. Hopefully, his paintings were safe with them.

Eli pulled into the driveway around four o'clock. "I came to pick up Dexter. We're going back to Greenville."

I smiled, leaned down, patted Dexter's head, and rubbed his ears. "I'm going to miss you, buddy."

"Is Dexter the only one you're going to miss?" Eli laughed. "Don't answer that."

I grinned. "Maybe Adam wasn't the only one who made quick judgments about people. It seems to me you aren't happy in Greenville. You could consider renting a condo here."

He stared at me, removed his ball cap, and smiled. "I could."

I laughed. "Stay here tonight and look for a place tomorrow. That way I get to be with Dexter one more night."

Eli smiled. "There's Dexter again. Nothing about me."

I smiled knowing that I had developed a trusted relationship with Eli.

At dinner, Eli asked. "What's on your mind? You have been extremely quiet."

"My mind has been racing all day. The storm, the cottage, and what you said about Adam at the cabin. Did Adam say anything other than he thought some things were being done illegally at work? Do you think the explosion was deliberate?"

"Things were a blur back then. I haven't told anyone about my conversation with Adam except you. Adam said that three others in the company had died from accidents. After the insurance company ruled that the water heater was the cause of the explosion, I didn't think about Adam's conversation again until we started talking."

"Eli, if Adam thought illegal things were being done, and three coworkers died from accidents, do you think the incident at the cabin was an accident? Adam could have been murdered, and if so, this would be a homicide case. Did Jack say anything?"

Eli walked around the table. He covered his mouth with both hands and then dropped them to his side. "Uncle Jack asked for the insurance report, but he never received it."

I poured another glass of Riesling and handed Eli a beer. "You need to tell Jack about your conversation with Adam. If Adam was deliberately killed, you owe it to your brother to find out what happened. Jack's a lawyer; I'm sure he'd have some leads about how to investigate all kinds of criminal situations. Maybe it was a plot to silence Adam. He could have been killed by a hired contract killer."

Eli's eyes widened. He shook his head and threw his arms in the air and yelled. "Wait! Wait! This is moving too fast. Why would you think any of this? I didn't think Adam was in trouble or that he had been murdered."

"Think back to your conversation with Adam. I'm only repeating what you said to me and it doesn't make sense. Think about it. Adam wanted to meet with you privately so he wouldn't be overheard. He told you about the three deaths of his coworkers that were being called accidents and about his discovery of illegal deals being made at the National Security Agency. You need to talk to Jack."

I went to bed trying not to think about how upset Eli was. He paced around most of the night. He didn't sleep. Neither did I.

Chapter 13

Friday morning, Dexter stayed on Eli's heels as he packed the car to return to Greenville. "Julia, I'll call you after my conversation with Uncle Jack."

I gave Dexter a quick hug and fluffed his hair on the top of his head. Dexter walked back and forth several times before he lay down at my feet. Eli's third call to Dexter to get in the car was in vain. Dexter had refused to move. I walked to the car and gave a soft whistle for Dexter to come. He took two steps and then retreated back to the front porch. He laid down spreading his paws out on the top step.

Eli turned to me. "You've spoiled him. He doesn't want to leave." He smiled and reached for my hand. "Would you like to keep him until I return? I'll come back in a couple of weeks. He'll keep you company and that will keep me from worrying so much about you."

"I'd love for him to stay. Are you sure you want to leave him?"

Dexter wagged his tail as if he understood our conversation. Eli gave me and Dexter a quick goodbye hug.

Midday, Dexter sat at my feet on the front porch while I opened my mail. There was an envelope from Christopher's Gallery. Frank, the curator, had forwarded the announcement from The American Impressionist Art Society saying Adam had won the Impressionist Award of the year. I immediately called Suzie, and within thirty minutes she and I were having tea in my kitchen.

"Julia, do you know what this means? Adam's paintings will be on tour in New York, Chicago, and Los Angeles. The award comes with a check for hundred-thousand dollars."

"What paintings? I kept two and sold the others because I didn't have room for them."

"You need to contact the Impressionist Society and inform them of Adam's death. I have the records of who bought his paintings. I'll contact them to see if they'll let the paintings be on display for a year. You can offer the owners a loner's fee out of part of the award money.

Since you own Adam's estate, they'll give you a release form giving you the right to display the paintings."

I looked out over the calm Atlantic and then back at Suzie. "I wish Adam were here to receive his award."

"I do, too. This is a high honor among artists. I'll pay tribute to Adam's work as a Charleston artist by reserving a corner in my gallery."

After Suzie left, I called Eli. "Hello Julia, Is everything all right? I didn't expect to hear from you so soon?"

"Yes, I wanted you to know Adam's art was chosen for the Impressionist Award. He's the artist of the year. His paintings will be displayed in art shows and galleries across America." There was silence on the other end. "Eli, did you hear what I said? Eli!"

"Yes, yes. Sorry, I'm shocked."

"I know me too. I wish Adam was here."

"Julia, on the way back to Uncle Jack's house. My heart won't let me leave you and Adam would want me to look after you. This afternoon I found a condo in Charleston. It's about three blocks from your house." My mind yelled stop! Was Eli moving to Charleston to protect me? I was an FBI agent. I didn't need protection. "Julia, I'll call you after our meeting."

My adrenaline was flowing with news of Adam's award and being anxious to know what Jack would say after Eli told him about his conversation with Adam.

The afternoon shadows had lengthened by the time I put on Dexter's leash and headed for our daily afternoon twenty-minute walk along The Battery. The storms were gone, and the end of November was feeling like a late Fall. The leaves on the sycamore trees were gone due to the storm and the time of year, and the high humidity level had dropped to a level low.

Friday morning, I wasn't expecting to see Eli at my front door. Before I could collect my thoughts, he blurred out. "You were right. Adam was murdered."

"Eli, slow down." I took a seat on the sofa and patted the cushion next to me. "Start from the beginning."

"After I insisted that Uncle Jack see the insurance report, he called to speak with the adjuster but the adjuster has quit and no one knows where he is or how to find him but the secretary pulled the cabin's report. It confirmed that the water heater had a burned-out element and wasn't functioning. That meant the origin of the explosion couldn't have been the water heater. Also in the report, there was information about several wires that had been run from the back of the cabin into the woods. Uncle Jack called the sheriff's department but they said the case was too old to investigate. He's now contacting the CIA. I don't know who knows what."

After a long sigh, "You need to understand, I was an FBI. I quit when Robert and I moved to Jacksonville. Most of my work was in the office collecting and analyzing data, questioning, and interviewing suspects, and investigating financial crimes. I was in the field a few times. My basic training was in Quantico. FBI women can't work in the field unless they are officers. I'm familiar with protocols if the FBI gets involved. Eli, they'll get to the bottom of Adam's death and why."

Eli sat speechless and stared at me.

Chapter 14

It was the coldest Charleston January on record since the ice and snowstorm in 2010. The freezing rain had fallen all day Tuesday and Wednesday, and all through the night, leaving the city in a frigid gridlock Thursday morning. All the bridges around Charleston were closed—the General William C Bridge, also known as the Westmorland Bridge over the Ashley River that connects Charleston to North Charleston, the Cooper River Bridge from Charleston to Mount Pleasant, The Don Holt Bridge over I-526, The Ravenel Bridge, the Isle of Palms Connector, and the Stono Bridge between John Island and James Island.

The DOT sand crews had worked non-stop throughout the night to keep the bridge over the Ashley River open. The ground was covered with tree limbs, which had fallen from the weight of the ice. South Carolina Electric and Gas had lost all power.

"Eli. I've got the ball rolling." Uncle Jack's voice was loud. I could hear the excitement in his voice standing a foot away from Eli. "I need you to come back to Greenville. The CIA and the FBI want to talk to you."

"Uncle Jack, did you know Julia was a former FBI agent?"

"No. Let me speak to her." Eli handed me the phone. "Julia, since you own Adam's estate, and you are an ex-FBI agent you need to go with us. You may understand what's ahead of us more than we would."

After lunch, I packed my suitcase. Eli insisted that I ride with him. "I don't want to depend on you to take me everywhere." I laughed. "I might need to go shopping. You wouldn't like that."

"If you need to go somewhere you can use my car. No need for us to drive two cars."

Snow and ice were piled three feet high on both sides of I-385, and traffic was at a standstill, ambulances and fire trucks inched by us. "Eli, there must have been a wreck. We've been sitting in gridlock for miles and over two hours. We're moving at twenty miles per hour when we do move."

When we approached an overpass, we saw an overturned van with all four tires pointing to the sky, a car on its side in the ditch, and an SUV in two pieces wedged between three trees in the woods.

I stretched my neck. "You know if the accident had been on our side of the interstate, it would have taken us more than six hours to get to Greenville and that doesn't count the times we have to stop to let Dexter run and pee. I'm glad now that you were adamant about us taking one car."

When we arrived at Jack's, I shook his hand. "Thank you for letting me stay here with you and Eli."

Jack gently patted my back. "You're becoming one of the family."

I awoke the next morning at seven o'clock to the aroma of coffee and bacon. Margaret, the housekeeper, must have come to work around six. I turned over and thought about this was my room when I came to Greenville. A smile covered my face.

At breakfast, Jack placed his hand on top of mine. "Julia, I hate to bring back memories of Adam in this way. I thought his leaving you the estate was going to be a simple transaction, and it should have been. None of us ever thought that Adam might have been murdered. Thank you for coming."

I shrugged my shoulders. "I never expected my life to be involved with Adam, especially in this way."

Jack pushed back his chair. "Okay, kids we have a ten o'clock appointment at the federal courthouse. We need to get going."

We stepped into the courthouse lobby to be photographed and have our faces and bodies scanned, including retinal scans and that wasn't enough, we had to stand arms outstretched, feet spread apart while gloved hands ran up and down our bodies. Then we were led to the elevator doors where two guards stood on each side. One guard pushed the button. We stepped off on the sixth floor, a guard gave a light one knock on a plain unmarked door and nodded without saying a word or a smile. A woman appeared, smiled, and said, "Follow me."

She gave a slight knock on a door across from her desk, then immediately opened it.

A tall man with a large belly, in his mid-fifties, stood, adjusted his suspenders, smiled, and shook hands with each of us. "Hi, I'm Bryan Wilson, head of the FBI. Ms. Haspel, the head of the CIA couldn't be here this morning. My office is in DC but I work out of this office on cases below the Mason-Dixon Line. The director here thought I should meet with you after hearing part of your story."

He offered us water, coffee, or a soft drink, but after we all declined, he motioned for us to sit at his round conference table. During the social preliminary conversation, Bryan established who we were—Jack, Adam's uncle and attorney, Eli, Adam's younger brother, and me the owner of Adam's estate. I gave him a little of my background of being a former FBI agent when the uniform was a black suit, white shirt, and a narrow black tie for everyone including women. We laughed about everyone looking like penguins.

I gazed around his office. On the wall over the credenza, hung a Ph.D. diploma from the University of Florida in criminal justice. His secretary returned with a legal pad.

Bryan smiled. "May I call you by your first names?"

Jack answered. "Yes."

We all nodded in agreement. I felt uncomfortable calling Dr. Wilson by his first name. A southern thing with elders plus his advanced degree.

Jack pointed to Eli. "Bryan, he had a conversation with Adam that didn't come to light until a few weeks ago. I had asked the insurance company for their report on the cabin explosion, which was never received. Last week I requested it again, and here's what came. There are some discrepancies." He pushed the report over to Bryan. "The three of us started putting two and two together. That is what has brought us to this meeting."

We all sat quietly while Bryan looked over the report. Bryan raised his eyebrows. "The report looks complete."

Jack explained the death was ruled an accident. After hearing the details of Eli's conversation with Adam, Adam being a CIA officer and working undercover at the NSA office, the insurance report, and the sudden disappearance of the adjuster.

Bryan removed his silver-rimmed glasses, reared back in his chair, and frowned. "If what you're telling me checks out to be true, the people involved in the killings are working for someone at the NSA." Bryan motioned to his secretary. She left the room. Five minutes later she returned and handed him a sheet of paper. "So far, it looks like no one has questioned the other three NSA deaths."

Julia ran her hand over her forehead. "Will the other three deaths be investigated? Will you try and find the insurance adjuster?"

"Yes, to both, you brought Adam's death to our attention. If our investigators find foul play and we determine this was an actual contract murder, this is a federal offense."

Eli put his hands in the air. "There are two federal agencies involved here. Will the FBI go after the NSA and the CIA?"

"Yes, if we find they have broken federal laws."

Bryan stood and reached out his hand to Jack. "Thanks for coming in. You'll be hearing from me." He shook Eli's hand and gave me a nod.

It was close to noon when we left the building. Eli said, "I am hungry."

The three of us walked to the next block and crossed the street to Stephanie's Coffee Shop. Stephanie gave Jack and Eli a hug. She gave me a quick pat on the top of my arm and smiled. "Glad to see you again, honey. Sit anywhere you like."

Jack ordered a hamburger, Eli asked for the lunch special and I ordered a salad. When the food arrived, I looked at my plate and pushed the lettuce around with my fork.

Chapter 15

The next morning after breakfast, Jack leaned his chair back on two legs. "I haven't been to the cabin since the accident, we should take a trip up to the mountain. Maybe there's some activity there."

I was apprehensive about the trip. I wasn't sure I wanted to go to the place where Adam was murdered. We arrived to find yellow crime tape surrounding the cabin and the sound of two Apache helicopters circling above. The quiet neighborhood on the side of the mountain wasn't quiet now with men dressed in black suits and others dressed in black pants and jackets with the yellow words "Crime Unit" printed across the back. People gawking with license plates from all over South Carolina had brought traffic to a slow pace.

Eli yelled. "Bryan didn't waste time getting the crime lab here."

An unmarked black car stopped next to Jack's car. A tall, thin man exited his car flashing his badge. "You people can't stop here."

Jack arched his shoulders back. "This is my cabin. My nephew died here."

The man propped his backside against his car's front fender. "No one can enter until we are finished with our investigation."

Jack pointed to the cabin. "Adam has been dead for over a year. What do you think you're going to find now?"

The man walked towards the cabin and turned to face us when he reached the front steps. "We never know what we're going to find and when."

The neighbor from the top of the mountain waved to Jack as she drove by. She stopped at the stop sign at the bottom of the hill then backed up and stopped next to Eli. "Jack, how are you? What's going on? Late yesterday afternoon and this morning people have been in and out of the cabin, and down the back of the mountain."

Before Jack could answer, Eli blurted out. "Adam was murdered here. The FBI is investigating."

She wrinkled her forehead. "I'm sorry Jack, I didn't know. Adam loved to come here and paint. I'm going to the grocery for lunch meat. I left the door open so the three of you should go up to the house. I'll make us sandwiches. It's lunchtime and there's no, no here."

Jack nodded and smiled. I was glad about the offer. The FBI people trampling around in the thick woods had stirred up a storm of mosquitoes and biting flies. The back of Eli's white shirt was black and I didn't have enough arms and hands to swat both of us.

Jack tugged on Eli's arm. "I don't think we should say Adam was murdered until we have all the facts. I know you are anxious, but let's keep our thoughts quiet for now."

After lunch, we returned to Greenville.

"Eli, I want to home."

It was close to nine o'clock when we arrived back in Charleston.

"Julia, I'm going to my apartment, but Dexter is staying with you."

I called Kevin to bring him up to date on everything that had happened after Hurricane Sharon. "Julia, why haven't you told me this before now? Are you and Eli in a romantic relationship?"

"No. He likes me and I enjoy his company. We're trying to find out if Adam was murdered or not. I'm involved because Adam left me his estate."

He laughed. "It wouldn't be because your FBI brain jumped back into action. Would it?

"I'm thinking about contacting my old boss." His silence told me, he was digesting my answer.

After a few seconds, he continued with why he called. "Are you going to New York to accept Adam's award?"

"I haven't thought about the award. I need to call the Impressionist Society and get the details."

"If you decide to go, I want to go with you."

My bed was my comfort zone and Dexter was the one constant thing in my life now. I couldn't believe it was almost ten a.m. when I woke with him licking my fingers. I opened one eye. He woofed. "All right boy, I'll get up and take you out."

I opened the front door and Dexter bolted pulling his lease from my hand. I was surprised to see my mail scattered over the front yard. I checked the clasp on the mailbox to make sure it was secure, and it was. I knew the wind had not blown the door open. Inside the box was a plain bright red envelope addressed to Julia Stone, there was no stamp and no return address. I opened the envelope to find a 2 x 2 white piece of paper with an email address on it. I stared at the paper wondering who would have scattered my mail. Dexter ran into the back of my legs almost knocking me down. "Okay, boy let's gather the mail and go inside."

I hurried to my computer and typed in 3and1for4@hotmail. I sat staring at the white screen before I typed "Who are you? Why did you scatter my mail?"

Two hours later, I hadn't received a reply. I called Jack.

"Julia, do you feel you're in danger?"

"No, I don't know anything."

"Someone knows where you live. I'd take it as a warning."

I cleared my throat. "A warning about what? Do I need to call Bryan?"

"You have nothing to tell him yet except your mail was scattered and you have a piece of paper with an email address. Wait a little while and see if you get a reply."

I stared at the dark screen and watched the minutes tick around the clock. Thirty minutes later, my email chimed.

What do you know about Adam's death? Do you know who killed him?

I typed. *I know nothing. Who are you?*

I'll contact you again.

I waited minutes before I shut down the computer.

Chapter 16

Tuesday morning, after talking to the receptionist at the Impressionist Society, I waited for the president of the society to return my call. Mid-afternoon, Ms. Zenfield gave me all the information on the awards ceremony. Her voice cracked. "I am sorry to hear about Adam's death. That explains why he never responded to our notifications. You can accept the award for him."

"I would be honored but I don't want to give an acceptance speech. Ms. Zenfield, will you get someone to speak?"

"Sure. I'll see you May fifteenth in New York."

Thursday morning the fourteenth of May, Kevin, Eli, and I flew from Charleston to Newark, New Jersey. As we started our descent, the pilot circled the Statue of Liberty giving everyone a close-up view. "Ladies and gentlemen, welcome to New York."

We boarded the train at the airport and made our way to the Waldorf Astoria Hotel in midtown. The front desk clerk greeted us as if we were royalty. When we arrived at our rooms, we each had a welcome basket filled with candies and fruit. Along with my basket, I had a large bouquet of red roses. At five o'clock we waited at the large mahogany bar in the Bull and Bear Steakhouse for Ms. Zenfield. She apologized for being an hour late and after all the introductions we agreed to call each other by our first names. Katherine tossed her head when she spoke which made her silky auburn hair bounce around her shoulders. She looked like a model and my age. At dinner, we talked about Adam's death and the unfortunate accident at the cabin, but Eli, Kevin I said nothing about a possible murder.

The Impressionist Award ceremony was at noon in one of the Waldorf's banquet rooms with a luncheon following afterward. Katherine gave an impressive speech praising Adam for his work. To my surprise, she announced that I would say a few words and handed me the award. The only thing I could think about was that Adam should be here. With tears in my eyes, I said, "On behalf of Adam

Robinson, I accept his award." I smiled and retreated from the podium.

After the presentation, Katherine asked. "What time is your flight?"

Eli laughed. "Mid-night. The only return flight we could get is the red eye."

She laughed. "Getting flights in and out of New York can be difficult sometimes. Do you have any plans before your flight? If not, I would like to give you a quick tour of New York City and I have extra tickets for the seven o'clock performance of 'Come From Away.' It's a Tony nominee for best musical. You might enjoy it. A good way to kill some time before you go to the airport."

Kevin replied. "That would be great. What's it about?"

Katherine smiled. "Well, on September 11, 2011, the isolated town of Gander, Newfoundland finds itself being the unexpected host of thousands of stranded travelers. Thirty-eight planes had diverted to this small town's airstrip. The tiny town was having an average day and now it had become an international sleepover. The people of Gander opened their homes, hearts, and bars to the travelers."

The limo pulled in front of the hotel. Katherine climbed in first facing the front of the car. Kevin sat next to her. She smiled and pointed to the rear seat. "The view will be better if you look through the back window."

As an onlooker, I noticed Kevin's eyes light up and his conversation with Katherine was one of knowledge. He was trying hard to impress her.

Eli almost put his head in my lap as he looked up at the top of the Empire State Building. With the traffic, it seemed like we sat still more than we moved. We did see the 9/11 Memorial and Little Italy. Eli and I wanted to see Chinatown, but Kevin said he didn't. I gave him a wink when Eli and I exited the car. Kevin stayed with Katherine while the driver drove around the block when we took a stroll through the center of Chinatown. Kevin and Katherine were smiling and laughing when the driver came back to pick us up. We arrived at the theatre at six and were back out in the limo by nine-thirty. At ten o'clock the driver pulled up in front of the American Airline terminal. Eli and I waited at the boarding gate for Kevin.

"You didn't want to get out of the limo. You and Katherine had a long goodbye conversation. You're smitten." Laughing I punched him gently in his left arm. "I don't know where you think this is going with you in Hilton Head and her in New York. What happened to you? You were going to play the bachelor life and never get married."

He put his hand over my mouth. "You talk too much. We both met her at the same time."

"I know but you can't stop grinning and you are giddy."

On the flight back to Charleston Eli read a book, Kevin slept with a grin on his face and, I contemplated going back to work for the FBI.

Monday morning, Dr. Wilson answered his cell phone on the second ring. "Bryan, this is Julia, how are you?"

"Fine, thank you. What can I do for you?"

In a strong and matter-of-fact voice, I answered. "You know my background as a former FBI agent. With everything that's going on with the Adam Robinson's case, I want to be reinstated. My experience and criminal background knowledge will be a great benefit."

In a questionable voice, he replied. "Are you sure about this?"

"Yes."

"If so, submit your application. You'll have to back through basic training at Quantico."

A week later, Bryan's number appeared on my phone. "Julia, your FBI application has been accepted. You report to Quantico next week."

My insides jumped like a kid with a new toy. "Thank you. You'll be proud of me."

The following Wednesday, I presented my passport, driver's license, and my official FBI identification card to the marine at the Quantico front gate. I was surprised at the debriefing the next morning how much I remembered. In combat training, I was amazed I could stay with the front runners in the one-and-a-half-mile run. I contributed my stamina to Dexter. Our running every day kept me in shape. The three-hundred-meter sprint made me a little winded.

The instructor moved around me in a circle. "Good. Stay on your toes. Right shoulder front. Perfect. Stand behind that chalk line and reach for the can on that post and return it, keep your feet flat."

I dropped my arms. I hurt from my shoulders to my calves. He yelled. "Boxing is about punching. You can't punch if you are not balanced. Keep your elbows close to your body. You have to keep the box closed otherwise you will hit every punch."

I kept my elbows in and threw a punch at the instructor. It was enough to back him up.

The instructor put his hand on my shoulder. "No more boxing—you've got it. Now don't forget how to throw a punch when you get under pressure."

When the eight weeks of training ended, I was one of 4,800 special agents. Not being in the FBI for eight years, I was labeled Condition Yellow, which meant I was on a relaxed alert but staying in a continuous awareness state of all my surroundings. My motivation through training was focused on finding Adam's killer and getting enough evidence to put Wesley Campbell behind bars.

I requested to be assigned to the Criminal Investigating Division (CID). This division looked for and interrupted financial networks that supported terrorist organizations.

I said goodbye to two instructors that had asked me to come back and teach the female recruits. "I'm on a mission with the FBI. Maybe in three years, I might consider coming back and teaching tactics, if your offer is still available then."

On the way back to Charleston, my brain bounced around how to start planning for Adam's case long with the excitement to be back in the FBI.

There hadn't been any word from Bryan since I returned from Quantico. Monday after Dexter and I had returned from our walk along The Battery, my phone ID showed the FBI number. "Good morning, Bryan."

"Julia, we have an update on the Adam Robinson case. Do you think you and Jack can meet with me at three tomorrow in my office?"

"Yes, I can be there."

I called Jack and Eli even though Bryan didn't say anything about Eli being at the meeting. Eli and I left Charleston early Tuesday morning. After a late lunch at Stephanie's Coffee Shop, the uneasy feeling returned again like we were being followed. I wedged myself between Eli and Jack. We walked across the street and entered the FBI building at two-forty-five. Each one of us was scanned again individually before we entered Bryan's office at three. Bryan sat behind his desk and motioned for the three of us to take a seat in the chairs in front of him.

"What I'm about to tell you is confidential between us. I can't give you all the details but I'll confirm that Adam was murdered. We found a whistleblower who wants to expose the killer. In cases like these, we may never resolve it, but we know it's political and there were a lot of payoffs."

I interrupted. "Do you think the whistleblower can be trusted?"

Bryan laughed. "As much as any of them can be. Based on the information he gave and what we were able to confirm Adam found large sums of money were being deposited in offshore accounts. I have international trade lawyers working on the case along with the homicide division, and an agent who specializes in old murder cases. There is money missing from an NSA account. I think that is what Adam found. This is all the information I can release to you at this time."

Jack stood extending his hand to Bryan. "Thank you. We appreciate you telling us what you could."

On the way back to Jack's house I still had the uneasiness that I was being followed.

The week after I returned from Greenville. I opened my emails to see one from 3and1for4@hotmail.com. I froze staring at the screen. *I know you have been talking to the FBI. I am watching you.* I quickly shut down the computer as if whoever sent it could see me.

I reached for my phone. "Jack!" My voice was high-pitched. "I received a reply from the email address I told you about. It said they were watching me. What do I do?"

"Call Bryan. He will instruct you."

Bryan returned my call a little before five. "Julia, it's a scare tactic. Probably in the next email, they will ask for money. Forward all the emails to me. We may need them in the future. Do you know for sure someone is stalking you? I can assign you an undercover agent if you think you are in danger."

"No. I don't feel threatened, but it's eerie."

"Stay in touch and if you change your mind about an agent let me know." There was concern in Bryan's voice.

I stewed for an hour and paced around the house before I called Eli. "Can you meet me on The Rooftop at the Vendue in an hour?"

Eli laughed. "Julia, I know your voice by now. You sound stressed what's wrong?"

"Can you meet me?" I yelled.

"Yes. I'll see you around six-thirty."

I ordered a coconut guava margarita and an appetizer of fish tacos at the bar while I waited for Eli, I watched several boats motor in and out of the Charleston Harbor, children playing at Waterfront Park, and the end of the workday traffic going home over The Arthur Ravenel Jr. Bridge, which was at a standstill. The downtown lights came to life at sunset. I jumped when Eli sat quietly down beside me. He ordered a gin and tonic and I pushed my taco plate toward him. Eli kept brushing my hair away from my face but the summer breeze kept being insistent.

"Julia, what's going on."

"Several weeks ago, my mail was scattered all over my front yard and in my mailbox was a small red envelope with an email address inside. I replied to the email and told Jack about it. There were no threats so there wasn't anything that anyone could do. Today the email said they knew that I had talked to the FBI and they were watching me. I called Bryan who offered me a bodyguard but I refused, but I have felt someone has been watching me for weeks."

Eli blurted out. "Why didn't you tell me? I--"

I interrupted him. "Jack knows about the envelope and I asked him if I should tell Bryan. He said there was nothing to tell. I'm not scared but I don't want people stalking me. In all my thirty-something years, I've never been watched or followed by anyone I didn't know."

We stayed at the restaurant until closing. I didn't want to go home.

Eli reached for my hand. "You shouldn't be alone at night. I'll stay with you."

"Let Dexter stay with me."

Before I crawled into bed, I tried to call Kevin. I hadn't talked to him in over a month. His phone sent me to his voicemail, which to my surprise answered, mailbox full.

"Morning, Sis." Kevin was cheerful on the other end. "I saw I had a missed call from you last night. What's going on?"

Using my goading tone. "I should be asking you that. It's not like you to have a full voicemail."

"I've been busy." His voice was childlike.

"Okay, Kevin, out with it. Where are you and what have you been doing?"

A pause followed which told me he was contemplating how to answer. Kevin enforced his business voice. "I took on a new client."

The way Kevin said it bothered me. I didn't want to press him. We had no secrets, but this was not like my brother.

Kevin laughed. "Sis, Katherine Zenfield, and I have been communicating since the Impressionist Award. I took on a new client in New York City to be able to spend time with her. She has also been to Hilton Head several times. We are testing the waters."

"Kevin, I must say you couldn't have surprised me more. What happened to my bachelor brother? However, I did see the spark between the two of you last year. How serious are you two?"

"Katherine is divorced. She said she would never marry again. You've heard those exact words from me." I heard the smile in his voice.

Then his voice changed along with the subject. "What have you heard about Adam's death."

"Nothing, at the moment. Bryan has several teams working on different angles with Adam's case."

I didn't want Kevin to worry so I said nothing about Adam being murdered or about the email address that I found in my mailbox. "Kevin, have fun and keep me in the loop."

I stared at the black screen on my phone, then smiled knowing my brother was happy.

Before the New York trip, we talked every day or at least every other day. But since our return, I was doing good, to hear from him every two weeks, and it had been almost a year since I had seen him.

Around noon, I answered the doorbell never expecting to see Kevin. "What are you doing here? Why didn't you tell me last night you were coming?" The shock had worn off. "Come in."

"I wanted to see you and I have lots to tell you." Without taking a breath he continued. "You know Katherine and I have been seeing one another since you accepted Adam's Impressionist Award. I've been traveling back and forth to New York from Hilton Head and I've taken on more clients in New York. I rented an office in a law firm and I passed the New York Bar. Katherine has also been traveling back and forth to Hilton Head. She tried to find a job with the State of South Carolina but that has not panned out. I'm going to move to New York"

I walked toward the kitchen. "Have you had lunch?"

"No."

He pulled me to the sofa.

"I had no idea you two were this involved. This relationship sounds serious. Tell me all about her and don't leave out any details. Are you hungry? How does a hot ham and cheese sound?"

"Great, and iced tea." He stood and pulled me to my feet.

He took a seat on one of the bar stools. "I've asked Katherine to marry me." Kevin's smile covered his face and his eyes twinkled.

I fixed our sandwiches and placed his in front of him and gave him a wink. "Are you sure about this?"

"Yes, very. We want a small ceremony. Our guest list is you and Eli. I was wondering if we could have the ceremony at the water's edge behind your cottage in Folly Beach."

"You could, but you knew that Hurricane Sharon destroyed the cottage. I haven't built it back."

His smile turned into a frown. "Okay, it was a thought. We'll find a place in Hilton Head."

I placed my hand, on top of his. "Have you set a date?"

"No. I wanted to talk to you first." The lines on his face grew deeper.

"I tried to give the lot to Eli, but he won't accept it. He's renting a condo close to here. I hate for him to pay rent when I could build a nice cottage and he could live at the beach. I still have a hard time accepting that Adam left everything to me. The beach was my calming place and I've given a lot of thought to rebuilding it. Let me talk to a contractor. If you and Katherine want to wait, you can get married there."

He laughed. "We aren't rushing to the alter today."

"I know but with all the construction still going on after the hurricane it could be at least a year or more before it will be finished."

We talked for a couple more hours before Kevin informed me, he had a six o'clock flight.

After he left, I called a contractor.

The next morning my phone woke me. "Hello."

Jack started talking ninety miles an hour. "Julia, I have a meeting with Bryan at eleven today. He said it was a consultation meeting. I don't know what that is about but I'll call you this afternoon with an update. Have you had anything unusual happen since you returned home?"

"No. Nothing. Everything has been normal. Did Bryan ask for me?"

Jack answered. "No."

At 5:00 p.m. Jack rang my doorbell. "Julia, we need to talk."

Grinning not sure if I should smile or be apprehensive. "Come in. Can I get you something to drink—tea, coffee, water, beer?"

"Not now maybe something later."

Jack sat in the oversized chair next to the bay window and I sat on the sofa across from him.

Jack's forehead became wrinkled when he talked. "Bryan said he was going to bring in an outside consulting firm as a subcontractor on Adam's case. They have used them before in old cases and when they needed to be discreet. Guarding Resolutions is a worldwide security company. They provide security for companies and individuals, and they investigate crimes for insurance companies. The FBI and the CIA have subcontracted with them in the past. They work worldwide. Bryan said the FBI had a full caseload and couldn't give Adam's case their undivided attention. He was certain Adam was on someone's hit list. Rebecca Miles is the owner of the security firm. She worked on homicide cases for the FBI for over ten years. Do you or did you know her?"

"No. Her name isn't familiar. She must've started after I left or worked in another territory. Remember I worked in the Charleston office. I don't know what territory she was assigned to cover."

Jack smiled. "She knew Adam. Bryan has met her. He thinks highly of her and her work."

I shook my head. "Why would someone leave the FBI and still do the same work in the private sector?"

"Julia, you know the government. There's a lot of politics that happen behind the scenes. Plus, she can make a lot more money with Guarding Resolutions. Bryan said she has solved a lot of old murder cases, some as far back as twenty years. Rebecca has charged through this dominated man's world like a bull. She's disliked by a lot of her colleagues but she gets the job done. She doesn't sidestep away from anything. And one of the best in her line of work. She has compiled a database of contract killers that is more extensive than the FBI's. Her resources are mostly snitches and informants. She believes in them, the odds are high that their information is accurate, and contract killers rarely get caught by the police."

"Jack, do you think she will want to talk to me?"

"I don't know, maybe. I have told you what Bryan told me. Now we wait and see what happens."

Jack and I were walking to the front door when the doorbell rang. Eli's name appeared on my phone. I opened the door. "Eli, why are calling and ringing the doorbell at the same time?"

"I drove by and saw Uncle Jack's car."

"Come in. Would you like a beer?" After I finished my Old Fashioned, we headed to Hyman's Seafood on Meeting Street for dinner. Later we sat in my living room and talked about all the scenarios involving Adam. I had another Old Fashioned, and Eli and Jack had a couple more beers. Eli went back to his apartment and Jack spent the night in my guest room.

Chapter 17

My phone woke me at seven. My body was slow-moving which reminded me that I shouldn't have had that second Old Fashioned last night.

"Ms. Stone, this is Steve, the contractor. Can you meet me at your Folly Beach property around ten?"

I jumped out of bed, and on the way to the shower, yelled for Jack to get up. After my shower, I called Eli. By eight-forty-five the three of us had finished breakfast. Goodbyes were said to Jack and he was on his way back to Greenville. Eli and I were on the road headed to Folly Beach. The big oak trees that once stood lining the main road into Folly were piled close to the side of the road. The island still looked like the hurricane had hit last week—buildings were in shambles, debris that needed to be hauled away was piled everywhere, fences looked like they needed to be mended and others needed to be replaced. The die-hards that had stayed looked weary. A lot of houses still had broken windows and others were abandoned and the crumbling facades on some houses were too damaged to repair. The FEMA trailers were still there but the tents had been removed. Folly Beach continued to look like a war zone.

Eli stopped in front of what was now my vacant lot. We arrived at the lot at nine-forty and Steve was on his third page of notes.

I stretched my hand forward. "I'm Julia. Nice meeting you Steve."

He smiled and pointed south. "Julia, there is nothing here to be salvaged. What studs are left are split and weather-beaten and as old as the concrete slab is I would suggest we start from the ground up."

I put my hands on my hips and gazed out over the water. "I agree. I know I have a postage-size lot but can I get a two-bedroom two-bath, kitchen, eating area, and living room on it? I would like to have the living area and kitchen all open and the bedrooms and baths to themselves."

Steve looked up from his notebook. "Let me check with the city and see what the lot restrictions are. I think you can. Do you have plans or do you want me to furnish them?"

"I need you to supply them."

He smiled. "It'll take me a couple of weeks." He climbed into his truck and leaned out the window. "I'll be back in touch."

After Steve left, Eli opened the car door and Dexter bolted toward the water. I ran after him to the water's edge but Dexter had sprinted almost out of sight. Eli spread a towel on the sand and we sat watching the waves drift to and fro until Dexter decided to come back and join us. It was like old times at the beach.

"Eli, after Kevin and Katherine's wedding I want you to live here. I don't want the new house to be vacant and I don't want you to have to keep paying rent."

"Julia, this is your cottage. I want you to live here or to be able to come and go whenever you want."

"Eli, my home is in Charleston. I have no desire to live at the beach full-time. I'll come and visit and if you need to go to Charleston you can stay in my guest room. Hopefully, the situation with Adam will be resolved and we both can have a normal life again."

A month later I had approved Steve's plans and the cottage construction had begun. By April, I had chosen all the colors, cabinets, appliances, countertops, and tiles. I was pushing for Kevin and Katherine to have a June wedding, but due to the building materials shortage from all the rebuilding and Steve's crews being spread thin. He said he would try but he couldn't guarantee a June wedding this year.

"Kevin, the contractor is running behind. Let's be realistic it's time that you and Katherine should find another venue."

"Sis, let me talk to Katherine. I want the wedding at the cottage."

Steve pulled a miracle and in June, Kevin and Katherine were married at the cottage. Katherine was beautiful in her off-white sundress and bare feet. A halo of white daisies with pink dianthus intertwined through her hair. Kevin reminded me of a wealthy beach bum with his navy-blue shorts and printed tropical shirt and bare feet. After the ceremony, the four of us headed over to St. James Gate Irish Pub. Eli and I stayed a couple of hours before leaving the honeymooners alone in the cottage.

The week of July the fourth, Eli insisted that I come and stay the weekend with him at Folly Beach. Eli had gotten permission from the city to build a small bonfire on the beach behind the cottage. We sat with our feet in the Atlantic watching the fireworks and listening to music from the local bars. After most of the crowd had dispersed, we went to The Crab Shack for a couple of lobster rolls and boiled shrimp.

The next morning at breakfast Eli laughed. "You forgot your sunscreen yesterday"

I looked in the mirror and saw my red face from yesterday's sun and wind.

Chapter 18

Eight months had passed and I hadn't heard anything about Adam's case until Bryan Wilson's ID showed on my cell.

"Julia, this is a quick update. Adam's case has been scrutinized. Bits and pieces have shown foul play but no concrete evidence. A Rebecca Miles will be calling you."

Two months after my conversation with Bryan, my phone rang with an unknown caller. I debated whether to answer it or to let it go to voicemail. On the sixth ring, I said, "Hello."

The female voice replied. "Is this Julia Stone? I'm Rebecca Miles from Guarding Resolutions."

I cut her off and answered. "Yes. I've been expecting your call. How are you?"

"I'm fine. Thank you. Ms. Stone, Dr. Wilson said I should give you an update but I also have some questions."

"Please, call me Julia."

Rebecca's voice turned into a matter-of-fact tone. "I've been informed that you are the beneficiary of Adam Robinson's estate and that you are an ex-FBI agent. Is that correct?"

I cleared my throat. "Yes."

Rebecca continued. "The CIA didn't find anything unusual on Adam's work computer. They gave it to the FBI and now the FBI has given it to me. My specialists were able to decode some of the embedded files. Financial statements and some offshore deposits were found, but I don't know yet where these originated, or to whom they belong. I don't know if Adam discovered this information on his own or if there was a whistleblower. This information can be one of our best leads. The FBI has been pressuring the IRS to finish its investigation into the tax returns of Wesley Campbell, who is the director of the NSA. It has been over a year and finally, the IRS findings have resulted in an indictment. According to the IRS report over two hundred thousand dollars of income wasn't reported in 2015 and 2019. Campbell could get a maximum sentence of 30 years in prison for embezzlement, but the FBI wants a murder indictment. There is evidence that indicates Wesley was involved in Adam Robinson's murder. I also understand Adam left you a safe deposit box. Do you still have the contents?"

I closed my eyes tightly remembering Adam's letters. "Yes."

Rebecca's voice was emphatic "I would like to see them. Is that possible? There might be some hidden information in them that you wouldn't have picked up on."

I whispered. "They were love letters to me."

Rebecca's voice was adamant. "Can I see them, please? We could meet at a quiet public place. Will you meet me tomorrow at the Charleston County Public Library?"

"Yes, when? Can Eli, Adam's brother, come with me?"

"For this meeting, I prefer it be the two of us."

I agreed to her request.

Late the next afternoon, I stepped out of the elevator on the second floor of the Charleston library. A woman in a navy blue suit that was standing in the doorway of the editorial room motioned me to her. Rebecca, wasn't anything like I had pictured. She was thin, mid-fifties with shoulder-length blond and grey-streaked hair.

After the pleasantries, Rebecca started her conversation. "Julia, everything has been moving forward on Adam's case. Some months, information moves quicker than others. You know I've been assigned to look further into his murder. It wasn't an accident. We know there was a reason he was killed. There are still lots of missing pieces but I'm going to keep working until I have a solution. I have a list of thirty-two people who work in DC offices and the NSA office, and I have the FBI's list that they compiled, but I don't know yet who might be a suspect. I'm still waiting for the CIA's list."

I glanced at the list and gasped. Anger welled inside me.

"Julia is something wrong?"

My mouth became dry. "Why is Eli's name on the list? He's Adam's brother. Eli wouldn't harm Adam."

Rebecca shifted to the front of her chair. "My understanding is you knew Adam, did you know Eli, as well?"

I felt my hands twisting my skirt. "No, I met Eli after I was named beneficiary to Adam's estate."

"Do you think Eli knew you were the beneficiary?"

I sat up straight in my chair and looked her in the eye. "No! No one knew but Adam's Uncle Jack. It was confidential between Adam and Jack and he told Eli after I found out. Adam and Eli were very close. Adam asked Eli to go with him to the cabin to tell him he might be in trouble. Adam had found something that he thought might put him in danger. He wanted Eli to be aware." I was almost yelling. "Eli wouldn't even imagine hurting anyone."

"Julia, I didn't mean to upset you, but we look at everyone, everything, and every angle. You know that. Can I see the letters?"

After Rebecca read a few letters, she asked. "Can I take these with me? I promise I'll keep them safe and get them back to you."

Reluctantly, I nodded yes.

Rebecca opened her briefcase and started to put them in. When I noticed an envelope in the stack that I hadn't seen before. I grabbed it. When I opened the envelope, a ring fell into my palm. I froze staring at the circle that was glistening at me.

My Dear Julia,

I never knew how joyous life could be until I met you. My heart skipped a beat when I saw you enter my booth. I had never felt anything like that before. You are my inspiration to paint non-stop. I cannot hide my smiles or my feelings. All I can think about is your warmness and my love for you. I pray you will keep my ring until I can officially place it on your wedding finger.
I will love you to the end of time.
Adam

Tears filled my eyes. Rebecca reached for the letter. I pulled away and tucked it into my purse. Rebecca withdrew her hand.

"Julia, I know this is hard for you but please let me and my team do our job. We're working for Adam's justice."

With tears running down my face, I walked away from Rebecca.

Arriving home, I never imagined being involved in a murder investigation and found myself frustrated with all the twists, turns, unclear information, and unknown facts surrounding Adam's death.

Eli was in my kitchen cooking lobster, shrimp, Dungeness crabs, and scallops.

"Eli, what are you doing? There's enough food here to feed the entire block."

Eli handed me a glass of Pacific Rim Riesling. "After you met with Rebecca today, you needed to come home to a special dinner. What did she have to say?"

I gave him a brief synopsis of the day including the new letter from Adam, but I

didn't tell him his name was on Rebecca's checklist.

Another four months passed before I heard from Bryan again.

"Julia, can you be in my Greenville office in the morning at ten? I've asked Jack and Eli to be there too.?"

The next morning at six-fifteen, Eli and I were on our way to Greenville.

Jack, Eli, and I were seated in front of Bryan and Rebecca.

Rebecca said. "I've contracted with a retired FBI agent who was a demolition specialist in the military. He now works undercover and gathers information from contract killers. He has an informant who owed him a favor. All the information we have to date is correct. Let's do some recapping." Rebecca looked at Eli. "We know there wasn't a faulty water heater at the cabin. Eli, did anyone know you and Adam were going to the cabin that day? Do you know what Adam wanted to talk to you about?"

Eli placed the palm of his hand on the table. "Not that I remember. On the way, Adam and I laughed and talked about our childhood and the pranks we played on one another growing up. Adam didn't want to talk about why he wanted to go to the cabin until we got there."

Rebecca continued. "The front door explosive charge was set several weeks before you and Adam arrived. The three CIA officers that were posing as insurance adjusters were murdered and so was Adam but we still don't know why and all this is connected yet. I've turned this information over to the FBI and the CIA. The next step is to find out who set the explosion at the cabin and why. Julia, you will be working with me."

Bryan smiled. "I was going to tell you this morning that you have been officially assigned to Adam's case."

Eli asked. "Why are you working with informants that are contract killers?"

Rebecca replied. "To get what you want or need sometimes there are tradeoffs, he got what he wanted from the informant and the informant got a new identity."

Eli stood and walked around to the back of his chair, gripping it with both hands until his knuckles turned white. "Rebecca, how trustworthy are all these informants that you're using?"

She gave a slight smile. "Money talks. We work in the shadows. Sometimes that is the only way we can solve a case. We don't have the guidelines that the FBI works under and the CIA has its own agenda."

I crossed my arms over my chest. "Rebecca, you said there wasn't anything on Adam's computer at the NSA, and the passcodes you tried only let you access the first layer of information. Do you know there's is a business in Texas that can break any code and hack any computer? I've used them before and had very good luck with them."

"Yes, that is where I sent Adam's computer and I have also sent another computer from the NSA office there. Wesley is doing illegal business and using the NSA as a front. We'll get him, be patient."

Eli asked. "What's the NSA's job?"

Rebecca replied. "The National Security Agency is an intelligence agency within the Department of Defense. NSA does global monitoring, collects, and processes information for foreign and domestic intelligence. It generates thousands of intelligence reports and intercepts communications from all over the world. They are responsible for Signal Intelligence, which tracks image signals from outer space and foreign countries. We have NSA offices in all Army headquarters bases around the world. They also control many military secrets and work with NATO.

Bryan cut in. "NSA has been having leadership problems. New directors were being appointed like a revolving door. Wesley Campbell has lasted longer than any of the directors. No one thought anything about Campbell firing his chief financial officer. But now I'm not so sure that the financial officer didn't approach Campbell about what he was doing. Eli, do you remember when Adam was shot on assignment?"

Eli nodded his head yes.

Bryan continued. "While he was recuperating from his gunshot wounds, the CIA moved him into the NSA in a ploy to get closer to

Campbell. Adam's master's degree in finance and his G-7 pay grade insured that he would be moved into the chief financial position."

Rebecca stood up. "Adam and I worked on several cases together when I was at the FBI. He was an expert in every job he was assigned to."

I listened and sat frozen, without emotion, nor a blink, hearing Rebecca talk about Adam. My bottom lip started to quiver and my cheeks became tear-streaked. I felt Eli's hand on my shoulder. I gripped his forearm. I know he felt my fingernails dig into his flesh.

Rebecca looked at me. "Julia, I hear you think you're being watched. As a precaution, I'm going to have a guard shadow you for a while. You won't know our man is there."

I couldn't say no to her and quietly acquiesced.

After Bryan and Rebecca politely refused Jack's lunch offer. Eli and I said yes and had a quick sandwich at Stephanie's Coffee Shop. Then Eli and I said our goodbyes to him and headed back to Charleston.

The next morning, I stumbled into the kitchen. Dexter was lapping away, his floppy ears were in his water dish, and of course, right afterward he had to shake his head sending water all over the floor and the lower cabinets.

"Dexter, stop!" He gave a soft woof and raced to the front door.

"Okay, okay, let me put on my shoes and grab a jacket."

I pushed the screen door open and saw a bright red envelope poked halfway under the doormat. My address was printed in big black block letters in the middle of the envelope and there was no return address. I picked it up and put it in my jacket pocket. I didn't want to be too obvious with my surprised look. I glanced around my yard and my neighbor's but I didn't see anyone or anything that looked suspicious. I coaxed Dexter to hurry to do his business and quit sniffing around. Back inside I opened the envelope, the words, "BACK OFF" were in block form on a small piece of white paper. I called Rebecca immediately.

The next day a man in blue jeans and a tan tee shirt knocked on my door. "Good afternoon, Ms. Stone. I'm Hector. I work for Rebecca. I'm staying in the house next door. If you need anything or are aware of something unusual please let me know immediately. May I see your phone? I'm going to put an App on it and all you need to do is tap it.

It'll buzz me and I can be here in seconds. Do you have any questions?"

"No, I thought I was safe and I didn't need you to watch over me, but now I'm not so sure. Thank you for being here."

"Ms. Stone, I assure you this will all be over soon."

"Thank you, Hector."

Hector being next door gave me comfort but it was still unsettling to think that someone was tailing me. I didn't tell Eli. He would have insisted on moving in with me.

Chapter 19

Spring break was in full swing on Folly Beach. Eli invited me to come to the beach for the weekend. When Dexter and I arrived, Dexter ran straight to the water. The FEMA trailers were gone and so were the downed trees and the debris. The hotels and a couple of B&Bs were open but only a few restaurants due to the owners moving inland.

One hotel had advertised a barbecue and two bands, Country and Hype, and had partitioned Folly Beach to close off the east end of Ashley Avenue for a stage. The locals needed some fun and the college students would party without a reason. Folly Beach looked to be coming back to life.

At midnight the partiers were still going strong. I tugged on Eli's arm. "This is great. It's good to be back at the beach. It's nice to be able to come to the beach whenever you want."

Eli put his hand on the small of my back and yawned. "Are you ready to go join Dexter? He went home at nine."

"All right, old man, we can leave."

At eight the next morning, Eli knocked on my door. "It's too early. Go away."

"I'll leave your cup of coffee on the dresser."

The mirror showed my puffy red eyes. I dressed, took my coffee, and sat next to Eli at the kitchen counter. "To live here full time isn't for me, but it's fun to come and enjoy the ocean whenever I want. The sunsets are beautiful and the sunset last night looked like Adam had painted it."

"I think Dexter has missed the beach too. He left early this morning and hasn't returned." Eli cleared his throat. "Julia, can we talk about us? You're fun and full of life, there's an extraordinary sense of peace when I'm with you. Do you feel the same way about me?"

I sat silent and still.

The knock at the front door made us both jump. Eli almost turned his plate of eggs and bacon over. My voice was curt. "What are you doing here?" I'm sorry. I didn't mean to snap. You caught us by surprise."

Rebecca rushed in and started her conversation without saying hello. "Julia, you know that we have had you under surveillance. Whoever has been watching you has followed you here." My body stiffened. Rebecca continued. "I have two FBI agents with me. This is Agent Caldwell. Hector is checked in at the B&B. We want to draw the person or people out."

"How?"

A scowl covered Rebeca's face. "This is a long shot but we need to see who is watching you and why. All you have to do is walk in a circle. We're watching your every move. Go to the hotel where the party was last night cut across the parking lot to the beach and walk back here. Stop and look up and down the beach as if you are looking for Dexter. You can even call his name. Take your time. An agent will be in the parking lot and Agent Caldwell and Hector will be on the beach. I want you to be noticed. Wear a swimsuit and cover-up. Are you game?"

"I guess." This wasn't my choice and the whole idea didn't appeal to me. "Can Eli go with me?"

"No. We'll all be close by and we're watching you from every angle." Rebecca sighed. "Don't ignore anyone, but don't be too quick to start a conversation either."

Mid-morning, I put on my sunglasses, adjusted my sun hat, wrapped a bright yellow, red, green, and blue beach towel around my waist, and walked out the ocean door around to the front of the house, then slowly headed towards the hotel. In the hotel parking lot, I made a sharp right turn towards the beach and stood at the water's edge. Looking out over the Atlantic was always peaceful and beautiful to me. For a few seconds, my mind was lost in the past with the memories of Adam. Then my brain made me aware of the presence of Eli who was watching me from his position on the beach. Several men walked past me giving me a stare or a smile, one tried to engage in a conversation but I showed no interest. A couple of younger he-men lathered in suntan oil, large biceps, and draped in gold chains attempted to goad me into some small talk. I acknowledged them with a nod and a hello but didn't give them the incentive to carry on a conversation.

The pang in the pit of my stomach kept me aware of Adam's death. Being with Eli and back in Charleston made me think the emptiness would be filled, but it hadn't. Eli was a trusted friend. He wanted more but that wasn't going to happen.

After an hour and a half, no one approached me. Dexter came running up the beach with his tail wagging and his ears flopping and stopped at my side. We ran into the water through the waves and past the breakers. About twenty minutes later, we returned to the cottage.

Rebecca said, "No luck."

"No. It was like trolling for men. Rebecca, there should be a better way. Why do you think they're watching me? I haven't been put on any assignments that would raise anyone's eyebrows."

She paced back and forth in the great room. "Well, you aren't trolling. We're only looking for one person. Let's wait until this afternoon and try again. We know you're being watched. A wild guess is they know you had a connection to Adam and we don't know what Adam found out. They may think you do."

I pointed out over the water. "Did you see the trawler out there offshore? He looks like he's trolling back and forth in the same place. He's moving too fast to be fishing. Maybe there's a connection to that boat."

Late afternoon I went back down the beach, laid a towel out on the sand, and waited. The sky turned from crimson to pink to purple and finally to a deep blue. An older man walked past me heading east pulling his dog behind him. He looked like he was trying to appear casual but his face showed he was looking for something or someone. The dog kept trying to go in a different direction, but he kept pulling his leash dictating where the dog would go. A few feet past where I was sitting, he turned and unleashed the dog, the dog ran to me. The man followed and stopped by mt side. He had a scraggly beard and a floppy hat that looked to be too big for his head. A gust of wind blew taking his hat down the beach. He had salt and pepper hair, (more salt than pepper though) dirty shorts, and flip-flops, that was too small for his feet. I took the bait and rubbed the dog's ears. The dog lay down next to my feet. The man smiled and looked up and down the beach but didn't make the dog move. "Nice evening." Then he tipped his hat, leashed his dog, and continued down the beach.

I was glad the FBI was watching me. The man had raised my suspicions. Immediately after the man walked away, a woman walked toward me with three dogs. Her bright pink and turquoise, big-brimmed hat, was flopping in the sea breeze. She stopped smiled and handed me a piece of paper without saying a word. Then she continued walking east down the beach.

The sun looked like it was resting on top of the water for a few minutes before it quickly disappeared. Back home Eli looked relieved. Rebecca said, "Julia, any luck?"

"Yes. Here's the note the woman gave me."

"Good. Agent Caldwell is with the man who stopped with his dog and another agent is with the woman who gave you the note"

I showered and sat on the sofa with my feet tucked under me and a blanket wrapped around me. Eli came and plopped down next to me. His face showed relief and the wrinkles around his mouth and forehead lightened. Both Eli and Rebecca were waiting for me to speak.

"The man started his conversation by saying he had been alone for twenty-five years, rather than asking me if I was alone. He wants me to go with him and some friends on a boat tomorrow. "I let him think maybe but didn't give him a definite answer."

Rebecca held up the small paper. "The man and woman were working together. I think she was used as a backup person if he failed. It gives the name of the boat *"Sea Witch"* and where it's moored, Mariner's Cay Marina. Be at the boat at 11:00 a.m. and it will return at 2:00 p.m."

Eli jumped up. "No! You're not going!"

Agent Caldwell opened the front door. Before anyone could say anything, he said. "I followed the man and his dog to a weekly rate motel." A man was waiting for him in the parking lot. He showed Rebecca and me the picture on his phone.

"I know this man. The FBI sent several of us out on a stakeout once." My voice had a sharp tone. "He's full of disguises, but the black ink skull and crossbones and dagger through the red heart is a tattoo that he can't change. I've had experience with bad men, but this one has no conscience."

Agent Caldwell reached for his phone. "I'll keep an eye on him tonight."

The next morning Rebecca joined me at my kitchen counter for coffee. "Julia, thank you for doing the job for us yesterday. I don't want you involved anymore. I know you're capable, you've helped us out. We'll handle it from here. You're not going on the boat today. Bryan's decision."

I took a sip of coffee. "What about the woman?"

"She's a local. She didn't know anything other than she was paid to give you the note."

"Can I go back to Charleston today?"

She smiled. "Yes. The FBI will follow the boat and I'm going back to my office."

My goodbye was short. Eli's was subdued.

I dialed the radio to an easy-listening station and pulled onto Highway 171. Three miles from Folly I saw an old rusted green pickup truck stopped in the middle of my lane. I tried to slam on the brakes but my car didn't respond. I gripped the wheel so tightly that my fingers hurt trying to keep all four tires on the pavement. I hit the brake hard again but the car didn't slow down. I stomped the emergency brake making the car skid but it still didn't stop me from hearing metal scraping and crunching as I slammed into the back of the truck sideways. I looked in my rearview mirror to see if any cars were going to ram into me. Sitting sideways I couldn't see anything but woods with tall trees. I looked in my side mirror. No cars, but a tsunami of SUV vehicles were coming up behind me. One SUV had stopped about twenty-five feet behind me and two men jumped from the vehicle. Bullets from an automatic weapon ricocheted off the pick-up truck and were pelting my windshield, glass was shattering and had scattered in all directions. There wasn't a window left in my car. I scrunched my body into a fetal ball on the seat telling myself not to panic. I pressed the heel of my palms against my eyes. Another rapid succession of heavy gunfire started again. The continuous stream of bullets hitting the metal car roof was deafening. I knew I was trapped. My stomach was in one big knot, my mouth was dry, and I couldn't swallow. The thought that I might not get out of my car alive raced through my mind. In FBI training we were taught that panic caused bad decisions and bad decisions made for bad outcomes that could be fatal. Nevertheless, my panic button was still on high. My stomach and heartbeat pulsed together. It was best for me not to think about what was happening now. I willed myself to survive. I directed my thoughts away from the present and concentrated on the past.

Adam—Thoughts of his paintings and the week we spent together brought me peace. I could still hear his laugh and see his bottom lip curl upward. I closed my eyes tighter and remembered his soft lips on mine and his arms engulfing my body holding me close. I could hear his voice telling me I was going to survive. I tried to imagine how different my life would have been if I had chosen Adam instead of Robert and maybe I wouldn't be in this situation now if Adam was alive.

Eli—Adam's older brother. Every time we are together, there's a reminder of Adam. I won't allow myself to fall in love with him. He has alluded to wanting our relationship to move forward but there is a gnawing inside that holds me back. Sometimes I find myself forgetting he's not Adam. His mannerisms, laughing, and walking are exactly like Adam's. He even curls his lip the same.

Kevin—my brother, married at forty, moved his law practice to New York City and loves the big city. He surprised me, I didn't think he would ever leave Hilton Head. I miss him but we have our own lives. Since his marriage, we are not as close as were once were, but he would insist on my moving to New York if he knew bullets were flying around me.

The silence from the ceased firing jolted me back to the present. I heard brakes squealing and voices in the distance making me concentrate on my predicament at hand. The voices grew louder. I peered out through the broken glass on the driver's side hoping to see one of the FBI's agents from the beach but instead, there were three men all dressed in black—shirts, pants, jackets, and caps—headed towards my bullet-ridden car. Behind me, the passenger door opened.

I screamed. "Don't shoot." My body stiffened and an earthquake shiver rolled thru my body. A hand brushed across my hair. My face was buried in my arm and hot tears burn my eyes.

"Julia, are you hurt?" Incredible relief entered my body when I heard Hector's voice.

"I'm okay. Where's Dexter? Who was shooting and why?"

He reached for my hand to help me out of the car. "Dexter is in my pick-up truck. Rebecca called in extra forces she was uneasy about who was watching you at the beach. They were following the cars behind you but none of us was aware that the old pickup truck was involved. None of us expected an ambush. With all our surveillance, this should have never happened. They have one person in custody, one won't live to see another day, but four have fled. Two FBI men are in pursuit of them now."

I heard more voices, I turned to see news crews running towards me, and more news vans and crews were flocking in from the north and east. There were more news reporters than FBI agents. Cameras were pointed at me from all directions. Agent Caldwell and two other men in black intercepted the local sheriff before he reached me. After a few words, the sheriff retreated and disbanded the news reporters.

Agent Caldwell "What was that all about?"

"Ms. Stone, we don't want any publicity about this incident. All of us are working undercover, we don't need the local police and we don't want the incident on the six o'clock news or them harassing you."

Hector called a tow truck for my car. Then guided me to his pickup truck. "I'll take you home."

The adrenaline rush was over and I was exhausted. I slept the twenty-five minutes back to Charleston.

Chapter 20

I woke the next morning in a fog, feeling very disturbed. My dream was more of a thriller mystery movie trying to solve Adam's murder. Dexter barked bringing me back to reality. He was in his favorite spot at the bay window watching the squirrels chase one another up and down a tree. I wasn't ready to dress and take him for a walk. I opened the back door and called him. "You can play in the backyard for a while."

I sat in my comfy chair, drinking my coffee, and thinking that going to the art exhibit in the park that Saturday should have never happened. My life would be a lot simpler now. It would have been easier to open a good book and read a good murder mystery than actually be involved in the middle of one.

Rebecca's name peered on my phone. After being at the beach with her and her FBI team I wasn't ready for a morning call. After the cordials, she said. "Julia, it's taken us a long time to decode Adam's phone notes, but we finally have. His notes were precise under the headings of:

Offshore deposits

Scamming money

Selling information to foreign intelligence agencies

No names of buyers at this point

Adam had reported the offshore deposits to the CIA and he also reported that several NSA security employees were aware of sensitive information was being transferred to an unknown source. They were trying to determine what and where the information was being sent. The FBI confiscated a computer from Wesley Campbell's office and sent it to their decoding department. I also know that the three insurance adjusters were working undercover for the CIA." Rebecca cleared her throat. "Their cause of death was listed under unusual circumstances. Campbell is more involved than we first thought. I've called my contacts at MI-6 to help find out who he was selling military and other confidential information to in Europe. Some foreign agencies don't always pay in money they give precious gifts. Campbell was connected to an auction house. I think he used them to turn the gift items into money. After Adam's death, the Department of Defense placed a retired CEO of an investment banking firm to fill Adam's position at the NSA. The FBI thinks he fell in with Wesley and the two of them were selling all kinds of confidential and military information and scamming the money together. There may be others even higher up than Campbell who is also involved."

I paced around the room.

Rebecca's voice had become tense but controlled. "A gunman with an AK-47 has killed three people entering the NSA building this morning. The shooter disappeared in all the chaos. We don't know who he is or where he's going to strike next and until I have more information, I'm taking all precautions to keep you safe. The email and note you received have me concerned. Julia, pack a small overnight bag. I'm sending Hector to pick you up. He'll be there in about thirty minutes. I'm moving you to The Francis Marion Hotel on King Street for a few days."

The next morning, I couldn't get the coffee maker in my hotel room to work. I threw on a pair of leggings and a sweatshirt and headed down to the lobby cafe. I stepped into the elevator, but before the doors completely closed a hand reached in. Two men and a woman entered. I stood close to the buttons and the door. No one said a word. The doors opened into the lobby. The woman wrapped her arm right around my waist like we were schoolmates. I felt a hard cold object dig into my ribcage.

The woman whispered. "Julia, don't make a sound and continue walking out the front door."

I glanced around the lobby to see a familiar face but there wasn't one. I smiled at the desk clerk, the lobby janitor, and the bell captain, but I didn't make eye contact with them. The doorman raised an eyebrow as we exited the building but he didn't say a word.

I was escorted to the north side of the hotel where a black SUV was parked in the loading zone. A man dressed in a dark blue jacket entered the back seat first, the woman gave me a slight shove into the back seat, then retracted the gun when she sat next to me. The driver closed the door, which sounded heavily armored. Then he slid in behind the steering wheel.

"Bulletproof?" I murmured.

The man next to me put a black hood over my head. I squeezed my eyes shut, feeling my erratic heartbeat, and tried to search my brain to remember what Quantico had taught us when we were caught in unknown dangerous situations. Remember deep breathing, holding my breath for three seconds, and repeating the process, squeezing my muscles and then letting them relax, and repeat the process. Remember happy places to go to block out the current situation. I was brought back to the present when silence filled the SUV. The vehicle stopped and the woman removed the hood. From what I could tell it was a short ride. We were in a row of storage warehouses with no names or numbers. The woman tapped the code buttons and the wrought iron gates opened. At the next set of gates, the driver punched numbers into a keypad. Outside the rusted iron door all kinds of debris were scattered, broken beer bottles, empty shotgun shells, fast-food wrappers, and empty tin cans that had bullet holes in them. The man that was seated next to me pulled a remote from his pocket and pointed it at the door. I heard the tumblers click and the door opened into a climate-controlled unit. All the windows were covered with blackout paint. The driver flipped on the lights. I slowly scanned the inside. All kinds of guns, whips, and chains hung on the walls. A small desk and a lamp were against the back wall. All my senses went on high alert. I didn't know if I was going to need to fight or try to flee.

I blurted out. "Are you going to kill me? Who are you? Why did you kidnap me?" My throat was dry. My words came out fast and strong.

The man who had been in the back seat with me pushed me into a straight-back chair. "I know your background and that you had a connection to Adam Robinson and Robinson had a connection to Wesley Campbell. I want to know what the FBI has told you about Campbell?"

I released my clenched fist and looked down at the red indents my fingernails had pushed into my left hand. I tossed my head making my hair clear my eyes. "Nothing. I know Adam was killed. I'm involved to help find Adam's killer but you already know that."

The woman put both her hands on my shoulders and pushed down hard and put her face two inches from mine. The old rickety chair rocked and squeaked. The door opened and a man walked in. She backed away. His dark blue business suit was wrinkled, no tie, and his white shirt looked like he had slept in it. His face was freckled, red, and blotchy like he had spent a lot of time in the sun. He was slightly bald and his nose looked like it had been broken several times. He had a long scar down his left cheek. He sat down behind the old small wooden desk that matched the chair I was sitting in. He opened his attaché case and tossed a file folder in front of him.

In a heavy foreign accent, he said. "This is from the CIA."

My voice didn't waver. "Who are you? How do I know you're telling me the truth?"

Without answering my question, he threw another question at me. "Do you expect the CIA to contact you?"

My tone was adamant. "No. Why would they? I've been in touch with the FBI."

He cleared his throat. "You left out the part about Rebecca Miles with Guardian Resolutions."

I moved forward in my chair. The man that was standing behind me clamped my shoulder with his hand and pulled me to the back of the chair. "Look, I don't know anything about Campbell. What I know is the CIA, FBI, and Rebecca are working on Adam's case. I'm sure you know my connection to Adam and his brother Eli. I don't know anything else."

He leaned back in his chair, it creaked and rocked sideways. "You know the KGB was replaced by the FSB in 1991, and the FSB has no restrictions. You were on their radar after you showed up in Greenville?"

"No, I had no idea." My tone was controlled and confident. "I don't know anything. For some reason, Adam Robinson left his estate to me and after that, my life has been turned upside down. All I knew about him is that he was an artist. I didn't know he worked for the CIA or the FBI or any other government agency."

The man sneered. "What if we told you Adam wasn't dead."

Without thinking I blurted out, "Now who's lying? Who are you? Who do you work for?"

He chuckled. "It's your choice to believe me or not. If I were you, I wouldn't tell Rebecca about this meeting."

In a sarcastic tone, I asked. "Why not?"

He picked up the folder and nodded to the other three. He looked at me and said, "Just don't if you want Robinson to stay alive." Then walked out the door.

Less than an hour later, the SUV stopped a block away from my hotel. The woman opened my door. "Remember you don't need to say anything about this little trip to anyone. That means no one. We're watching you."

I looked in all directions as I ran up the street to the hotel entrance but the street was empty, and there was no movement in the shadows. If someone was watching they must have been on a roof or well hidden somewhere. I stood impatiently at the elevator door waiting for it to open.

For the next three days, I didn't leave my hotel room as I waited anxiously for Rebecca's all-clear call to return home.

The day after my kidnapping, Rebecca called. "Julia, the man on the beach who wanted you to go on the boat is the same person who was sending you the notes and scattering your mail. We found the evidence in his apartment along with Russian documents. There were a few bills of sale but they didn't say for what. That's all we know at this time. We don't know yet why you were targeted. The CIA took him into custody for questioning and then turned him over to the FBI. I have no proof of anyone else watching you. I'm removing Hector as your guard."

I was trapped between a rock and a hard place. This was not over and Hector didn't need to be pulled away, but I was afraid to say anything about the trip to the warehouse. Hector knocked on my hotel door as I put the last piece of clothing in my suitcase.

The eerie feeling made my skin crawl. I was uncomfortable and tried to think of a way to keep Hector. We were silent on the way to my house.

Chapter 21

I sat gawking for several minutes before yelling. "Hector, my front door is off its hinges!"

"Julia, wait in the car."

My body tensed watching Hector disappear through the front opening. Tears started streaming down my cheeks, I moved to my porch rocker and waited for Hector to surface.

He returned with an ax in his left hand. "Julia, every door in your house has been axed, and your house has been ransacked. All your kitchen knives are stabbed upright into your dining table. There are several window panes broken and your linen closet items are in the middle of the hallway. Whatever they were looking for they didn't find it."

Sitting on my sofa with my knees up to my chest, I watched the waves splash over The Battery wall while Hector called Rebecca. After a short conversation, Hector handed me his phone.

Rebecca's voice was stern. "Julia, you need to make a decision. You can go back to the hotel or you can go stay at Folly Beach. Wherever you decide Hector will be close by. I'm sorry Adam's death has involved you to this degree." Rebecca, still didn't know about the SUV trip, but I wasn't going back to the hotel. "My job is to protect you."

"I will talk to Eli and let you know my decision."

Eli answered on the first ring. "Would you like to go with me to Folly Beach for a week?"

I heard the laughter in Eli's voice when he answered. "Yes, of course. I'll meet you there."

Steve, my contractor who rebuilt my cottage after Hurricane Sharon, arrived a little before lunch. After surveying all my doors, he handed me the repair estimate. "Julia, I can put up temporary doors for you tonight. I hate having to give you a bill for your damage."

"Steve, you don't work for charity. I wouldn't let you not charge me. I'm going to Folly Beach for a few days. You will have the house to yourself."

Steve smiled and shook my hand. "I'll call you when I'm finished."

After Steve left, I repacked my suitcase and drove to Folly Beach.

The week at the beach was spent playing in the water with Eli and Dexter. I also had lunch a couple of days with Suzie. It was our catch-up time with what was going on at the Atrium Art Gallery. The beach was my fun place it kept my mind from dwelling on my house in Charleston, the abduction from the hotel, and the fact that I was on someone's tracking system.

At breakfast, Eli asked, "Julia, I heard you moving around in your room early this morning. Are you leaving?"

"Steve finished my house yesterday, it's time for me to go back to Charleston. You questioned me hard yesterday about my return to the FBI. Last night you barely said two words to me."

"Julia, I didn't mean to upset you. I don't think you've been realistic. You didn't need to go back to work." He looked away. "Adam wouldn't have wanted you to either."

Anger rose from my toes up my body. "Eli, you don't control me."

He stayed on the sofa when I said, "Goodbye."

It hurt when he threw Adam's name at me. I don't know now if Adam is dead or alive.

The morning after returning from Folly, I was and finishing my breakfast and swallowing my last drop of coffee when I heard a murmur of voices on my front porch. Rebecca was on the phone pacing back and forth and Hector was walking up the front steps.

I gave Rebecca a half-smile, but before I could say anything she disconnected her call and blurted out, "Julia, I know about the ambush yesterday, and you being taken from The Saint Frances Hotel. One of the men we have in custody confessed to kidnapping you and the man that was killed was the driver of the SUV that took you from the hotel. They work for a Russian FSB agent. Why didn't you tell me? How am supposed to protect you if you aren't honest with me? Were you hurt? I thought we had everything under control."

I reached for the door. "Come inside Rebecca."

"You were a very good agent for ten years and thought situations through. Surprises are not in your being, you research all and any information before you react. You keep a cool head. But you should have confided in me. Did they take you because you are an agent or they thought you knew about their operation? She placed her hands on her hips and paced back and forth. Why, Julia, Why? Give me some answers."

"I don't know why? They had all kinds of files from the FBI and the CIA. They said Adam wasn't dead. Rebecca, let's keep this quiet. It could be a lie."

My doorbell rang. "Bryan, what are you doing here?"

The four of us sat in my great room, Rebecca, Hector, Bryan, and me. Bryan opened his briefcase and pulled out a folder. "Julia, after reading all the reports, the situation with Adam's death involves more people than any of us ever imagined. It seems we have stirred a pot of bad people who want Wesley Campbell dead. The latest info is that the CIA received an anonymous tip that led them to a pile of boxes in a highly secure area in the basement at their headquarters. Wesley's fingerprints are all over one of the metal index card boxes. The box is full of hand-printed names of some of the best-known hitmen. At the Hoover Building, the FBI is analyzing the handwriting. If it is Wesley's, I know he is tied to the murders, we just have to prove it. We don't know how he knew these old files were there but it's likely that the person that leaked this information had worked for the CIA years ago and knew that the boxes had been overlooked when everything went digital."

He handed a thumb drive to Rebecca. "See if you can get your people to penetrate the passcodes. My techs have spent two days trying to break the encryptions, and when they did break through they found two more hard drives with another layer of encryptions. People are dead because of Campbell and so far, I haven't found enough proof to put him away."

Rebecca piped in loudly. "He's betrayed his country and the NSA for money. He's responsible for the deaths of four CIA officers that we know of. Isn't that enough?"

I sat forward in my chair and propped my elbows on my knees, putting my fists under my chin. "How long do you think this will take before you can convict him?"

Bryan leaned back in his chair and folded his hands behind his head. "I don't know but I want any loopholes. He has to be connected to the deaths without question."

Late that afternoon I was rambling through the kitchen trying to decide what I wanted for dinner, with everything that had happened my appetite was on hold, but I knew I needed to try and eat something.

Hector rang my doorbell. "I want to give your house one more once over before I retire for the night." After he had checked all the doors and windows he said, "Julia, everything is secure. Buzz me if you need anything."

"Hector, what are you having for dinner?"

"A take-out meal from Cracker Barrel. Would you like to order something?"

"I was going to have a salad and a glass of wine. But if you eat with me, I'll order a meal."

I reached for my phone, but my pocket was empty. I checked my purse, but it was the same story. Hector went to check his car. "Julia, it's not there. When was the last time you used it?"

"I don't remember. I guess at Folly Beach."

Hector dialed my number, but we heard nothing.

Hector called Eli at the beach, Eli called my phone and then called Hector back. "Everything is quiet here."

I paced back and forth. "Maybe it's still in my car."

"Julia, you can't stay here without any way to contact me."

Hector started punching at his phone. "I put a tracer on your phone. It's in your car at the junkyard."

Hector picked up our dinners from Cracker Barrel.

I looked up from my plate. "You know you have been with me for over a year now and this is our first meal together."

Hector stood, gathered up what was left from dinner, and disposed of it in the trash. I heard a pounding on the front door. Hector motioned for me to stay in the kitchen.

When he opened the door Eli charged in, sidestepped Hector, and headed to the kitchen. Hector stayed on his heels.

"Eli, what are you doing here?"

"You don't have a phone. You're not staying here by yourself without a way to call for help. I'm staying with you until you find your phone."

Hector added the emergency app to Eli's phone, then headed next door for the night.

The next morning at seven-thirty Hector rang my doorbell. "I'm going to the junkyard. I'll be back shortly."

When Hector returned, I put my phone on charge. I saw I had three voicemails—Rebecca, Eli, and an unknown caller. The unknown must have hung up when it went to voicemail. Hector was almost at the front door when my phone rang. An unknown caller showed on my ID. Hector turned reached over and hit the speaker button. I said. "Hello."

The phone went silent. Hector had a concerned expression on his face. He quickly grabbed the phone from my hand.

"Hector, what's wrong? What's bothering you?"

"It's what's not bothering me that would be more accurate. Julia, I think someone may have hacked your phone."

Hector popped off the back of my phone and pulled out a tiny black chip. "I'm going to put a scrambler on your phone. Your voice might sound different and your incoming calls may sound far away."

Thirty minutes after Hector removed the tracking chip. Rebecca called. "Julia, the auto repair shop owner informed me when he was closing up last night, he saw a man sitting in your car. When he started towards him, he bolted. He ran after him, but the man jumped in a dark blue sedan and sped away. He said he was about six feet tall, dressed in all-black clothing, and with the darkness, he didn't get a good look at his face or the make and model of the car. I'm sure he put the tracer chip in your phone. Can you meet me in Bryan's office around two this afternoon?"

Hector followed us to Greenville.

Eli and I passed through security and sat down in Bryan's office at two-thirty. After the cordial greetings, Bryan rocked back in his chair and spoke. "Julia and Eli, I have called the forensic unit out to fingerprint your car. They are more thorough than the sheriff's department. Also, this is not official yet, and not all the agents at Langley agree with my opinion that Campbell is working with several people that helped him embezzle over a hundred million dollars. He has several accounts in the Grand Cayman Islands banks. If anyone suspected something or questioned him, they either disappeared or were found dead in what seemed to be a suspicious accident. The CIA has a significant relationship with the Grand Cayman Island banks. If they can prove money laundering the banks will cooperate. The Cayman bank has turned over a collection of investments that Campbell has made along with his bank statements and tax records to the CIA. The CIA has enough proof to arrest him for stealing federal funds, but I want him on murder charges. Murder carries a death sentence. Money laundering only prison time and then he will be free."

I wrapped my arms tighter around my body as I listened to Bryan. I lowered my head. "All I want is justice for Adam."

Bryan slapped his hand down hard on his desk. "And we will get justice. I promise. We have found requisitions made every two months over the last year from Campbell asking for new computers. Rebecca still has people working on hacking the ones we seized. We are hoping there's more on those computers than just offshore deposit info. I have to make sure that all the dots connect to everyone that may be guilty. I don't want anyone to slip through the cracks on this."

I was quiet most of the way back to Charleston. Eli let me have my downtime.

Chapter 22

It was completely unprecedented for the CIA to take the lead in collecting intelligence in a case like this. That was the NSA's department or the FBI's, but under the circumstances, nothing was running true to normal. The FBI was coordinating with the CIA and both divisions were analyzing all the compiled data and working together to produce and implement a strategy. They were making sure all the "i's" were dotted and the "t's" were crossed and it was loophole tight.

My phone rang. "Hello, Rebecca."

"Julia, I'm on my way to Warsaw. I'm sending MI-6 Rawls to Charleston to be part of my added security team with you. He's worked for me on cases like this before. He speaks fluent Russian. His mother is from Chita, Russia, but his father is American. Rawls is all business. Don't take it personally. I'll see you in a couple of days."

When I heard a car pull into my driveway, I opened the front door. A tall man dressed in a black suit with coal black hair was paying the Uber driver. He gave me a half-smile and introduced himself.

Rawls was polite but not friendly. "Ms. Stone, I gave Rebecca the name of a Russian assassin. She will return with him. The assassin works alone. She has a list of other informants who work undercover. For now, the CIA operations are continuing as usual.

Rawl's phone rang. "Okay, I'm scrambled and secure." Then he hit the speaker button.

A voice announced. "This message is coming from the Secret Intelligent Service and the Director of the CIA."

Rawls responded. "What are my instructions?"

"We think Wesley Campbell may not be who he says he's. He faked all the paperwork he submitted in his application for employment to NSA."

Rawls cleared his throat. "I ran him through the international criminal data system but found nothing. Do you know who he is? Have you contacted Interpol?"

My phone rang and I recognized Rebecca's voice even though it sounded strange. I hit the speaker button. "Julia, do you know the last time anyone saw Adam? When was the last time you saw him?"

Rawls cut in. "Is that why you are in Warsaw? Do you think Adam is there?"

Rebecca's voice was sparse and broken. "Rawls…you … in Charleston.. keep your … to ground. Contact …. resources pursue any suspects."

Rawls disconnected the call and called Rebecca back. "Can you hear me? Your conversation broke up. Rebecca, can you hear me?"

Rebecca answered without static. "Yes, are you in Charleston? Don't let anything slip by you. Keep your ears to the ground. I sent you a new list of contacts. Contact them and pursue any other leads and suspects. If you think there is a trail follow it. I'm taking the next flight back to D.C. to meet with the head of the CIA at the Pentagon. I'm boarding the plane now, call Bryan and ask him to meet me tomorrow for breakfast at eight-thirty at the Crystal Marriott."

After the phone conversation, I sat on my sofa, unable to stop the tears from flowing. I looked at Rawls. "What information do you have that makes all of you think Adam is alive? He's not!"

Rawls answered impatiently. "Ms. Stone, we are doing our job. You're emotionally involved and not thinking straight."

A week later, Jack and Bryan rang my doorbell. "Gentlemen, come in. This is a surprise."

I offered them coffee, tea, or a soft drink but they declined. Jack shoved his hands in his pockets and walked around my kitchen like he had ants in his pants before he spoke. "Julia, Bryan thinks you are in a more dangerous position than we realized. He wants to send you to a safe house. He needs everyone back in the field concentrating on finding Campbell. People aren't who we believe they are and until identities can be verified, we need you safe."

Bryan sat in my overstuffed chair and cleared his throat. "Julia, a Supreme Court justice has been murdered. Campbell had a case before him last year. You may be in danger until we can find out his and others' true identities. We don't want to be worrying about you. We're sure he has had a dozen or more people killed. I think Adam found out more than we know at this time."

Jack sat across from me on the other bar stool. "Julia, you'll be fine. When all this is over your life will be back to normal. I promise you that."

"Normal? I'm beginning to wonder what is normal. What about Eli?"

"I talked to him yesterday. As you would suspect he's upset with me and Bryan. He said he understood why he couldn't see you, but it didn't make things better." Jack continued. "Eli called Bryan, but he wouldn't agree for him to be with you."

I brushed my foot across the floor, not lifting my head to look at Bryan. "I know why you didn't. Eli's name was on Rebecca's list of suspects. She wouldn't listen to me. She said everyone had to be checked and rechecked, but that's crazy. Eli didn't kill Adam."

Bryan answered. "I know. It's protocol since Eli was with Adam at the cabin. I'm sure he will be cleared."

The next week, I boarded a private twin-engine Cessna bound for Miami. I had agreed to go to a safe house and Bryan had allowed Jack to fly with me and stay until I was comfortable and settled, then he would fly back to Greenville.

The SUV that had picked me and Jack up at the airport stopped at the massive wrought iron gates. A buzzer sounded and the gates opened. The fourteenth-century Spanish Monastery was iconic in the Miami area. Mass services were given at 10:00 a.m. and 4:00 p.m. on Sundays. No one entered the walls beyond the vestibule except the priest and the nuns.

Sister Margaret met us when the SUV came to a stop. She reached for my hand. "Everyone here that has any contact with you is vowed to secrecy. I'll take you to your cottage." She turned to Jack. "Father Mulcaudy is the only priest here. He'll be with you shortly." She was spry but walked with a tiny limp. She relied on her cane and looked to be in her nineties. "You have no restrictions except you can't leave the grounds or talk to anyone but the priest or the nuns. You don't have to participate in any activities or go to mass or confession. You can eat in the dining room with the nuns or you can have your meals brought to you."

We entered a small cottage. A strong lavender odor overwhelmed me. Everything was plain—concrete walls, a sofa, and an end table in the living room, a small bedroom that was big enough for a single bed, and a nightstand with a small lamp that cast a dim shadow across the room. Sunlight streamed through the glass-paned door in the living room.

"Julia, I'll see that you get a TV." Sister Margaret opened the back door and pointed. "You have your own private garden."

I walked along the main path through the gardens stopping every few feet to look at the lush foliage. It reminded me of a tropical jungle. Every color of orchid spilled over the brick wall. "Sister, I've never seen so many different varieties and colors in a rose garden and the old banyan trees are gigantic." I laughed and pointed to the other side of the garden. "The male peacocks like it here too. They are strutting their colorful tail feathers and squawking for a mate."

Sister Margaret smiled. "We have a great gardener. You can give him a nod but you can't talk to him. Priest orders. The gardens are meant to be a place of peace, so that goes for you, too. Don't think about throwing any parties." Her laugh was hearty and her eyes sparkled.

I laughed. "Don't worry. I'm not in any mood to celebrate. But I'm grateful for your help."

She turned towards me when she reached the cottage door. "I'll meet you in the dining hall at five for dinner."

I watched her cross the gravel path and disappear into the monastery.

I strolled past the gardener every day as he weeded the flower beds without speaking a word. I spent most of my days writing. I jotted things down that I never wanted to forget. When Jack later asked me what I had been doing all day, he smiled and said I should also write down the things that I wanted to forget.

At noon every day, the priest always led me from my cottage to the dining hall. I could've done without the idle chit-chat and was glad when Jack joined us. The tall windows in the vestibule allowed the sun to give an outdoor feeling and they framed the spire of the church across the way.

It had been a long week for me and for Jack. In the morning, he would be leaving. We said our goodbyes.

Around midnight, two low-flying helicopters awakened me. The sound faded, then before long, it sounded like one had returned and was hovering over my cottage. Automatic weapons started firing. Laying in my bed without moving a muscle, I expected another round of gunfire to break out. The eerie silence was lasting way too long for my comfort. I ran to Jack's room to find it empty. I stopped in the hallway and thought about how my world was becoming more and more dangerous and complicated and how trouble kept piling on more trouble. I turned and ran through the dining area into the south wing where the nuns slept, hoping they were okay, but entering their room my eye caught two men passing by their window climbing down a rope from a helicopter to the roof of the next building. Running to the vestibule suddenly my ears rang from another explosion that brought the ceiling down. Large chunks of cement rubble lay everywhere. I crawled under a table in the hallway and stayed frozen and immobile waiting for the second story to collapse. Screaming at the top of my lungs to make someone hear me proved to be fruitless. The kitchen exploded in the next few seconds. Smoke hung heavily in my section of the building. As old as the building was there had to be gas lines running throughout the wall and floors. I made my way to the outside courtyard to find debris everywhere but found no sign of anyone or bodies. Another explosion came from the other side of the building, I started running to the front gates when a man tackled me from behind. I grabbed for his hair but he caught my hand and twisted my arm behind my back and pinned me to the ground. He was dressed in solid black—shirt, pants, hood, and shoes. He slammed his boot vigorously into the small of my back. I tried to suck in a breath but couldn't. My third cough allowed me to take in a little air. Hearing a trigger click, I covered my head with my arms waiting for the shot. Next someone pulled on my hands, it was great to hear Jack's familiar voice.

"Julia, are you hurt?"

"My back hurts but I'm not aware of anything else hurting at the moment." When I stood a piercing stab shot through my left side. I thought that one of my ribs had punctured my lung and hoped not again. I had that same sensation years ago. My breaths were still shallow. "Red was everywhere. Is that my blood?"

Jack answered. "No."

"The gardener...where's the....my head started spinning and wooziness overtook me. I stumbled over a loose brick at the edge of the pathway. Jack grabbed for my arm but it was too late, I was already in forward motion. My ears heard the thump on the pavement. With my knees pulled up to my stomach, I tried to force myself to move but couldn't. My right wrist hurt. I was in pain physically and emotionally.

Jack got me to my feet and guided me to the entry gates. "When you see the gardener, you can thank him. He took a bullet for you."

"Where is he now?"

Jack's grip tightened. "He was taken to the hospital."

When we reached the gates I looked back at the monastery, flames were now rising throughout the building—windows, roof, doors, and walls. A figure was running on fire. The screaming stopped and a ball of fire lay on the ground. Sirens and red and blue lights were flashing from all directions—police cars, ambulances, and fire trucks. Yellow flags marked footprints that littered the immaculate grounds and blue uniforms looked like a beach wave coming ashore.

My head was throbbing and nausea set in. My wrist was hurting more now and so was my rib cage. Then everything went black.

Stirring enough to see a paramedic standing over me, and in a conscious state, I surmised the feeling of being on a gurney and saw the red-lighted emergency room sign as we passed under it. The long hallway looked like a high school fire drill. Everyone was running from room to room and from one person to another. An orderly parked my gurney next to a man who was covered with a blood-soaked sheet. The gurney across from me had a sheet spread completely over a body. I was able to process that the body under the sheet was deceased, and on the gurney next to me was the gardener.

I gave him a half-smile. "I understand you saved my life, that should be me lying there."

He let out a soft moan. "You'd be in the morgue. I'm lucky his gun misfired, but his knife didn't miss. My comfort right now is that he's suffering from a broken right knee. Being shot in Afghanistan and having worked hundreds of murder cases still nothing shields me from seeing my own blood."

"I'm Julia., but you know that. We were instructed not to talk to one another but under the circumstances, I'm sure that request doesn't exist now. You're in so much pain because of me. Do you know anything about the nuns and the priest?"

"No, there has been no news. But you're right I don't think previous orders will be enforced." He gave a slight smile. "I'm Agent Brett Jones, FBI. I've been in excruciating pain before and had lots of rehabilitation but this pain is worth it. I did my job you're still alive."

The words "thank you" were almost out of my mouth when an orderly whisked my gurney into the operating room.

I woke up in a private room with the surgeon explaining, "The bullet sliced across your rib cage, you are lucky there was no damage to the right lung. The pain you're experiencing is from a broken rib that pierced your left lung. You are going to be fine."

Two FBI agents were placed outside my hospital door around the clock. After a week of convalescing from my injuries, the hospital discharged me, but moving around was going to be slow-paced. My rib cage was taped to the point that I almost couldn't breathe and my right arm was in a sling with a three-quarter-length cast.

Chapter 23

When the orderly pushed me through the hospital's front doors, Bryan was pacing back and forth on the sidewalk. "Julia, I'm sorry. We thought we had you in a safe place. Langley has agreed to let us move you to a new location in Colorado. You'll need to get used to the 8,000 feet altitude, but the acclimation shouldn't take long. You will always have CIA officers and FBI agents with you." He gave a half-smile. "If we need to, we'll bring in the military."

I laughed. "I'm not worth all those taxpayers' dollars." My tone turned harsh. "Bryan, can I see Eli? Does he know what happened? Rebecca wouldn't let me tell him goodbye."

"We are still trying to verify everyone's identity. There are so many channels to go through now but I'll see what I can do?"

I scowled. "Jack and Rebecca should be able to clear Eli."

Bryan gave a long sigh. "Julia, under the circumstances we are moving as fast as we can. This entire situation isn't simple. We still don't know who is who and who works for whom. I have a CIA plane that will fly you to Colorado. At the small airport, you'll look like another tourist coming to the mountain. There will be no uniform personnel on board."

I boarded the plane on the private jet runway at the Miami airport and was flown to Colorado with the CIA's Special Activities Division (SAD) with one CIA officer on board, David Carter.

Officer Carter looked at his watch thirty minutes after takeoff. "We'll arrive in three hours at the Gunnison airport."

When we landed, an SUV and two FBI agents met me. Everyone looked like the Michelin men in their white snowsuits. We drove up the mountain and beyond Crested Butte and continued up the winding mountain road. Heavy clouds had settled over the mountains. The cold gray sky made me shiver when I stepped out of the SUV. The snow and wind were worse than the weatherman had predicted and the sky didn't look like it was going to clear anytime soon.

"Officer Carter, you said I was going to be housed in a chalet. This is no chalet, it's a giant mansion made of wood and stone."

I buried my chin in my scarf and ran up the flagstone steps to the front door. Officer Carter moved past me and unlocked the door. He punched in the code disarming the security alarm. I entered the foyer which was a good-sized space in itself. I stood still absorbing what my eyes were seeing.

I yelled. "This place looks like a furniture showroom."

The furniture sat on luxury cowhide rugs. The double-pane glass floor-to-ceiling windows gave the effect that I could reach out and touch the mountains. I stood in awe looking out over the Elk Mountain range in the Rockies covered in new snow. The fireplace covered half the wall on the left side of the room. I ran over to it, but I couldn't stand that close too long or the roaring fire would engulf me.

"If there wasn't a fire, I could stand completely inside it and not touch a single stone." Officer Carter laughed.

I glanced over to the other side of the room. The dining table had twelve chairs and sat on a large leather rug. The table was covered with platters of cheeses, rolls and crackers, and a large compote of fruit.

After the shock of where I would be staying wore off, I rolled my suitcase into the master bedroom. I had started unpacking when I heard voices shouting. The closer I inched to the kitchen the louder and angrier the voices became.

I yelled. "Men! Stop!"

They stood in silence for what seemed like minutes but were only a few seconds.

My voice was firm but calm. "Gentlemen, what's going on?" To my surprise, Agent Jones turned around. Our eyes locked. I assessed him from across the room. It was the first time that I had noticed how fit he was—strong shoulders, well-developed chest, muscular back and he stood over six feet tall. The work he had done in the gym for physical training showed. My heart skipped a beat when I saw his broad smile. He looked flawless and I was smitten. His thick black hair and deep-sea blue eyes emphasized his high cheekbones. I had thought about how Brett's recovery was many times after leaving the hospital but I never thought that I would meet him again.

Brett smiled. "Officer Carter and I think you would be safer in the master bedroom on the second floor. The other three agents think you have the right to stay where you choose."

Upstairs one bedroom was furnished with two double beds, two dressers, and an adjoining bath. The other bedroom was the same except it had two queen beds. The master king-sized bedroom was between the two bedrooms. All the beds had sheepskin rugs next to them. Brett took the master downstairs and Officer Carter took the room with the queen beds. At three a.m., I was awakened by laughter, hollering, and what sounded like a girl's pillow fight. The sound system was vibrating the entire house. I grabbed my robe and ran to the stairs. I was halfway down when Brett came out of his bedroom.

Before I spoke, he yelled, "You guys cut the noise. The billiard table is not in the garage, it's under the stairwell in a rec room in the middle of the house."

All four of them gave a slight bow toward me and said in unison. "We're sorry." Sleep wasn't in my forecast now. I walked into the library behind the rec room. Every wall was covered with bookshelves, there must have been over ten thousand books waiting for someone to read them. It was hard for me to choose one.

Brett walked in and smiled. "Sorry, about the noise."

I took a book from the shelf. "Have you read *The Water Keeper*? Charles Martin is one of my favorite authors."

He chuckled. "No, I have enough mysteries and conflicts daily. TV is my thing."

"That way you don't have to think." I laughed.

"You're right." See you in the morning.

For two weeks, the five of them, three FBI agents and two CIA officers took day and night shifts. Agent Jones slept very little staying on guard on both shifts. Officer Carter took a walk on the mountain every morning and night. On the last Monday of the second month when I came downstairs to breakfast, the voices in the kitchen went silent when I entered.

I looked around the room. "Where are Agent Jones and Officer Carter?"

The three agents at the table looked at one another before one answered. "They went for a jog."

I knew something wasn't right. "There's nowhere to jog here except down the mountain. There's too much fresh snow for them to do that."

The CIA officer pointed to the window, jumped from his chair, and yelled. "There he is!"

A man in a tight-fitted black shirt and black pants ran across the deck, jumped over the patio sofa, and fell over the cedar rail.

Agent Jones was on his heels, he ran down five steps hit the landing, turned, and ran down ten more steps, then fired his gun at Officer Carter. One agent in the house pulled his gun from his shoulder holster and stretched his gun out in front of him and ran after Jones. We heard a gun fire.

Another agent pushed me down behind the kitchen island. I heard two more gunshots but the agent on top of me didn't move. I heard the great room door open with a bang.

Then Agent Jones yelled. "All clear."

The FBI agent pulled me to my feet. Jones's chest was heaving in and out showing his lungs were working extra hard to pull in oxygen. He stood tall and looked out over the mountain without saying a word.

My heart along with my entire body warmed watching Brett. He looked regal and confident. He was about a foot taller than me. I told myself Brett's line of work put him in physical danger on most of his assignments and that would be difficult to deal with on a daily basis. I didn't give any thought to other agents when I was working at the FBI. It was a job with fellow workers, not a job to get personally involved in a romantic relationship. I hadn't inquired if Brett was married or not but he had been in the FBI for twenty years and that was hard on any marriage. He was doing his job. He was protecting me.

I made my way from the library to the great room. Agent Jones was pacing back and forth watching his feet put one step in front of the other. "Here's what we know. Campbell hired, bribed, or somehow coerced Officer Carter to work for him. We knew there was a leak but we didn't know who. Julia, that's why I was posing as the gardener at the monastery to protect you. Bryan, Rebecca, and the FBI Director narrowed down the person to three after the convent was attacked. We moved you here to be sure our suspicions were correct. I didn't want it to end this way. A helicopter is on the way to pick up Carter's body." Agent Jones was still talking when I heard the whirring rotors beating the thin cold air. "You are safe, we're all going home tomorrow."

I stared out the window watching rain and sleet hammer the helicopter. Agent Jones touched my shoulder. "You've seen enough."

"Not yet. I want to make sure they get Carter's body, but in this weather, I'm not sure it's worth losing a helicopter and three men."

The pilot hovered over the treetops. He had the advantage from above to find Carter's body. One man was being lowered down by rope with a basket attached. A gust of wind caused the helicopter to flap and lean slightly sideways. The man with the basket swung in circles a couple of times but managed to hang on. When the helicopter was back in position another man was lowered. Agent Jones touched my shoulder. "It's time to go."

After two and a half weeks in seclusion on the mountain, it was good to be back in Charleston. The day did seem strange with no officers and agents wandering everywhere and hovering over me. I had to admit to myself, I did miss Brett, and if our paths ever crossed again there would be more than a platonic relationship.

I welcomed my old boring life and was enjoying my breakfast when Bryan called. "Julia, can you be at my office around one?"

I arrived in Greenville at 1:15 p.m. and breezed through security. Bryan and Rebecca greeted me when I stepped off the elevator.

Bryan smiled. "We were going to the lobby to wait for you."

"Sorry, traffic was heavier than usual"

When we entered Bryan's office his conference table was scattered with papers.

Bryan spoke first. "Julia, you're here because we needed to make sure you weren't being followed."

Rebecca spoke. "I put a tail on you to make sure. You're in the clear."

Bryan continued. "This is an update briefing. You know Campbell offered Officer Carter money to work for him, Wesley has been missing for almost a month now. We have officially terminated him from the NSA for being AWOL at work. We need to get the NSA back to its high standards again. He knows we're looking for him and all his conspirators. I hope within the next few weeks someone will report his whereabouts and we can charge him with Adam's murder."

I sat forward in my chair. "Why would he surface? He knows several agencies are after him."

Rebecca said, "I've got undercover people who think they know where he is. When we capture him, he'll be sent to Quantico for interrogation and psychological testing."

Bryan chimed in. "He'll cooperate if he thinks he won't go to jail. This gives us more time to make sure we have an ironclad case to charge him for Adam's murder and possibly others. We will keep a close tag on him to see who contacts him or who he contacts." Bryan smiled. "Eli has been cleared."

On the way back to Charleston my mind was still clinging to the events that had happened in Miami and Crested Butte. I pulled into my driveway to see Kevin sitting in my rocker. Before I could put the car in park, he sprinted off the porch, opened my door, and pulled me from the driver's seat.

"Where have you been?" I've been calling you for a couple of weeks. I couldn't find Eli. Jack told me you were safe and not to worry but that is all he said. I've been going crazy and Katherine almost divorced me. I couldn't think straight, eat or work. She didn't agree that I should fly here until I knew what was going on."

"Kevin, I got home yesterday. Why didn't you call me last night or this morning? I'm sorry. So much has gone on with the CIA and the FBI trying to find Adam's killer."

Kevin kicked the grass with the toe of his tennis shoe. "What does that have to do with you?"

He followed me through the front door to the kitchen. "Would you like some iced tea?"

We sat on the sofa with our teas. After Kevin was brought up to date, tears welled in his eyes. He sat silently mulling over everything I had said.

"I don't know what I'd do if I lost you. Where's Eli?"

"I'm not sure but I know he'll be calling shortly."

After our take-out dinner, we were both exhausted. We made it an early night.

"Sis, I feel better this morning. I still don't like the idea of you going back with the FBI. Don't ever disappear again without giving me a warning as to what is going on and where you are going. I have a flight this morning. Don't fix breakfast, I'll get something at the airport after I return the rental car."

"Kevin so much was going on last night with our conversation and I was tired. Can't you stay a few days?"

"No, my clients are calling me and I still have to settle things with Katherine. It'll be a lot easier now when she hears about your adventures."

I stood in the driveway watching Kevin leave when Eli pulled in.

Chapter 24

Eli jumped from his car, picked me up, and twirled me around before setting my feet back on the ground. "I know I should've called first but you had me worried out of my mind. No one would tell me anything."

I couldn't look Eli in the eye. We stood staring out over the Atlantic. "I'm safe. Rebecca thinks she knows where Wesley Campbell is and when Bryan arrests him, he's going to send him to Quantico. My body and mind have been consumed trying to find out if Adam is alive or dead."

Eli lowered his head. "Julia, drop this whole thing. If Adam is alive he'll surface one day. You need to stop putting yourself in danger. Quit the FBI."

"Well, you have no say."

The look on Eli's face told me that no matter what I said he would never understand.

Bryan called. "Julia, Dr. Maxwell Alexander, Director of FBI, in Europe needs our help. I'm sending you to Russia. You'll get flight schedule emailed to you shortly."

"Eli, Bryan is sending me to Moscow. You'll hear from me often."

I flew from Virginia to New York changed from a military plane to TWA's late-night flight to Berlin then the next morning flew into Moscow. I entered Lubyanka Square and stood looking up at the tallest redbrick office building in Moscow before entering. Dr. Maxwell Alexander's name was listed on the fourth floor.

When I exited the elevator the receptionist smiled and buzzed Dr. Alexander.

"Good morning, Julia, you've had a long flight. This meeting will be short. You've been sent here to follow the paper trail of Wesley Campbell that worked at the NSA. I'll be available to you at all times. Under your previous circumstances of being pursued, you need to wear a disguise for your first assignment. Your flat will be under surveillance twenty-four-seven. My door is always open and if you need anything let me know. My assistant, Carla, will show you to your workspace."

I followed Carla into what looked like a prop room in a theater. She rummaged around in some boxes for a bit. "Here Julia, shove your hair under this short red wig. Do your make-up heavy like a call girl, and wear these thick, black-rimmed glasses. Don't worry the glass is not prescription. You'll go by the name of Shelia Beck."

I laughed. "I look like a streetwalker waiting for the next call. I don't know what's worse being used as bait on Folly Beach or this."

She smiled. but didn't have a clue about what I was referring to.

"Carla, this building seems to have more security than usual. Is there a reason why?"

She walked towards the door and started down the hallway. "This was the former KBG, now PSB building, needless to say, all the security systems are still in place and the FBI added more when they moved in. This building is tighter than a drum. Here's your work area. If you need anything, let me know."

I read through all the emails that Dr. Alexander had forwarded to me and then sent all the correspondence to the appropriate divisions. After I had worked at my computer for a couple of hours, I noticed a man three computers down watching me. He had entered the building this morning behind me. Several times when I casually glanced his way, he quickly looked back at his computer screen as if he was absorbed in his work.

His skin was well-tanned like he had spent every day on the beach. He had small beady black eyes and weighed over two hundred pounds. He looked to be in his mid-thirties and was dressed in blue jeans and a black sweatshirt. To me, he didn't fit the FBI profile.

At three o'clock, I erased the browsing history and shut down my computer. I needed to find my flat and a welcome bed after being awake for thirty-six hours. Looking back to my desk through the glass door from the elevator, the overweight man was still watching me while talking on his cell phone. I opened the front door of the FBI building seeing a man standing by a red Audi talking on his cell phone. At the entrance to the parking garage, where my rental car was, another man dressed in all black clothing, was talking on his phone. At the other end of the garage, another man was talking on his phone. He was over six feet tall, and on this warm sunny day, he had on a black rain slicker. I started to go back into the FBI building and talk to Maxwell, but being here for only a few hours, I didn't want him to think I couldn't handle my job.

My imagination ran wild after my experience on the road back to Charleston from Folly Beach. He could've had a shotgun or any other kind of gun or weapon or even a taser under his raincoat. I hurried to my car, jumped in, locked all the doors, and made my way to the exit sign. When pulling onto the street, instantly a white Mercedes pulled up behind me. Scanning my rearview mirror, the three vehicles that the men were standing beside earlier were now behind me. I turned west and saw an alley running north and south. The last car that had been behind me turned into an alley and angled his car to form a barricade. My heart raced, I was going to be herded into a trap.

I wasn't frightened but pulled my .45 out of my purse for safety measures, and laid it on my lap. At that moment, sirens and red flashing lights pulled in behind me. The next traffic light turned red in my face. Split seconds ran through my head, run the light or stop. I made the decision to stop.

A man in a police uniform knocked on my window. I yelled. "Show me your badge."

He showed me his badge and his personal ID. I rolled down my window.

He spoke in English but had a heavy Russian accent. "Shelia, Dr. Alexander called me. He said you were being followed when you left the FBI building. We'll escort you home."

I smiled and rolled my window up and followed him. Another patrol car pulled in behind me. They escorted me to my front door.

All the houses on the street looked the same—brownstone, one-story, and gabled roofs. Inside my flat, I pushed the deadbolt closed. After the click one officer said. "Goodnight, Shelia."

It was going to take me a while to get used to the name Shelia.

Chapter 25

On the block where I was staying, five houses were sandwiched next to one another. I was safe behind my bolted door in a small four-room brownstone. The living room housed a small TV, sofa, one side table, and a stuffed chair. The kitchen had French windows in the small bay window with a small round table and two chairs. The back door from the kitchen led into a small courtyard that was surrounded by a tall thick hedge. A canal flowed behind the hedge. The bedroom was painted lemon yellow with a double bedspread covered in yellow roses. A handheld shower was attached at the top of the tile over the tub. The bathroom wouldn't accommodate two people at one time.

A knock on the front door made me jump. I yelled. "Who is it?"

"Maxwell Alexander." The voice replied.

I unbolted the door to find Dr. Alexander holding two bags of groceries. "You haven't had time to shop and I know you're exhausted from your trip. This should get you through the night and breakfast tomorrow."

I smiled and reached for the two bags. "Thank you. You're right. I'm too tired to go grocery shopping. Would you like to stay for dinner?"

Dr. Alexander answered. "No thanks. You get some rest."

I leaned against the door and listened to the stillness of the house, then I tossed my coat on the bed and went to the kitchen to empty the grocery bags. Dr. Alexander had done a great job at shopping—coffee, milk, salad fixings, eggs, salad dressing, cheese, and ham. My stomach was growling. I chopped some lettuce, tomatoes, and black olives, then grated a little bit of the Swiss cheese. The salad was all my body needed in its exhausted state.

The next morning, the shower soap Maxwell had in my groceries smelled like lilacs. I wiped the steam from the mirror and was pleased to see no bags under my eyes after all the flights yesterday. Dressing in the two items of clothing that I retrieved from the "prop room" yesterday, and then repacking my bathroom items, I was ready for work. Not knowing if I was being followed or not, or if someone might try and break in, I didn't want to leave anything behind. I lifted my suitcase into the car trunk. The groceries were still in the pantry.

There was a piece of paper under my windshield wiper. The note read:

We *know who you are and why you're here. I'm a Russian official. I have important information that you would be interested in under the right conditions. I will meet you at 11:00 a.m. at Osteria Mario Italian Restaurant in Lubyanka Square.*

Damir

'Right conditions' meant money. The information that was being offered could possibly be incorrect. Arriving at work, I went straight to Maxwell's office.

"Julia—or 'Shelia' in your case, you know you have to verify and track all leads. I'll do a background check on Damir."

At eleven I was seated at the back of the restaurant next to the kitchen. The area was small and crowded with tables and chairs. The location wasn't the best but when I looked around at the crowded bar, my table was good. "Sir, is there a back door?"

"Yes madam, only staff." His accent was heavy and his English was broken.

The back door had an obstructed view from my table. I didn't care what he said, if I needed it I could be out the back before anyone could stop me. I tried to look like a regular patron and not stare constantly towards the front door while sipping my tea.

After being out in a field operation only a couple of times in Charleston, this was the first time I was given an assignment in this type of work, but I was willing to do anything if it helped find Adam's killer.

Damir was prompt. He looked like a young college student. Maxwell had said he was in his mid-forties. He had no wrinkles, was tall, in a tailored suit, clean-shaven, crew-cut black hair, and had black eyes. His attitude was smug and coercive as he attempted to impress me to gain my trust to get whatever he wanted. To me, he was a pretentious jackass, but he had my attention.

He pulled a file from his briefcase and pushed it toward me. It had my full history and Adam's. From what I read, they had Adam under surveillance for a few years.

Damir ran his hand through his hair. "Go to the Leningradsky Railway Station Wednesday night at nine alone, someone in a tan trench coat will meet you where the Brown Circle and Red Line intersect. At that time of night, this area will be deserted. Wait on the last bench on the platform. You should be the only one there. You will get the information you want."

I met with Maxwell after lunch. "I'll have several men in the surrounding area that afternoon. Wear a shirt that has an upper arm pocket, you will be wired and you will have a small wireless speaker in your ear."

I departed the Brown Circle Line at 8:45 p.m. I sat on the last bench, as ordered, and pulled my flat ivy green cap down to cover most of my face. After the next train stopped on the Red Line a man departed on the other platform. He propped himself next to a column. Adrenaline shot through my veins. More than thirty minutes went by before anyone spoke to me through my earpiece. "Do you see the man in the long black coat across from you? He's with us."

"No one told me I had a spotter." I was antsy and wanted to move to the shadows. "It's been over an hour and he hasn't shown."

The streetlight over me went dark. I heard Maxwell's voice. "Everyone, stay alert."

The spotter on the other side of the platform wandered towards the train schedule at the end of his platform. My thinking was that the man who was supposed to come with the information either chickened out or he had spotted the other agents. Either way, I was on assignment and my adrenaline was still at an all-time high.

Maxwell said, "We've been stood up."

I answered. "Can't we wait until twenty-three hundred?"

"If you aren't ready to hang it up, we'll wait."

A few minutes later, Maxwell announced. "There's a shadow moving towards you, Shelia."

An elderly woman with a limp and a cane approached me. In a frail voice, she asked in Russian. "Dearie, do you have the time?"

My Russian wasn't good, but I knew the word time. I answered. "10 o'clock."

She smiled and said in English. "Would you share your bench with me?"

She didn't look like a contact person or if she knew anything about our meeting. Maybe she didn't have any information that could help us. I took the chance and said, "I'm authorized to compensate you for any information."

She took in a big sigh and looked at me as if she didn't care. "Call me Linda. I know you were expecting a man but I've been in this business a long time. Let's go have a beer. Leave your men here."

Maxwell approached us and looked in the direction she pointed. In Russian, he said, "I'm Maxwell Alexander. You don't know my face but you do know my name. "May I join you since you know I'm here?"

She tapped her cane twice and started around the corner from the rail tracks. There was a small pub tucked away on a side street. The old high ceilings, a couple of rows of long wooden tables, and a small fireplace on the back wall gave patrons a warm welcome. The three of us sat on benches at a wobbly table. After two beers, she handed me a manilla envelope. "Here's the dirt you asked for. I can get you more but my fee will go up."

Maxwell snatched the envelope from my hand. Linda and I sat silent while he sifted through the papers. He laid the contents on the table in front of her. "Linda, how sure are you about this info? Comrade Lenz is an FSB agent that Wesley Campbell sold satellite coordinates to. It unscrambles high government officials' private phone lines including cell phones. That's only part of the information he sold. We have worked on several cases. I had no idea he was a traitor."

Linda whispered. "Maxwell, I'm giving you what I know. There are so many people involved and Campbell has contacts throughout Russia and Germany. He has had several people killed that got in his way. Same scenarios—bodies found in dumpsters, shot three times in the chest, and their middle and index fingers cut off on both hands." She reached for the envelope. "Take it or leave it but give me my rubles. The London CIA office is sitting on the same info. No one wants to act on this for fear of starting a turf war within all the agencies."

Maxwell nodded. I handed the cloth pouch of rubles to Linda.

Chapter 26

The next morning, I ditched my wig, make-up, and glasses. It was good to look in the mirror and see Julia again. After the meeting with Linda last night, Maxwell thought I wasn't on anyone's watch list. Linda was running info and watching her own back, Damir was the go-between-guy setting up meetings.

When I unlocked my office door, I saw a red file folder lying on my desk with a note attached. *Top Secret. I'm at the FSB office. Scan and send all the contents to Bryan.*

When Bryan answered his phone. Homesickness welled up inside me. "Julia, it's good to hear from you. How are you doing? I was worried that you might be in over your head or in trouble." There was relief in his voice.

I cleared my throat. "Did you get the documents I sent? Campbell has been selling information ever since he started at the NSA. Several FSB agents have been lining their pockets like he was. They sold what info he gave them to other countries, Germany, England, Italy, and China that we know and there could be more."

"Julia, The Soviets thought they were the only ones with the information. They found out that Campbell was involved with other FSB agents in selling the information to other countries. We have him under surveillance and lockdown at Quantico. He's being allowed visitors. We're speculating a big payoff and Campbell may be splitting it with others. We're watching the situation closely. We don't want any conflicts over this with other countries. We're making sure now there's not a leak in the CIA. We're going to move in on his accomplices in Germany and Russia at the same time."

After lunch, Maxwell summoned me to his office. "Julia, you have done all you can here. The FSB, the CIA, and the FBI are cleaning house. I'm sending you to Germany this afternoon. You need to find out who the informants are there."

I boarded Lufthansa Airlines at 3:00 p.m. for Berlin. The two-and-a-half-hour flight gave me time to pull my thoughts together. My contact person in Berlin was named Finn. After departing the plane and collecting my luggage, I waited for over an hour at the baggage claim before a man in his thirties approached me and flashed his badge.

"I'm Agent Hans Finn, FBI. Everyone calls me Finn. Sorry, to be late. As you know, work comes first. A team had to be assembled. We have an operation run tonight. Let's get you checked in at the hotel. I'll brief you on the way."

The Marriott Berlin hotel lobby was empty except for the clerk. I checked in and turned to Finn. "Where is everyone? It's unusual for a hotel this big to have no one here. Even the lobby bar is empty."

Finn didn't answer. We kept moving toward the elevator.

At 9:30 p.m. Finn, twelve agents, and I boarded an unmarked FBI van. Finn said. "My orders came in from Quantico about an hour ago."

It was hard for me to tell which direction we were going. I have always been a north, south, east, and west person but I couldn't get my bearings in the darkness. All the houses we passed were in a row, like a small American subdivision. We had been driving a half an hour I heard the gravel crunch when the tires left the pavement and turned onto a rutted road. The vehicle bottomed out a few times and tree limbs brushed the van. At the top of the hill, there was an open grassy field. We had to be somewhere out in the countryside. Finn saw smoke drifting from a stone chimney, he slowed the SUV within a hundred yards of a small brick cottage.

Finn checked his gun and asked everyone else to do the same. "I don't like working in the dark. The cloud breaks will give us a little light. I wished we could've arrived here at dawn, but that didn't happen. We have to move now. We're to arrest four suspects, a Saudi, an African, a German, and a Russian. Seven of you are going with me through the front door the rest of you go through the back."

The minute the van stopped, the doors flew open and all of us hit the ground. Finn flipped his night goggles down and so did the rest of us. We were loaded in heavy gear—Kevlar vests and helmets, ammo—my adrenaline compensated for the extra weight. Finn gave the hand signal to move out. Half ran to the back of the house and the others started to the front door. I stayed close to Finn.

One man ran ahead of us and came to an abrupt stop at the crumbling first step. He looked back at us. "I see gray ground wires running everywhere."

Finn yelled. "Back away slowly."

We heard the team in the back enter the house. We ran in behind them into a narrow hallway. The inside was sweltering from the small fireplace filled with burning logs. We checked the two bedrooms and the closets. In the third bedroom under the bed, I pulled out a briefcase. Inside there were passports, driver's licenses, and $10,000. in American cash. There was one entry visa into the Soviet Union. I followed Finn who was tracking a trail of blood. He forced the bathroom door open. All four of our suspects had blood running from their mouths.

Finn yelled. "Put your hands up!" No one moved. Finn repeated the order in German and Russian and another agent repeated the order in Arabic and Swahili. Still, no one moved. Finn yelled again. "Where are the others? One tried to crack a smile and mumbled. "I killed Agent Robinson." His head flopped sideways. The others sat silent. They were committed to dying without saying a word.

Finn turned to me. "They've downed Cyanide tablets. There's still another Soviet somewhere. I think there is cell service here, go outside and call for a team of medics to take the bodies away."

I ran out outside and everything went black.

Slowly, I woke up in a dim-lit room. The floor was hard and cold. My neck and the back of my head hurt. In fact, my whole skull hurt. I tried to lift my head and knew in an instant that was a big mistake. My head fell back onto the floor. The pain hammered away in full force. I was conscious of coming back from a black hole. The good thing was being alive. I tried to recollect who hit me.

Someone shook me. I opened my eyes to see Finn. Everything looked fuzzy and the room was spinning. I reached for the back of my head feeling a huge lump. I yelped when I touched the spot. "Who karate-chopped me?"

Finn shook me again and rubbed both my arms. "We're in a barn, you're safe. We are moving to a safe house"

I gave a half-smile. "I would hate to find out what a not-so-safe house was. Seems like they are few and far away. The monastery was supposed to be safe and so was the house in Crested Butte."

Finn smiled. "You're safe now. One of our agents is missing, he's the one who clobbered you. He escaped and we know now that he was the mole at Langley. He has been helping the Soviets get in and out of our country. You weren't at a safe house when you were attacked from behind.

I looked at Finn. "Who can we trust? It seems everyone—FSB, FBI, NSA, and CIA—has people selling confidential information."

Finn smiled ruefully. "Trust your team. It's the bond that holds us together. You have orders to return to Langley."

The next evening, my head was still sore but all my functions and thought processes were working. I was flown from Berlin to Rhein-Main Air Base Germany in Frankfurt.

On our descent the pilot announced. "The main runway is closed for a couple of hours. The field we have to land on isn't lighted and there's no moon tonight. The rain is heavier than predicted we may be landing in a waterlogged field."

The landing was smoother than I expected, a Private driving a hummer met me at the plane's steps. His frown showed his apology. "Ma'am, sorry about the conditions."

Two hours later, I was on an air force plane headed back to Langley.

After I was debriefed, I walked out of the CIA headquarters at midnight. I was exhausted but I smiled when I saw Finn waiting for me. "What are you doing here?"

"I've been summoned to Quantico. If you need anything let me know." Finn smiled and squeezed my hand.

We hadn't talked about specifics but we knew we had an agreement. We would watch one another's back. We didn't know who was a mole and who wasn't anymore. We didn't know who we could trust at Langley, the Pentagon, or Quantico.

Finn gave me a quick hug. "It's good to be on the same side."

I smiled. "Is this where we cut our thumbs and become blood brothers and double-dog swear."

Finn laughed. "No, I faint when I see blood."

We both were still laughing when he got in the back seat of the FBI car.

Chapter 27

I'd been to four cities in three days and the return to DC had been a twenty-two-hour weather storm flight from hell to Langley. Bryan had left a message that he was flying in from Greenville last night and for me to meet with him this morning at seven-thirty at Langley. After we had said our hellos, Bryan's cell phone lit up, and mine vibrated. I had switched it from airplane mode to vibrate without realizing it. I immediately switched it to ringer.

Bryan frowned. "This is not good."

We learned at the same time that Agents Brett Jones and Hans Finn had been shot at Quantico, but not dead. Immediately Bryan called for a helicopter. Fifteen minutes later we landed on Quantico soil. Major General, Richard Harrison, the head of Quantico, met us on the tarmac. Those that knew him called him Dick.

Dick gestured towards the flashing blue lights. "You got here fast, Bryan. I talked to you an hour ago. The ambulance has already taken Brett and Finn to the base hospital."

Bryan smiled. "It's easy when you have the government escort at your disposal, but seriously we were about to start our meeting when you called." Bryan turned and pointed out over the base. "No doubt this was an inside job. Were there any witnesses?"

"One cleaning crew member." Dick nodded toward the crime scene.

I asked Dick. "Have you called the forensics team?"

"Yes, they're on their way."

We walked towards the crime scene; blood was splattered all over the pavement. Dick pointed to the overhead cameras. "You know we have the best surveillance system. We're tracing back from midnight to the present. We have six video monitors on each camera."

We went inside the building. The cleaning man was perched sideways on a table in the breakroom.

Dick sat in a chair next to him. "What's your name?

"Sergeant Brown, sir." He moved into a chair across from Dick and Bryan.

Dick's voice was calm. "Is my information correct that you never saw the shooter and you didn't hear any shots?"

"That's right sir. My shift was over. I was standing at the front door putting my cart away. I looked up and saw both men lying on the ground. A black car pulled around the side of the building. I ran out the door and around the corner, but the car was already out of sight."

The three of us walked to where Sergeant Brown said he first saw the car and then to the side of the building. A person dressed in total black from head to toe moved towards us. A muffled voice said, "Julia, meet me in the George Bush Building cafeteria at 11:00.a.m. Ask for Kelly."

Before I could answer or ask any questions the figure took off running and disappeared behind another building.

Bryan said, "I don't believe this. Dick, you need to call a security meeting. We have major espionage agents and spies working all over the world. Somehow, they have infiltrated our military."

Three military jeeps came to a screeching halt surrounding us. Corporal Meriweather jumped out and saluted Dick. "Sir, there have been two more shootings at the front gate."

Dick jumped in the jeep and headed south. Two helicopters swarmed overhead. The churff sound of the whirling rotors was in tune with my heartbeat. Surveillance drones hovered overhead. I couldn't believe how everything had changed in the last thirty minutes.

Bryan and I headed to the cafeteria and arrived at five to eleven. We showed our IDs to the guard at the door. Bryan said, "We are looking for Kelly."

He pointed to the back of the room where a woman sat alone. She looked to be my age, thin with copper-colored hair that was pulled into a bun it clashed with her bright red dress. The long white pearls added contrast.

She looked startled to see both of us. She pointed at Bryan. "Who are you?"

He answered, "Bryan, head of the FBI. Who are you?"

She picked up her phone and scrolled through the screens as if she was looking for something. She looked up at me. "I know you and I know Adam."

"Stop!" My voice was loud. Several people turned their heads. "You *knew* Adam. Adam is deceased."

In a sarcastic tone, she answered, "Whatever you say."

Dick walked in and pulled up a chair, then tossed a file folder on the table. "Kelly, how did you get on base?"

"I know people and I have credentials." Her tone was sarcastic.

Dick slammed his hand down on the table. "You need to be careful what you report or I'll arrest you for murder."

Bryan and I looked at one another. Bryan picked up the file lying on the table, smiled, then said, "I know who you are now. You were banned from the military as a correspondent ten years ago. Now you are digging up all kinds of dirt on people and maybe even blackmailing some."

She replied indignantly, "You don't know what you're talking about."

Bryan responded, "I don't know if you do the blackmailing yourself but would bet you have come close to participating in it. You deal in dirt, and extortion, and go after the high in command. The government is not going to pay you but I'd love to know what you have on Wesley Campbell?"

"That worm. Don't believe a word he says. He has contacts all over the world and he uses all of them as leverage to pay him big money."

Bryan sat forward in his chair and picked the file up. Opened it and tossed several newspaper reports and clippings from her columns in front of her. "Where did you get your information to report this? You alluded to documents being sold for money."

She cackled. "You don't know much, do you?"

Bryan placed his hands flat on the table. "I know more than you think. There are forces involved that you haven't even thought about. You need to talk. I'm after one person. Wesley Campbell."

She stood, took a few steps, then turned around. "You don't think I don't know about the CIA, FBI, and the NSA's involvement?"

Her pace was quick as she headed for the front door.

I ran after her. "Kelly! Kelly! Wait!"

Her pace increased to almost a trot. She entered a waiting car in front of the building with a government license plate.

Chapter 28

Dick, Bryan, and I headed to the front gate. Military police cars and trucks passed us with their lights flashing and sirens blaring. Bryan turned and looked at me. "Julia, call Rebecca. See if she knows anything about what's going on here at Quantico."

When we arrived, all the chaos looked organized. Uniform personnel was swarming like bees. It looked like everyone on base was there. Yellow crime tape was being run in all directions. Paul, the name of one of the marines on duty at the gate, was being questioned. The paramedics had already bandaged his left arm.

Dick said. "You two come with me."

Bryan and I followed Dick into the building behind the guard gate. The video feed from the surveillance cameras showed a civilian wearing a blue ball cap sunglasses and a black leather jacket driving a black Audi sedan. A stack of printed photos of the driver was lying on the security desk ready to be distributed.

Paul entered the security office from the guard gate. Dick pointed to a chair in front of the desk. "Have a seat, son. Tell us what happened."

Paul answered. "Yes sir. There were three of us in the guard house. I was standing behind the guard on duty. We were getting ready to change shifts. When the car pulled up, Kyle, the other guard, asked for his ID. We both thought he was reaching for his wallet when he pulled a gun and started shooting. He hit Kyle in the neck. I squatted down but not before the second bullet grazed my left arm. Then the next bullet hit the other guard. I held him in my arms for a few seconds before he took his last breath."

Dick handed Paul a photograph. "Have you ever seen this man before?"

Paul's eyes widened. "Yes, he was in the car with Wesley Campbell from the NSA when he came on base to be locked up. I remember because the man was dressed the same that day as he was today."

Dick turned to the security marine. "Get me the footage on July 12th."

The security man nodded. "That may take a bit, sir. But I'll find it."

After they had walked outside Bryan turned to Dick. "I want to talk to Campbell."

After lunch, We drove over to the brig. I stayed behind the two-way mirrored glass listening to Bryan. "Mr. Campbell, this is a courtesy meeting. I'm giving you a chance to tell me what's going on."

Wesley leaned back in his chair and in a sarcastic tone replied. "I have nothing to say. How would I know anything? I've been here for a month and a half."

"You might want to avoid being executed or life in prison. This meeting could save your hide. Have you thought about that?" Bryan was pacing. He stopped behind him. "Let me put it another way. The first one to talk could cut a deal. You know there are so many people involved and someone is going to crack."

He sat straight up in his chair. "A deal. What's that going to get me? I'm not stupid."

"Campbell, this offer stands until the first one talks, after that no more deals. Who knows? Someone could betray you. There could even be a contract out on you." Bryan's voice was stern.

There was no change in Wesley's expression or his voice. He still sat rigid. "There have been rumors." He cocked a half smile.

Bryan shouted. "Rumors!" He stood next to Campbell. "What kind of rumors?"

I could tell by Bryan's body language he wanted to attack him, but he kept his cool.

Wesley looked up at Bryan. "People might think they know what happened but they don't know why." He sat there with a smug grin on his face.

Bryan walked to the door. "We're done here. There's no deal."

Bryan and I met Dick outside. Bryan shook Dick's hand. "Julia and I need to get back home. I don't think there's anything else we can do here. You're on a trail. Stay on it."

I sat quietly on our way over to the airfield waiting to see if Bryan was going to say anything. We boarded the plane headed to Greenville. Bryan sat silent.

On our descent, Bryan slammed his hand down on his knee. "We do whatever we need to do to get the job done. Sometimes it works and other times we have to find another avenue."

"Bryan, there are days like this. We'll get him."

We landed around 3:00 p.m.

I arrived back in Charleston at 6:30 p.m. It felt like midnight. All I wanted to do was go to bed. I stepped out of the shower and looked at the clock. 8:00 p.m. The doorbell rang. Throwing on a robe, I hurried to the door. Eli rushed in and swept me off my feet, swirled me around, and set me back down. "I missed you. I didn't know if you were alive or dead. Uncle Jack said he didn't know anything either, other than you were on an assignment."

"Come sit on the sofa. I'm fine. It's been a long four months."

"I drive by your house every day. Your lights on tonight surprised me. I'm sure you can't tell me where you've been or what you've been doing?"

"Eli, you know all that's classified." I stood and started towards the kitchen. "Would you like something to drink?"

He smiled. "No, all I want is you."

"Eli, I've run into conversations multiple times over the past several months indicating that Adam is not dead."

Eli's voice was curt. "Who said that? Who have you been talking to?"

I stared into Eli's eyes. "Several people overseas."

Eli's hard expression softened. He lightly chewed on his bottom lip. "They don't know what they're talking about."

"Well, it's been an eerie feeling. Like they had recently seen him."

Eli stood in front of me and pulled me to my feet. "I'm sorry. I know your job has been hard and emotional."

"Eli, I'm the one who's sorry. I know how close you were to Adam."

Eli's grin looked like it was frozen. "Can I give you a hug?" I stepped next to him. He smiled. "You know this is where you belong"

I pulled away and lowered my head. "I'm not ready for a relationship at this point. Right now, my job comes first."

He walked to the door and placed his hand on the doorknob, turned and faced me. "Good night, Julia."

With tears in my eyes, his taillights were blurry.

My caller ID showed Rebecca's number. "Hello."

She talked fast and the inflection in her voice changed almost after every sentence. "I know it's late but I wanted to bring you up to date. Some of Campbell's contacts have turned against him. A lot of them thought they were the only ones he was dealing with. Since he has been at Quantico, the word on the street is that his contacts think, he's going to rat them out. I've heard there is a contract out on him."

Her information confirmed what I already suspected. "Well, that doesn't surprise me and it explains why Quantico was attacked. Keep me and Bryan informed. We'll talk tomorrow."

The next morning at 6:30 a.m. my phone ringing woke me. My hand fumbled around on the nightstand knocking it under the bed. By the time I retrieved it, my voicemail dinged. "Sorry, Bryan, my phone fell on the floor."

"Julia, a plane will be waiting for you at eight o'clock at the Charleston Executive Airport on St. Johns Island. Agent Jones will pick you up at Langley Air Force Base. The two of you are going to question Caleb Johnston a professor at DC University in Washington. Agent Jones has all the information. He will brief you on the way."

Brett looked good after all he had been through. The knifing, gunshot wounds, and whatever else I didn't know about. We were working and my professionalism needed to stay in tack. He had no idea how much I wanted to give him a big hug. He had saved my life more than once.

Brett parked in front of the Student Union Building. He yelled. "There he is. The man in the black leather jacket with the brown satchel. I'll take care of this." Brett jumped out of the car and ran towards Professor Johnson. I stayed on Brett's heels and yelled. "I'll be your bodyguard."

Brett came to an abrupt halt, looked at me, and laughed. "I've always wanted one of those."

Brett turned and waved his credentials. "Dr. Caleb Johnston. I'm FBI. You're under arrest."

"Arrest? For what?"

Brett and I stood on each side of Caleb. Brett continued. "Four accounts of murder."

Dr. Johnson shouted. "Murder! I've never killed anyone. I don't know what you're talking about!"

I pulled the satchel off his shoulder. Inside was a blue ball cap, sunglasses, and a Colt .45 semi-automatic pistol.

I looked up at him. "We have you on camera in the car with Wesley Campbell and a second time at Quantico the day the gate guards were shot."

Dr. Johnson yelled. "I want a lawyer!"

Brett read him his rights.

By this time a crowd of students had gathered and were shouting. "Murderer! Murderer! Murderer!

Dr. Johnson yelled. "Go away. There's nothing to see here."

Brett put his hand on the top of his head and gently pushed him into the back seat.

Dr. Johnson retorted. "I was working for Colonel Weatherford. Someone has to take a stand and act on corrupt people. I fought in Kabul. I know about conflicts, corruption, and selling your country out. Campbell is the one who needs to be arrested."

Brett didn't waste any time driving to Alexandria. He and I made sure the federal holding facility processed Caleb Johnston correctly.

It was close to midnight when I made the seventeen-mile trip from Langley to the Element Hampton Hotel. At six the next morning, my body instantly told me I hadn't had enough sleep. I turned on my side with my mind racing forward. There was no way I was going back to sleep. I grabbed my phone and scrolled to Kelly's number. After my second cup of coffee, I decided to make the call.

Kelly answered on the first ring. "I knew I would hear from you. I didn't know how long it would take, but you surprised me by calling so soon."

"I want to know what you know about Adam Robinson."

Kelly laughed. "And if I tell you, what are you going to give to me in exchange."

"I know who was behind the Quantico shootings."

The silence lasted for a minute or so before Kelly replied. "Are you trying to appeal to my soft side? You know I don't have one."

I laughed, and then in a stern voice said, "Give me the names that Wesley Campbell sold the NSA documents to. The FBI or the CIA wants to charge him with Adam's murder. In return, I'll give you the name behind the murders at Quantico before it hits the news."

Kelly's silence lasted more for than a minute before she said, "I can give you that information but it's not going to lead you to Adam's killer. From now on you will be my inside source."

My voice was harsh. "Give me the information. I'll make sure you'll remain anonymous. As far as a source that depends on the contents."

After Kelly's conversation, I smiled. Maybe, at last, I was going to find justice for Adam.

Chapter 29

My mind digressed through everything that had brought me to this point in my life. I would still be in Jacksonville if Robert were alive. Trying not to dwell on Adam's death, I thought that Kelly's idea that Adam wasn't dead was far-fetched. It seemed that Eli had dealt with his brother's murder by closing his dental practice and disappearing for a while. He and Adam were close, Adam would've contacted him if he was alive.

My caller ID showed Agent Jones. "Hi, Brett."

"Julia, have you talked to Bryan?" His voice was strong and agitated.

"Not today. What's going on?"

Brett took in a long breath. "Major General Richard Harrison, the head of Quantico, called a press conference informing everyone he had removed Colonel Weatherford from the head of the Security Battalion at Quantico. Dick said it was due to a loss of confidence in his ability to command. He made his decision based on the incident at the Quantico gate. Weatherford had been an officer for over twenty-five years. He was charged with several violations under the Uniform Code of Military Justice. Dick said his relief was due to a deadly event involving firearms on base a few years ago when two soldiers were killed. Now Caleb Johnson is a hitman for him. Quantico is governed by an order requiring all military personnel on base to register personal firearms and store them at the base armory, off-base, or in non-barracks family housing under high-security conditions. This order applies to all personnel except for those required to carry concealed handguns in the execution of their duty. State-issued concealed carry permits are not recognized on the base. Security Battalion oversees personal weapons registration and enforcement of the weapons order for Quantico. Weatherford violated gun laws on government property. He also said, last year a civilian construction contractor smuggled a shotgun onto the base. Dick didn't mention anything about the guard gate shootings in his press conference. He only talked about past incidents."

I listened intently to every word. "Brett, we have no idea how deep the layers go and who's all involved. Did you know Adam Robinson? He worked for the CIA and was working undercover at the NSA before he was murdered."

Brett replied. "No. I didn't know him but have heard his name mentioned many times in the last year. Julia, Bryan is trying to prove that Campbell put a hit contract out on Robinson. I think he may be behind the Quantico shootings and set up a diversion to escape."

My phone buzzed. "Brett, Bryan is calling me. Thanks for the update. We'll talk later."

Bryan's voice was controlled. "Julia, there's a meeting at 2:00 this afternoon in room 210 at Langley. I'll see you there."

Before I could answer, the phone went dead. I showered and dried my hair. Put a navy-blue suit on from my suitcase and grabbed a sandwich in the hotel bar.

I arrived at Langley expecting a full meeting with the CIA and FBI agents who had been at Quantico but entering the room there were ten agents, half representing the CIA, and half the FBI and Dick Harrison. Everyone seemed to be working in groups. They all had the appearance that they had been working all morning—ties were loose, the ones in long sleeves had them rolled up, and every table was covered with file folders. All the folders had a CIA or FBI seal stamped on the front.

"Bryan, am I late?"

"No. We've been working on some files since seven a.m. Take a seat."

Bryan walked over and placed a thick file in front of me.

I opened it and gasped. "Bryan, where did Adam's file come from?"

"How well did you know him?"

I was puzzled. "Not well. Why?"

He pointed to the file. "Take a look."

I thumbed through it looking at all the assignments Adam had worked on, dates, places, and, people he had arrested. My pulse raced and my heart started beating faster when I saw my name. I closed the file and pushed it away.

Bryan turned and told everyone to take an hour's recess.

I heard the agitation in Bryan's voice. "Did you know what cases Adam was working on? Did you work on any of the cases with him?"

I was puzzled and wrinkled my forehead trying to figure out where all this was coming from. "Bryan, no. We were friends, that's all. I spent a week with him in Charleston when he was exhibiting his art at the Spring Art Festival. He told me he had committed to doing an art show for a year traveling throughout France. I didn't know he was CIA. I married a naval officer and moved to Jacksonville. My husband died five years later and I moved back to Charleston."

Bryan walked around the table with his hands folded behind him. "Don't you think it's odd that Adam left everything to you after being with you for a week?"

"Yes, I tried several times to give it to his brother. Eli wouldn't take it. Jack said it was Adam's instructions. It couldn't be changed. Why these questions? You knew all this back in Greenville."

Bryan leaned across the table. "Listen carefully and tell me the truth. There is evidence that Adam might be alive. Have you seen him?"

"I'm sure my face showed a deer in the headlight look. "No."

Bryan's phone buzzed. He checked his message. "We'll talk later."

He abruptly left the room.

As far as I was concerned my work at Langley was finished. I went back to the hotel, packed, and made a flight reservation to Charleston for 8:00 p.m.

The next morning, I didn't want to discuss Bryan's conversation with Eli over the phone but I needed some answers. He answered on the third ring.

"Eli, where are you? We need to talk."

"Good morning to you too, Julia." He laughed.

"I'm sorry. Where are you?" My voice was tense.

Eli's tone changed to an inquisitive one. "What's so urgent? I'm in Folly Beach. I decided to try painting again."

Before he could say another word. I blurted out. "I'm on my way. See you in thirty minutes."

I was in shock when Eli opened the cottage door. Every inch of the floor, walls, and every nook and cranny was covered with paintings. "Eli, what are you doing?"

He walked to the kitchen window and stared out at the Atlantic. "Concerned and worried. Trying to figure out where you were, what you were doing, and if you were even alive."

Dexter ran out of the bedroom hitting me full force, knocking me down on the floor then landing on top licking my face. I wiped his saliva and hugged him. "Dexter, I need you."

I stood up still rubbing Dexter's ears. "Eli, these paintings look like Adam's work."

Eli moved away from the window and looked at me. "Why not? He taught me. You know that." His tone was curt.

His paintings were professional and as good as any well-known artist's. "Eli, have you talked to Suzie at Atrium? She would be glad to take the beach scenes."

"No. All I wanted to do was paint. Adam taught me it's good therapy and keeps your mind sane. You are welcome to any one of them."

I looked at the one he was in the midst of painting. "You need to sell them, not give them away."

He walked over to a painting of Dexter. "Here you take this one."

I smiled and ran my fingers over the painting. "It looks exactly like Dexter running down the beach. His front paws were outstretched and his tail was flopping in the breeze. I love it. Thank you."

My mood changed when I sat down on the edge of the sofa. "Eli, there has been a lot going on this past eight months. I've been all over Europe and have spent a lot of time at Langley. Things are heating up in Quantico about people seeing Adam. Is there something you would like to tell me? Have you seen Adam?"

Eli shifted from one foot to another. "Why would you ask me that?"

I looked at Eli with a glaring stare. "Because if he's alive, he might have contacted you. I think there's a lot you're not telling me."

Eli walked back to the window and stood for a few minutes in silence watching the waves. "It's lunchtime. Let's go have seafood. You can ask me anything you want, but I don't know what else I can tell you."

"You can tell the truth and answer the question."

The hostess pointed to a table overlooking the ocean. Before I could get settled in my chair, another waiter set two glasses of water in front of us. "Would you like to order a drink from the bar?"

Eli was quick to answer. "Yes. I'll have a martini and the lady will have an Old Fashioned."

"Eli, it's the middle of the day."

"Julia, the way you started your conversation from the time you walked into the house, I think, I'm going to need a drink."

A few minutes later, the bartender sat our drinks in front of us. "Julia, it's been a while since you've been here."

I kept my composure, but I was shocked to see Brett bartending.

The waiter brought our lobster dinners. I sipped my Old Fashioned and stared at Brett behind the bar. The bourbon warmed me from my throat to my chest or was it the sight of seeing Brett?

Eli leaned forward. "Well, tell me why you think Adam is alive, and what has stirred all this up?"

The next ten minutes felt like twelve hours. "Rumors from reliable sources say they have seen Adam in several places throughout Europe. I can't believe you wouldn't know Adam was alive as close as the two of you were?"

Reluctant to hear his answer, there was no choice, I had to ask the question. "Were you in Quantico when the two soldiers were killed and when the guards were killed at the gate?"

"No." He took a big swallow of his martini. "Why would you even ask me that?"

Keeping my tone down, I asked. "Was Adam there? Eli, do you work for a government agency?"

Eli pushed his chair back from the table. "No and no. Julia, why all the questions?" He was almost yelling.

I stared as hard as could into his eyes. "Because things aren't adding up about Adam."

At that moment, a man sitting behind Eli had white foam oozing from his mouth and fell to the floor. His appearance was like that of the men in the bathroom back in Berlin. A shot of adrenaline ran through my veins. I felt sick and scared at the same time. My Colt 45 was in the car.

Brett grabbed my arm and pulled me outside. A black SUV slid its tires coming to an instant stop. Brett opened the back door and pushed me in, then he followed. He pulled me next to him and held me tight. Eli was left standing on the sidewalk.

"Brett, what's going on? I was pressing Eli for answers about Adam?"

Brett gave a half-smile. "You and Eli are on FSB's radar. The inside talk is that they think you know where Adam is. Folly Beach has been crawling with their agents for the last two days tracking Eli. Rebecca called Bryan and Bryan called me. There were several of them in the restaurant. I don't know why that one was poisoned unless he didn't do something he was supposed to, like kill you."

This made me even more confused. "Why would the FSB poison one of their own? There's more to this than we know. Why would they want to kill me?"

Brett answered, "They've been trying to infiltrate the CIA because of Campbell and Adam. We think they're looking for a mole to use. Maybe, Eli. My guess is they were going to get to him by telling him Adam was alive. I don't know who's doing what to whom at this point other than Campbell is at the center of it all."

I frowned. "Eli doesn't work for anyone."

I'd been busy talking to Brett that I hadn't noticed where we were going. I looked out the window to see my house. "Brett, my car is in Folly Beach."

Brett pointed to the house next door. "And Hector is there."

My head was spinning. I tried to fathom Wesley having Adam killed, and Adam being alive.

Chapter 30

The July heat had hit Charleston and the sun was setting later in the day giving the sky a cotton candy sunset. Hector waved and waited on my front steps for Brett and me to get out of the SUV. Inside I offered everyone iced tea but no one accepted.

Brett exhaled and leaned back in my big comfy chair. "Someone came to me from special ops several months back telling me Adam was alive. You asked me earlier if I knew Adam. Our paths crossed once in France on a joint assignment of CIA and FBI agents. I was made aware several months back that he had worked undercover in the NSA. That was our first clue that Campbell was involved in giving confidential information to the Russians and from there it has snowballed into where we are now."

Hector's phone rang. I heard Rebecca's voice. Then mine rang. Bryan's voice sounded tense. "Julia, I'm letting you know we have enough evidence to arrest Campbell for selling US secret intelligent and confidential digital satellite information."

My energy level rose. "Where do we go from here? How long can you hold Wesley at Quantico?"

Bryan chuckled. "For quite a while. We could move him to an unidentified jail somewhere and keep him in isolation. You know government papers and people get lost all the time."

When Hector ended his call, he said, "Hey, guys we need to turn on CNN."

The news commentator was babbling about a contract killing. I glanced at Hector. "What's he talking about?"

Brett switched the channel over to NBC. The anchorman reported. 'A CIA officer is dead. Speculation is that it was a contract killing." Wesley and Adam's picture appeared on the screen.

Brett yelled. "Who would have leaked that?"

I responded. "Kelly."

Brett jumped up and grabbed his phone. When Bryan answered Brett yelled. "Kelly leaked Adam's death to the media."

Brett turned to me and pocketed his phone. "Bryan knew, he has her at Langley now." He cleared his throat and put his hands on my shoulders. "Eli has been picked up and is on his way to Langley for questioning."

I ran to the bedroom. Grabbed my suitcase. Dumped my clothes on the bed and threw clean blouses, skirts and pants, and underwear in. I returned to the living room with tears in my eyes. "I'm going to Langley."

Brett grabbed my arm. "We'll go to Langley. I called for a flight."

The plane turned onto the runway without slowing down, instantly we were in the air climbing fast to the level attitude.

At 1:00 p.m., a car was waiting for us on the tarmac at Langley. We were escorted to the observation area next to the integration room. The two-way mirror allowed us our privacy although Kelly knew her responses to Bryan's questions were being recorded and she was being watched.

Kelly was composed and her answers were direct. "I've known Adam for twenty years. We were friends and worked together as CIA agents. I was offered a correspondence job that paid more. There were rumors at one time that Adam had a torrid affair with another agent. Sylvia was in love with Adam. He was polite and nice to her but that was as far as it went on his side She tried to get the same contracts that he had, but Adam's boss wouldn't allow them to be together on the same assignment. Sylvia was transferred to another CIA division on the west coast. After retiring, I became a freelance news reporter and lost several ties with the CIA and Adam, but Sylvia knew he was at the NSA. She tried to get me to publish Adam's contract jobs to break his cover. She was in a lover's revenge mode. I suspect she contacted Wesley based on the fact she knew Adam was working undercover in his office. Who knows if he made a deal with her or not, she was killed in a car chase in Moscow. I heard Adam was dead, but I didn't believe it. He's too careful and smart."

Bryan slowly paced around the room for a few minutes. "Where did you get your information that Adam was alive?"

Her body stiffened "I don't give out my sources."

Bryan sat across from her and leaned his chair back on two legs. That was his usual position when he was in a tense meeting. "So, you're telling me, you're confident enough in your snitch that the information was correct, but you won't diverge where it came from. You know we could get a court order."

She laughed. "You could but you won't. Adam and I knew everything about one another almost to the point that we could finish one another's sentences. We know one another's mannerisms and voice pitches and how each of us is going to respond in every situation. I know Adam is not dead."

Bryan walked to the door. "Kelly, be careful what you report."

Kelly left.

An officer pushed Eli into the room. I gasped seeing him in handcuffs.

Bryan yelled. "Uncuff him. Who gave that order?"

The soldier stood at attention. "No one, sir. I was told to bring him to the integration room. My apology, sir."

Bryan shook Eli's hand. "I'm sorry. Security has been tightened around here."

Eli sat down with a puzzled look. "Bryan, why am I here?"

Bryan's voice was professional. "You passed the polygraph test except on a few questions about Adam. Now tell me where he is?"

My face had question marks all over it. "Brett, does he know?"

Brett shrugged his shoulders.

Eli answered in an above-normal tone answered. "Adam's deceased. I saw his charred body."

Bryan stood. "You saw a charred body. Has Adam contacted you?"

Eli folded his arms on the table and rested his head downward. "Not until last week. Wesley has been lying about everything." He raised his head. "Adam had to make him think he was dead. He made me promise not to tell anyone. He's been watching Wesley's every move and has been in Moscow and Berlin tracing the information that he sold. Adam thought he had a better chance of convicting him if Wesley thought Adam was dead."

"Where is Adam now?"

In a low voice, Eli answered. "I don't know. He was in Grand Cayman."

My face felt hot. I turned toward the door. Brett grabbed my arm and stopped me from leaving the room.

Bryan released Eli.

When my temper calmed, I wanted to be alone.

Brett left me in my hotel room and went down the hall to his.

Chapter 31

My body hadn't had enough sleep the next morning my entire being was tired and sluggish. I poked my head in Bryan's temporary office at Langley, he motioned me to sit while he ended his conversation with Ms. Haspel, the head of the CIA. Bryan had said hello to me when Dick from Quantico called.

I heard him say. Bryan, I need to see you and Julia in my office immediately, and now wouldn't be soon enough."

Without hesitation, Bryan answered. "Dick, we'll be there within the hour."

Bryan closed down his computer and reached for his suit coat. He wiggled into it as we hurried to the front of the building, where a car was waiting to drive us to Quantico.

We walked into Dick's office around nine-thirty. "Good morning, Bryan, and Julia. Sergeant Ronald Cook was the person on the midnight watch that helped Wesley escape. He had a money transfer of a hundred thousand dollars deposited from the Grand Cayman Islands to Sgt. Cook's bank account each month for the last three months. Three hundred thousand total. Sgt. Cook has gone AWOL. I know there are more people involved but I don't know who they are at this time. I'm sure others have had money deposited into their accounts. I have sent Brett to the Grand Cayman Islands."

Bryan rubbed his hand across the top of his head. "He chose sergeants because they hadn't seen that much money. Cook didn't use his head. He violated federal laws under his oath and now can be tried for federal fraud."

I frowned. "All he thought about was the money and not the consequences. He'll get a life sentence."

Dick moved his chair back away from his desk. "I've locked down the base. No leaves are being granted and no one enters unless they have a confirmation from the President. This is worse than the circumstances under which the major general was dismissed. I thought everything was under control."

Bryan said. "Dick, with all the agencies involved, it's bigger than any of us could have controlled."

Dick curled his lip up giving a cracked half-smile. "If you are trying to make me feel better it's not working. I have Sgt. Cook mug shots in all airports within a hundred-mile radius, roadblocks at the state lines of Virginia and Maryland, and his house in New York is under surveillance, including all known relatives. Bryan, you and Julia have full reign to do anything you need to do. Let's get Campbell back in custody and I'll take care of the military personnel. All information we find and that Brett finds, we'll forward to you."

Dick's phone rang. He held up a halted hand. His face took on a deep frown when he slammed the receiver down. "That was the surveillance team. There has been no activity at Cook's home. They had a warrant and entered the house. There was no indication that anyone had been there in quite some time. All closets were empty, the kitchen cupboards and pantry were empty, and the garage had shown no evidence of a vehicle."

Dick stood up and shook both our hands. "Thank you for coming. We'll stay in touch."

I turned towards Bryan as we walked down the building's front steps to the car. "How did things get so fouled? Last week Wesley was in custody, the military was doing their job, and we were trying to find out if Adam was actually alive. Those duties seemed simple compared to the events that have transpired in the last couple of days. Now everything has fallen apart."

Bryan smiled. "Julia, you know with our jobs nothing is ever simple."

Bryan opened my car door. We were saying goodbye when his phone rang. Bryan waved his hand for me to stay. "Hi, Brett." Bryan put his phone on speaker.

I laughed. "Hi, Brett."

Brett's voice was in a business tone. "Adam was coming out of the Grand Cayman bank this morning when he saw me. He darted in front of a tourist bus. I lost him for a bit but found him at the airport."

Bryan interrupted Brett. "Are you sure it's Adam?"

"I wouldn't be making this call if it wasn't."

My body stiffened.

Bryan cut Brett off. "We don't have any agents in Grand Cayman at the moment. Do what you can."

Brett's voice was loud. "Bryan! Adam is with me! Our arrival time at Ronald Regan Airport is 3:00 p.m. We'll be at Langley around four."

My nerves were on edge when I entered Bryan's office at 3:45 p.m. After saying hello to Bryan and Mrs. Haspel. Brett and Adam walked in.

Bryan looked at Adam. "Okay, you have a lot of explaining to do. Start when you and Eli went to the cabin."

Adam cleared his throat. "The cabin door blew off knocking me backward. My face and arms were burned. When I stood, the charred body was lying in the doorway. Knowing that Wesley was behind the explosion and the only way he was going to be caught was to go underground. I put my ID in the body's pocket and took his, then ran down the hill and through the woods. I hitched a ride on the other side of the mountain to the hospital in the next town. Telling the driver that my car had caught fire along with all my ID."

Bryan shook his head. "Adam, you weren't thinking clearly. Continue."

"Well, at the time, I had no idea that Wesley had killed anyone and how involved he was with the Russians. In my mind, if he thought I was dead I could maneuver incognito and bring him to justice." He turned and faced me. "I left you everything because I didn't know if Eli was alive, but I knew everyone had to think I was deceased and I knew I could be killed at any time. I hopped a private plane to Grand Cayman, found a counterfeit back room, and had him put my picture on Sean Walker's ID. I rented a small place until my face healed. A witch doctor gave me a concoction to rub on my face and arms to help the scaring." Adam laughed and raised his hands. "Good stuff, you can't tell I had any burns."

My heart was heavy and hurt that Adam chose to give up the life he knew. Thinking about the desperate path that he decided to take and how he had turned his world upside down for his country made tears dribble down my cheeks. He could have easily resigned from the CIA or told his superiors what he knew at the time.

Mrs. Haspel sat forward in her chair. "Adam your intentions were good but your judgment was skewed. Bryan and I understand your decision to assume Sean Walker's identity, but you didn't follow protocol. The situation in Russia right now has deteriorated. We have confirmed information that Campbell is planning an assassination of a Russian senior official. You need to go make it look like the official was killed by an FSB agent. You'll be briefed on the way to Moscow. We'll continue your farce charade of you being dead until you return."

Mrs. Haspel said her good-byes.

Bryan looked at me and Adam. "I'm going to give you two a few minutes."

He and Brett left the room.

Adam turned toward me and reached for my hand. "You know we both knew we were in love with one another after the week we spent together. There were many times that week that I wanted to tell you how much you were loved, but the time never seemed right. Through my sources, I tried to keep tabs on you. When you went back to work for the FBI, that made our lives more complicated. I loved you then and I love you even more now. Is there any way, we can make up for the years we lost?"

I had no words. I tried to stand but my legs were paralyzed. The tears hadn't stopped, in fact, they were flowing even more if that was possible. Adam squeezed my hand. After a few minutes, my composure returned. "One can never turn back time. It took me a while to get over you even though you were still in my mind. I've started to move forward, there's no way we can go back now."

Adam let go of my hand. Numbness still covered my body when I walked out of the office.

The flight back to Charleston was turbulent allowing me no sleep.

In my exhausted state, I tossed and turned and couldn't find a comfortable place on my mattress. I tried to make myself fall asleep but that didn't happen. Needless to say, it was a long night of digressing.

My mind raced thinking how it must have been for Adam, as it was for the rest of us. A strange sense of stillness and serenity finally drifted over me. I was now at peace that Adam was alive.

Chapter 32

I was finishing my ham and eggs when I heard Dexter barking. Eli knocked on the back door. "I didn't expect to see you this morning."

"I went to Greenville last night to pick up Dexter. Uncle Jack insisted I spend the night. Do you want Dexter or are you off to who knows where?" His voice had no emotion only a straight monotone.

I gave him a slight smile. "No, I'm not going anywhere at the moment. Would you like some coffee?

"Yes, please." Eli walked to the window and watched the waves. "Strong wind this morning." He turned towards me. "Can we talk?"

I didn't know what to expect but handed him his coffee and went to the sofa. Dexter had made himself comfortable at my feet. Eli took his time doctoring his coffee with cream and sugar before he came over. He was doing everything in slow motion.

"Julia, I should've told you that Adam called me, but I was trying to process everything from the cabin explosion to now. When Adam and I got to the cabin, we heard noises inside. Adam told me to go around back. That's when the cabin blew up."

Dexter ran to the front door barking. I opened the door to see Agent Caldwell jumping out of the van and ripping his headset off. I hadn't seen him since the Folly Beach stakeout.

Hector came running from his house yelling. "They ran behind Julia's house!"

Another van pulled next to Agent Caldwell and an agent yelled. "It's a cell phone here in Charleston! It's a burner phone, no, ID! It's within five blocks!"

Agent Caldwell repositioned his headset. "Kelly is talking to Rebecca. She knows where Campbell is."

I felt the blood drain from my face. "Does that mean Wesley's close by? Where is Rebecca? How is Kelly involved?"

Hector grabbed my elbow and escorted me toward my house. "Julia, he's close. You've been on his radar. We need to let him think he can get to you."

A gunshot sounded and Hector pulled me down on the porch before he took off running toward his house.

Agent Caldwell yelled. "It came from the right side of Julia's house."

A man bolted onto the porch and grabbed me. Eli ran out onto the porch. "Let her go!"

Eli walked towards the man who had my arm twisted behind my back. Hector ran from the left of his house and yelled. "Stop. Drop your gun."

I moved my right leg between his right and left and gave his right leg a jerk with my foot. He stumbled to regain his balance. I broke loose.

Hector put his gun on the man's back. "Turn around slowly. Now tell your partner to drop his." Hector jammed the man's ribs with his gun. "I have no problem shooting you. Do it."

All the agents had their guns pointed at the men. Agent Caldwell stared at the assailants as he retrieved their guns. "You didn't think you were going to get away with her, did you?"

Eli put his arm around my waist and pulled me next to him.

One man looked like a wrestler, and the other one was small-framed with long bleached blond hair. Suddenly, the smaller man took off running down the middle of the street. Hector pulled his trigger. The man fell and lay crumpled on the pavement not moving.

Agent Caldwell poked his gun into the heavyset man's temple. "Now I suggest you talk if you want to survive. Who's paying you to kill her?"

"I don't know." The man's lip quivered. You're a federal agent you can't kill me."

Hector approached the would-be assassin with his gun pointed at the man's face. "I'm not an agent. Talk!"

The man's voice was low. "He was paying me $10,000. Five now and five after she was dead."

Hector yelled. "What man?"

"I don't know." Hector shot him in his left foot. "Wrong answer. You do know."

Hector waved the gun across the man's face. "Who hired you?"

"I don't know. He had an accent, maybe Russian or German."

Agent Caldwell pushed a picture on his phone of Campbell in his face. "Have you seen this man?"

The man nodded. "Yes, he handed the money to a man to give it to me when she was dead."

Hector came face to face with him leaving only a couple of inches between them. "Where were you when he gave you the money?"

He closed his eyes and tilted his head up at the sky. "A warehouse. I don't know where. I was hooded and there were several codes used before we entered the building."

I gasped. "That sounds like the same warehouse I was taken to here in Charleston."

Agent Caldwell secured the men's hands with plastic ties, then Hector secured the man in the van. He picked up the man in the street. "Where are you taking them?" I asked.

Agent Caldwell laughed. "Away from you." Then he said. "They'll eventually be housed at Quantico."

Three police cars pulled up in front of Agent Caldwell. He hurried over to the first one before anyone exited their cars. He flashed his badge and said a few words. The police cars drove away.

Agent Caldwell approached me. "Julia, you'll be fine. We combed the area and didn't find anyone else. You could have Hector stay with you tonight."

"I'm fine. That's not necessary. Thank you."

I ran into the house with Eli on my heels. I grabbed a glass and shoved it under the water dispenser on the refrigerator door. I was so thirsty that it seemed like minutes before the glass filled. I looked at Eli and then handed him the glass. I filled another glass for myself.

I sat back in my favorite chair and motioned for Eli to sit on the sofa. "We have some unfinished business. In a stern voice, I said. "I still don't understand why you didn't tell me Adam had contacted you."

Eli took several sips of water and stared at the floor. "I'm sorry, Julia. I thought you would be safer if you didn't know."

I sat silently trying to calm my insides. I was upset with Eli and he knew it. He said nothing. I took Dexter for a walk out the back gate over to White Point Gardens and sat on a weather-beaten wooden bench trying to clear my mind, then threw a small pebble into the pond. The heat within me wasn't cooling. I picked up a handful more and threw them into the water as hard as I could. My sobbing had stopped. Robins, cardinals and blue jays were flying from tree to tree and I wished I had a bird brain and could fly away. The wind rustled the tree leaves sending the sweet flower scents toward me. I turned my head toward the ground and watched the pigeons scratch in the dirt looking for morsels of food. Then without any warning, uncontrollable tears were running down my cheeks like a waterfall, soaking the front of my shirt. A man's shadow appeared behind me making me jump. Eli stood towering over me, his arms outstretched for me to jump into them. That didn't happen. He said down at the other end of the bench. It seemed like hours before either one of us spoke.

"Eli, my car is still in Folly Beach. Will you take me?"

He smiled. "Of course."

On the way, his voice was soft. "Adam knew his life was in danger. He said that on the way to the cabin, but he didn't want to tell me all the details until we got to the cabin. I know he was going to tell me about Wesley selling confidential intelligent secrets to Russia. When I looked into the cabin after I climbed back up the hill, I saw the charred body. At the time I had no way of knowing that it wasn't Adam."

"Eli, I know Adam's disappearance has been hard, especially when you thought he was dead. He's back now and all of us can return to a normal life."

The long day had caught up to me. At midnight, the heat lightning danced across the sky. I couldn't sleep thinking about how Eli was having a hard time accepting Adam being alive. He was still obsessing about why Adam let everyone think he was dead. After seeing how hurt he was, I had to forgive him for not telling me that he had talked to him.

The warm water in the shower running over my head made my body relax as if the events of my day been washed away. I crawled into bed and glanced at the clock. The blue light showed 12:30. If my phone didn't wake me I could get at least seven hours of sleep.

Chapter 33

I buried my head under my pillow hoping the phone would stop ringing. On the seventh ring I answered but not in a coherent state at 2:18 a.m.

I heard two voices talking at the same time. "Bryan? Mrs. Haspel? Wait slow down you two. My brain's not in gear."

Mrs. Haspel answered. "Julia, I'm sorry."

Bryan's voice was deep. "Julia, It's been a month since Adam went to Russia and we haven't heard from him. We're sending you and Brett over. You have a flight at nine this morning out of Quantico. I'll send a plane to pick you up in Charleston at seven a.m. Brett will brief you on the flight to Russia."

The rest of the night I tried to analyze what had happened with Wesley's thugs and why he had sent them after me. Had he put a trail on me, and knew that Adam and I had talked? After all the chaos was over yesterday and they were in custody, I thought my life would be another ordinary day today.

At 5:00 a.m., I took a hot shower trying to get my body and mind awake and ready for the day ahead. I was packed by 5:30 a.m. and knocking on Hector's door with Dexter in hand.

The flight to Quantico was quicker than I had remembered. Maybe it was because Russia and Adam were occupying my mind. As soon as the plane landed, Bryan, Mrs. Haspel, and Brett met me.

On the way across the tarmac to the next plane, she brought Brett and me up to speed. "This information came from Adam two weeks ago. We know it's out of date, but it's all we have at the moment. The secret satellite intelligence information that Campbell had sold to Russia is now in Western Siberia. We think a rogue FSB agent is trying to cut off Germany's oil supply to gain what information Campbell sold to Germany. Brett, you're flying to Berlin, and Julia you are going to Moscow. Brett, you and Adam will meet up with Julia in Moscow after you confirm the information with Germany's

BND agents. Julia, Maxwell will have your orders. Work as quickly as you can, but there's no time frame. Accuracy is more important."

"What's Adam doing in Berlin? He went to Russia. Then to Paris." I stared out the window trying to put all the details in order.

Brett shifted in his seat and faced me. "Adam is trying to get the Russian Mob in Paris to corporate with us but last night four mob members were killed in a rush-hour traffic accident on Champ-Elysees Avenue. The surveillance camera showed two men dressed in black from head to toe on a black motorcycle pulling up beside the mob's SUV and throwing a bomb under it. The vehicle blew nine feet into the air. Chunks, bits, and pieces flew everywhere stopping traffic for hours." He cleared his throat. "The Paris news has been quiet but the BBC News channel reported that a Russian Mafia leader in St. Petersburg was gunned down the same time that the SUV exploded in Moscow."

I looked through the clouds at the ground as they descended into Berlin. "I think Wesley knows we're closing in and he's panicking. If the mob catches him, we'll never see him again. Maybe we need to find the people Wesley sold the information to rather than trying to track him down. The Mafia will take care of him when they find out how many governments he's sold classified information to. You know all this has to do with money. Who can sell the information to whom and get the highest price? The governments think they are getting secret information. Don't they know we change our codes and redirect secret information almost every hour? It's the agents in charge that's going to end up with the money."

I said goodbye to Brett in Berlin. "Be careful and stay safe."

He gave me a light kiss on the cheek. I wanted more but this wasn't the time or the place. With so much happening and us chasing around the world, there hadn't any private time for us.

Within the hour, the plane had refueled taking off for Moscow. It was after midnight when I checked into the Moscow Marriott Imperial Plaza.

At 6:00 a.m., Someone was tapping on my door. "Good morning, Julia. I'm Jock from Maxwell's communications division. I'm here to set up a secure telephone for you."

He walked over to the desk and set down a large brown box. "This box will scramble your cell phone to outsiders but Maxwell can hear you. I understand you're expecting a call shortly from Langley. You're all set. Have a good day."

I walked behind him to the door. The phone had a shrill ring. I put the medal key in the side slot like Jock showed me. A voice announced. "Call is being synchronized." Then followed by. "Line is secure."

Dick's voice came in strong and clear. "Julia, I hope you had a good flight." Before I could answer he continued. "I'm emailing you a list of bank account numbers. I think you'll find a trail leading back to Campbell. The Cayman bank clerk who was handling his accounts turned out to be an FSB agent. There are other names on the list too. Get Maxwell to run down the employee names. I will talk to Maxwell later today."

Before my 8:00 a.m. meeting with Maxwell, I handed him the list of names and told him Dick would be in touch later this morning. At eight, Maxwell introduced me to two FBI agents and two CIA officers from Berlin. Maxwell pointed to the back of the room. "Julia, take a seat next to Finn. I've handpicked all of you because you're the best in your fields. Everyone will have the same equipment. Over on the table, you will find your kits, try everything out." He laughed. "But don't fire any weapons in here."

The Kevlar vest was heavy. I was familiar with it and remembered it was filled with the half-inch steel plates in the front and back. I could handle the MP5 if I had to but I liked the Beretta 9 MM. The handgun was more to my liking. Also included were two spare mags. One of the Berlin men inquired about an AK-47.

Maxwell looked at him and in his strong voice answered. "This is what's being issued."

At that moment Adam and Brett busted through the door.

Watching Adam my mind flashed back to the week with him in Charleston. Seeing him now brought back memories that I thought I had forgotten. Maybe I still had feelings and I wasn't ready to let go.

Without acknowledging anyone in the room, Adam went straight to the point. "Langley is trying to build an international security case against Wesley. He's broken a whole slew of rules, international laws, and codes."

I said, "This was already an international security case when Wesley sold our documents to Russia and Germany."

Adam answered. "You're right." Then he continued as if I hadn't said a word. "A Russian citizen traveling to Berlin tried to sell some of the documents to the European Union. If they get sold to the union that makes it easy to sell all kinds of information to different countries."

Maxwell leaned back in his chair. "Adam, do you have a name or do we know who this person is?"

"Ivan Kostya."

Hans Finn, one of the Berlin officers, who had been wounded in the Quantico attack, chimed in. "I know him. He worked undercover for me in Rome on an assignment several years back. He's good at his job but he only wants to be paid in gold and he will only agree to a job if he talks to the person who's going to pay him."

Maxwell sat forward in his chair, propped his elbows on the table, then clasped his hands together. "Finn, what else do you know about him?"

"He was born in one of the smallest towns in Russia, Suzdal. He's short, mid-forties, bald, smart, and wears expensive clothes. He speaks fluent English."

Maxwell pushed his chair away from the table. "Adam, what do you think?"

Adam paced back and forth then walked to the back of the room. "Go for it. We may find out more than we know now and it could be possible he knows where Wesley is hiding."

Maxwell nodded to Finn. "Set it up."

For the past two weeks, I had been working on my laptop in a temporary office on the eleventh floor of the FBI building in Moscow and still, no one had heard from Finn. Wednesday morning, Adam and I were about to walk up the steps of the FBI office building when Finn and another man flanked us.

Adam whispered. "That's Ivan Kostya."

Then Finn said. "Keep walking. No talking."

Ivan turned to a sharp left and we followed. At the back of the building, the private courtyard was surrounded by a tall green holly hedge in front of a wrought-iron fence. Adam and I sat on a concrete bench, Finn stood on our right and Ivan stood facing us.

Ivan stared at Adam. "Are you the one paying me?

Adam nodded. "Yes."

"How much?"

Adam replied. "Depends on if your information is correct and how much you know."

"I'll tell you where Wesley is but I want my gold first."

Adam stood. "That is not the way we work. I assure you that you will be paid. You can take my terms or leave."

Finn nodded to Ivan.

Adam sat back down.

Ivan placed his left foot on the seat of the weathered bench in front of us. "I spent the last involuntary week in Wesley's presence.

Adam raised his eyebrows. "Were you kidnapped or working undercover?"

"Undercover. He wanted to sell me US secret documents. He was asking for more than the European Union pays and they pay big for information."

Adam cleared his throat. "Let me get this straight. Do I understand that you are buying secret information from Wesley, selling it to the European Union and now you are offering up him to me for payment in gold?"

Ivan said. "You got it. That's how I make my living."

Adam stood. "Have you agreed to his price?"

"Not yet. Wesley thinks I'm negotiating between him and the European Union."

Adam sat down next to me and stretched his legs out in front of him. "Where does all this stand now?"

Ivan cracked a half-smile. "I was taken back to my hotel in Berlin. I haven't given Wesley an answer yet."

Adam leaned forward and placed his hands on his knees. "Okay, pass the word that you will pay his price, you give me the location and the time that you are going to meet him."

Ivan frowned. "My gold?"

Adam stood. In a gruff voice, he answered. "When we get Campbell, you'll get paid. Get me the time and place."

Ivan exited through the path in the green hedge.

Finn said, "Thanks for not blowing my cover. He doesn't know I'm working with you."

Adam took two steps forward. "I'll try to keep your secret but no promises. He's going to end up in the US Army Regional Correctional Facility in Mannheim. Have a good day."

Chapter 34

I had finished my rib-eye steak and ordered another Old Fashioned in the Grand Alexander Restaurant, in my hotel. I knew it was known for its French cuisine, but I wanted a steak. Brett entered and immediately made his way to my table.

My eyes widened. "What are you doing here?"

He smiled. "Protecting you."

I laughed. "And you think I need protecting?"

Brett's watchful eyes showed no emotions. "Yes, everything is going to come to a head tomorrow."

The waiter sat my Old Fashioned in front of me. I looked at Brett. "What do you want to drink?"

Nothing." His eyes roamed around the room.

I touched the waiter's arm and looked at Brett. "He will order." Then winked at the waiter.

Brett smiled. "Why not? Tomorrow could be our last day. I'll have a Gin and Tonic."

His face was drawn. "Brett, what's going on?"

The waiter returned. Brett clinked his glass to mine and smiled. "Here's to tomorrow with Campbell in custody."

My mouth fell open as if I was looking at him for the first time I zeroed in on his words and wondered why he would allude to this may be the last time we might see one another.

Brett reached for my hand. "I thought about you all night. I couldn't get you out of my mind. This morning when I opened my eyes, I still remembered your soft lips, gentle hands, and your kiss. I looked away from him trying to control the heat welling up inside me.

The waiter brought my tab. I signed it, smiled, and handed it back. Brett pulled out his wallet. I pushed it away. "This one's on me." We laughed knowing the FBI paid.

He reached for my hand and gently pulled me to my feet. "Can I walk you to your room?"

In the elevator, his eyes traced my body from head to toe as if he was assessing every inch of me. The heated rush overtook me again. The older couple in the elevator smiled at us when they exited on the 5th floor. I smiled back. Brett's heavy wisps of breath in my left ear and the scent of his cologne were making it hard for me to resist. I wanted him, all of him. He cupped his hand in mine. My body stiffened watching his eyes dance as he engulfed me again from head to toe.

He ran his index finger over my lower lip and whispered. "Say yes." Before I answered his mouth was on mine and his fingers were intertwined in my hair. His lips were persuasive. My heart raced and pounded. I felt his chest move with every breath. He gently teased and nibbled my lower lip. I smiled and returned his kiss letting him know that I wanted more. He drew me closer when the elevator doors opened on the 10th floor.

I fumbled with the lock, my lips still pressed to his. He picked me up twirled me around and never let go of his mouth on mine until we reached the bedroom. My body ached for his touch and attention. My passion was so high now that kissing wasn't satisfying my need. He mumbled something but I didn't understand what he said or cared. At this moment, I didn't want to talk. I wanted him. I felt his firm, strong hands softly caressing my breasts. I didn't expect to feel his need or mine. My senses were tingling at an all-time high. He gently forced me onto the bed, unbuttoned my blouse with one hand and with both hands inched my skirt up to my waist. I held my breath feeling his gentle power. My pulse hammered and my body arched. Without speaking, he rolled to his side and drew me next to him. My body was still shuddering inside. He stroked my hair and nibbled at my ear until I was calm. He reached over and lowered my skirt. He whispered. "Are you okay? You didn't say no."

I sucked in a deep breath but I couldn't find my words only nodded yes. My body was serene and content. I wanted him to stay close and for this moment to never end. Everything was perfect.

He gently pulled my head to his shoulder. "It's late. I need to go. We have a big day ahead of us tomorrow."

He stopped at the door, held my face in his hands, and gave me one last goodnight kiss and a hug. I leaned against the closed door. Robert and I made love regularly, but during our seven years of marriage, I never experienced a night like this.

After Brett left last night, I forgot to close the bedroom drapes. I woke to the bright morning sun that lit up the ceiling-to-floor windows. A tightness filled my chest when the flashback from last night with Brett consumed my mind. I knew this was the man wanted. Then I recalled his conversation about today that it could be our last. I pushed that thought from my mind. This wasn't going to be our last day.

My phone rang. "Good morning, Maxwell."

There were no pleasantries. He went straight to the point. "The names on the list of FSB employees in the Cayman Islands you gave me are working for Campbell."

I answered. "There were also several shell corporations with the same ID number that belonged to Wesley. That was a slip-up on his part or someone who set up the accounts. One account has over two million dollars in it and another one with over three million."

His voice was in capture mode. "We're going to get Wesley Campbell today. Be in my office as soon as you can." He laughed. "Now would be good."

I was the last one to walk into Maxwell's office. The men stood until I took my seat. I nodded. They didn't need to stand but I enjoyed the respect. Everyone was dressed in their combat clothes, including Adam and two Berlin agents. I smiled at Agent Finn. I didn't know the other Berlin agent. To my surprise, I saw Brett sitting next to two FSB Russians. I avoided eye contact with him and quickly put on my Kevlar vest and checked my guns. Maxwell was barking orders as fast as he could talk. His anxiety was building and running wild through his body.

Adam announced. "Ivan told us that Wesley is supposed to be in Chinatown. We will head down Ilyinka Street southwest away from Red Square."

Maxwell pointed. "Adam, Russian officers, and Julia in the first vehicle. Brett, Finn, and the other Berlin agents are in the second SUV. You have been fully briefed. You have your orders, go!"

We pulled onto Ilyinka Street. A black car pulled up next to Brett's vehicle. Adam's voice was gruff. "Get ready. We have company." A black SUV had pulled up beside us. I yelled. "They have guns."

Our SUV was armor-plated and all the glass had three inches of bulletproof material between the layers. It would take a tank to destroy us.

Adam's voice was calm. "Don't do anything unless they fire first. It could be an escort."

Before Adam finished his sentence, we heard shots coming from behind us.

Adam looked in the rearview mirror and said, "Another SUV has pulled up behind us."

One Russian officer was in the front seat with Adam and the other one sitting behind him. The Russians cracked their windows and fired at the unknown SUV beside us. Their armored windows looked like spider webs. The Russians in our SUV kept pelting the other vehicles with rounds until their windshield shattered and all the side windows on the right side were busted.

Adam called out on the walkie-talkie "Are you guys, okay?"

Brett's voice was loud. He must have had his radio turned all the way up. "Yes, they weren't equipped for us. Not sure what kind of armor they have. But it doesn't match ours. They are still behind us and one is on the phone."

Adam was calm. "They're calling for reinforcements."

Brett confirmed that. "Two more vehicles are coming in behind us."

Adam floored the gas pedal and swerved left, cut across two lanes of traffic, and entered a side street. I looked back to see Brett make the same move. The two cars behind us continued down Llyinka. Adam drove four blocks on the parallel street. I kept watching them at every cross-street block. They made a right turn back onto Llyinka.

Adam pointed ahead. "They'll turn around and head back towards us. Keep your guns ready."

The two Russians reloaded their guns from the spare magazines. Adam's voice was strained. "Here they come. Headed straight at us. There is a gun pointed out the back right window and one out the front on the left. Everyone hold on, and brace yourselves."

The car flew past us unloading as much ammunition as they could. Adam floored the gas pedal and the brake at the same time making the SUV do a three-sixty. He split the two cars traveling towards us destroying their side view mirrors. He bounced off a parked car, gunned the accelerator again, and rammed the back right quarter panel crunching it into the back seat of the enemy's oncoming vehicle. The driver then lost control and spun into a parked car. Adam kept moving forward.

Brett called Adam. "No one is moving in the car you creamed."

"Brett, where's the other car?"

"Don't know. I haven't seen it."

Adam looked in his rearview mirror. "Keep your eyes peeled. Their reinforcements could appear any time."

Adam put his foot on the brake and slowed the SUV to a snail's pace as he approached the gates to Chinatown, then inched thru slowly.

I yelled. "Adam, do you know where we are?"

He laughed. "Do you think I'm lost? We're on Kitai-gorod Street. In one of the oldest parts of town in Moscow."

"Adam!" I shouted. "We are on the backside of Lubyanka Square. I had lunch back at that café the first time I was here.

"Julia, you're turned around. We are in Chinatown. I am looking for Sretensky Monastery."

Brett called Adam. "Why are we in Lubyanka Square? We are in the back of headquarters. The monastery has been closed for years."

Adam answered. "This is where Ivan said he would have Wesley." He stopped the SUV at the gates of the monastery. One rusted iron gate was off its hinges and propped up against a concrete pillar and the other rusted one was still attached but hanging by one hinge. Adam moved the SUV inch by inch up the cobblestone driveway to the front door and stopped.

Adam's voice was low. "Is everyone ready? Be alert. I don't know what we're walking into."

Brett and his men stood by Adam's door. "Adam are you sure this is where we're supposed to be?"

"Yes. Stay alert." His tone was curt.

Adam pushed open the squeaky heavy wooden door. The musty air smelled like stagnant water. The windows were so dusty and cloudy that we couldn't see the trees outside. The small windows at the top of the ceiling on the north side were cracked and full of cobwebs. I moved to the mahogany staircase. My first step went through the rotten wood. I could tell from underneath all the filth that the house had been something to behold in its day. For a quick moment, I imagined how the beautiful oak beams and huge stone fireplace looked when it was new. I was brought back to the present when the Russian politsia charged in with their guns drawn.

"Hands up. Stand still. What are you doing here?"

The commanding officer marched toward Adam and stretched out his hands as if he was going to frisk him.

Adam stood at attention. "You're not touching me."

The tension in the room mounted.

Ivan yelled in Russian from the top of the stairs. "Halt!" then rattled off several sentences without taking a breath.

The officer backed away and yelled for his men to retreat.

Chapter 35

While I was waiting to spring into action, I was hyper-aware of the twenty-pound Kevlar vest weighing me down. I was trying to stay calm but my stomach was in knots, my adrenaline was high, and my anxiety was at a peak. I knew I was flanked by my team but that didn't stop me from thinking a bullet could still kill me. Looking around at my team their faces were as tense as mine. Adam nodded. All eight of us charged through the door.

Adam met Ivan halfway up the staircase. I moved closer to Brett still avoiding any eye contact with him. A long round of automatic gunfire came from upstairs, I hoisted my MP5 over my left shoulder and pulled out my Beretta 9MM.

Ivan shouted. "Everyone, wait here."

Adam yelled. "I'm going with you, Ivan." He turned to Brett. "Stay here."

Ivan nodded to Adam. "Come ahead."

Brett moved halfway up the stairs. I pulled on his left sleeve. "I'm going with you. No discussion."

The sound of an AK-47 fired emptying its magazine. The two FBI Russian agents flanked me on both sides. One agent pushed me to the floor the other one covered me with his body tucking me under him. Now I couldn't breathe with the Kevlar vest and the agent. I pounded my fist on the floor. He stood up and offered me his hand.

I was furious. "You aren't here to protect me. We are a team. We are fighting together."

Another round of intense gunfire sounded. Then silence filled the air.

Adam and Ivan appeared at the top of the stairs. Adam yelled. "Is anyone hurt?"

We all answered in unison. "No."

Ivan started down the stairs. An AK-100 fired and the next thing I saw was blood and brain matter exploding from Ivan's head. I knelt in his warm blood, closed his eyes with my fingers, and folded his arms over his chest. Adam turned and fired two shots hitting one of the Russian attackers in the chest. He slowly tumbled down the stairs and came to a stop at my feet.

Adam walked down with the butt of his gun close to the Russian's face. "You have one chance to live here. Who's behind the attack." The Russian mumbled. "The London Mafia." Those were his last words.

Adam followed me to the door. I stepped over three Russian enemy bodies. One had been shot in the chest, and two others had been shot in the head.

Adam turned and looked at the bodies. "I don't know how many were upstairs or who they were. They all jumped out the window when the shooting started. Campbell could've been one of them but I'm not sure." He turned his head and scanned the entire area without blinking. "There's nothing more we can do here. Let's head back to headquarters."

Outside we were engulfed by darkness. We started putting our equipment in the back of the SUV, when bullets started flying toward us in all directions. My team scattered. I ran from the back of the vehicle to the back seat. Halfway around the SUV several bullets hit my back. I dropped the MP5. The Kevlar vest protected me but the impact knocked me down, I struggled to get inside the SUV. Lying on the floorboard, I reached for my MP5 but remembered it was lying on the ground outside the SUV. My heart pounded, my stomach was twisted in knots, and my palms were wet with sweat My beretta was in my hand but I couldn't tell from which direction the gunfire was coming.

Slowly, I moved to the seat, and raised my head. The outside was filled with orange-red blasts and sounds of AK-47s. I eased out of the SUV and headed towards the last blast of fire. Coming around the corner of the building, I ran into an FSB agent. My force and surprise made him drop his AK-47. Remembering my boxing instructor's words. "Use your overhand right for the element of surprise." I threw a right stiff punch to his left cheek and followed it with a left cross to his right cheek and boxed both his ears at the same time. His arms were longer than mine and he grabbed a hand full of my hair and pulled my head back. I lunged forward ramming my head against his nose. Blood splattering everywhere, I knew it was broken. He was still holding onto my hair. With my left hand free, I swung my fist as hard as could and hit his right cheekbone, backing him up again. He moved forward and I reached between his legs and grabbed his crotch. He gasped in agony and let go of my hair. I kicked him at the end of his sternum paralyzing his diaphragm. He gasped and fell to the ground. I stood over him with my gun pointed at his head.

Two black SUVs came to a halt at my side. Their brakes locked and clouds of dust billowed into the air through the headlights. Someone yelled. "Go! Go! Go!" Four men in each vehicle with FBI jackets over their vests hit the ground running. The first group ran to the right of the monastery and the other four ran to the left. They had no idea what lay ahead, all they knew was that a CIA operation had been compromised.

Maxwell exited from the second Escalade. "Julia, your combat moves were impressive."

"Thank you, sir. I argued with an instructor at Quantico who made me take boxing lessons. I kept telling him he was wasting his time and tried to convince him his instructions would never be needed." I laughed and looked around at our surroundings, then said. "Maxwell, what are you doing here?"

"I changed the code from 5 to 4."

I took a step forward and winced. His eyes were full of concern. "Julia, are you hurt?"

I stood still for a second before trying to stand at attention but my back was not going to have any part of that posture.

"I didn't think I was. There's no blood a round hit me in the back but I am fine. Why did you change the code?"

Maxwell put his hand on my shoulder and turned me around. "Your vest is ripped and pieces are missing but I don't see any blood. The vest did its job."

Maxwell pointed north. "Do you know how close you are to headquarters? I heard the gunfire. You know Code 5 is an undercover operation. You needed help that's why I changed it to 4. Have you seen Campbell?"

"No, Adam and Brett are inside. Ivan is dead. I don't know what the circumstances are now."

A round of bullets pelted the SUV where we were standing. He pushed me to the ground. "Maxwell, do you see the two shadows moving across the front of the monastery?"

I stayed on the ground in silence next to the SUV with my arms wrapped tightly around my body.

Maxwell grabbed my MP5 and started shooting as he ran toward the corner of the building. There was movement in the shadows, "Two men are behind you."

Maxwell stopped, turned, and fired. I ran to Maxwell's side on the south side. Both men were in FSB uniforms soaked in blood. One man was gasping for breath, the other one had a death rattle.

Brett yelled. "We're coming out. Don't shoot."

Brett and Adam appeared with three Russians in handcuffs. Adam handed Maxwell three AK-100 machine guns.

Maxwell asked. "Did you find Campbell?"

Adam pounded his fist on the SUV hood and took a few deep breaths to bring his rage under control. "He got away along with the other four FSBs. Finn and his agents are dead. Ivan knew the Russians but I'd never seen them before."

The caged van that Maxwell had called for arrived. Brett gave the Russians a hard nudge pushing them inside, then padlocked the door. Maxwell ordered two agents to take the Russian prisoners back to the FBI compound.

Twigs snapped and dry leaves rustled behind Adam. Adam turned and fired. In the moonlight, a body took several unsteady steps towards us with his AK-100 pointed at Adam. Adam had the advantage, he fired again. The body fell against the ruin of a stone column and then slumped to the ground.

Adam and Brett ran towards the front door. I grabbed my MP5 and emptied the remaining bullets at a shadow on our left.

Adam yelled. "All clear."

As Maxwell and I entered, a grenade ricocheted off the heavy-timbered closed door.

A helicopter rose from behind the building. Its searchlight waved across the windows. Maxwell said. "It's about time they got here. I called for backup when I arrived. They should've been her twenty minutes ago."

Adam turned to me. "I never expected this raid to be a seven-hour nightmare."

The frigid cold wind blew through the bullet holes in the windows. Snow had started to fall. The snowflakes glistening under the street post lamps making them look like crystals of glass. Shivering, in a whisper I said, "We're lucky they got here this quick."

Maxwell wasn't happy. He grunted.

A man yelled. "Maxwell we're coming in."

After they charged through the door. Maxwell did a quick roll call. "Two's missing."

One man answered. "With all the firepower that's been around us, ten survivors out of twelve isn't bad."

Maxwell radioed the helicopter. "All clear." He turned to the rest of us. "Let's go."

Adam floored the SUV down the driveway. He sideswiped the old, rusted monastery gate tearing it the rest away from the stone column. The column burst into pieces scattering concrete into the street. Adam stopped across the street next to the curb. The Black Hawk released a rocket into the building. The deafening blast rocked the ground. The explosion sent bricks, stucco, wood, water, and fire into the air. Most of the windows were shattered from all the gunfire, but glass still cascaded through the sky. Black smoke billowed upward covering the stars and flaming ash drifted to the ground. The air reeked of wet soot and burned flesh.

It had been a long night. The commando raid had lasted longer than any of us anticipated and the combat was more intense than anyone had expected. My body and mind had experienced a mixture of tingling excitement, flowing adrenaline, pain, and weariness. The sunrise was a welcomed sight as we arrived back at headquarters.

Chapter 36

It was noon when one eye slightly opened. Rolling from my left side to my back, the pain almost made me scream, I would try everything to keep from going to the doctor. There was no way my body was going to get involved in a therapy regime. My father always said my stubbornness came from my grandfather. Carefully, I swung my legs to the side of the bed and sat up without too much difficulty. Placing both feet evenly on the floor and keeping my back straight, I gave an upward push and winced. My back was sore but the pain was bearable. One last push and to my surprise there was very little pain. Looking at the clock, the digital numbers showed 12:26. That wasn't too bad it only took me twenty-six minutes to get out of bed. I laughed to myself.

There was a tapping at the door. "Just a minute!" I yelled to whoever was on the other side.

I had no problem walking, but I wasn't hurrying either. Brett looked no worse for the wear.

"What are you doing here? You should still be in bed."

"I had to see how you were." He gave me a quick soft kiss on my lips. Picked me up and twirled me around.

I gasped.

He frowned. "Did I hurt you?"

I forced a smile. "My back and ribs are sore."

"Julia, I'm sorry. I should've known better."

"It's okay. Would you like coffee?" I'll call room service for a pot and scones.

He reached for my hand. "I've had several cups of coffee already this morning. How about lunch?"

I smiled. "How about soup and a sandwich? Is that alright?"

Seeing no enthusiasm, I pressed the room service button and ordered the soup of the day and a chicken salad sandwich and a hamburger."

When the phone was back in the receiver, Brett laughed.

I sat on the sofa, patted the cushion next to me, and smiled. "We were lucky yesterday."

Brett brushed a strand of hair away from my eyes. "Early this morning in bed, I retraced everything over in my mind. You work great under pressure. You're a good agent but I was afraid you were going to be shot or killed. I don't know what I would do if something happened to you."

"Brett, we know the risks. This is our job."

"I know but I can't keep the last time we spent the night together out of my head." He walked to the window and looked out over Moscow. "You are etched in my memory banks. You have affected me more than any woman ever has. I want more nights like the last time we were together and you with me all the time." He walked toward me and kissed the scratches on my neck and face, then engulfed me in his arms. "I've missed us."

My body shuttered. It was wonderful to have him hold me again. We hadn't had an intimate moment since the last time we were in Moscow. His mouth brushed across my right cheek. My body went limp and I allowed my weight to lean against him. My body shivered and my heart pounded. He moved his hand up my back to my hair. His thighs pressed against mine making me feel his hardness.

He kept whispered. "I want you." His kiss was soft, playful, and gentle.

I was taken completely by surprise and never expected him to be so affectionate. By the time I had gathered my wits. His lips had parted mine. Exploring deeply and leisurely. I allowed myself to become involved and responded to his pleasure. My libido was experiencing a roller-coaster ride and didn't want it to stop. My limp body waited for the next breathtaking burst. He manipulated his tongue over my lips and cupped the back of my head in his hand, then gave one last driving force with his tongue parting my lips. My knees wobbled, and my entire body shivered. I had been conquered and never wanted this moment to end.

Brett slowly released me. I tossed my head back and looked into his dancing eyes. "Wow!"

He walked to the door. I pointed to a slice of pound cake. He gave me a wry smile. "Thank you but no. I've had dessert." He smiled and kissed me again. "Time is not on our side today but I had to see you." He laughed. " Thank you for lunch."

Brett's hug was strong and reassuring. "If you need anything let me know." He gave me a butterfly kiss on my right cheek and closed the door behind him.

At first, it was hard to admit to myself how much Brett meant to me, every time we were together, he left me wanting more.

Five minutes later, there was a knock on the door. I opened the door wide and said, "What did you forget?"

I was shocked to see Adam standing there with a bouquet of red roses and white lilies. He rushed in. "Julia, I had to see for myself that you were all right." I'm sorry for busting in unannounced."

"Thank you. The bouquet is beautiful. Can I offer you something to drink? Tea, coffee, soft drink?"

"No, nothing. Thank you." He walked over to the window.

I slowly sat down on the sofa keeping my back straight, then motioned for Adam to sit. "I've been slow-moving this morning, but I'll be fine. Adam, where do we go from here? Ivan is dead and Campbell is who knows where by now."

Adam propped his left leg over his right knee. "Right now, our hope is with the interrogation team. Maybe they can get the captured Russians to talk."

Both our phones rang at the same time. We answered. Maxwell's voice was tense. "You need to get to the office immediately." The phones went silent.

Adam looked at me and smiled. I laughed and said, Maxwell doesn't know we're together."

I stood. "Okay, work is calling. I have to take a shower. I'll meet you in Maxwell's office."

Adam wrapped his arms around my shoulders. "I'm glad you're better." Then he kissed the back of my hand.

After he left, I stood in the shower letting the hot water pound my back, and thought about the day we met. My mind was etched with so many of Adam's memories—the day him in White Gardens Park at the art show, meeting Eli, and then finding out that Adam was deceased and now alive.

I needed to call Jack and ask him to remove my name from Adam's estate. And now to complicate things more, Brett was running through my mind almost every waking moment.

My muscles relaxed. I wanted to stand under the water for hours. Knowing Maxwell, he would not start a meeting without everyone being there. He hated repeating words or fielding the same questions when someone was late. I surprisingly dressed without any back pain and scooted out the door.

Chapter 37

I was the last one to enter Maxwell's office at 3:00 p.m. Adam and Brett were already seated at the conference table. Two marines were standing at attention against the back wall. Their faces looked like they were frozen. Maxwell cleared his throat and introduced the head of the FSB, Igor Turgeuer.

Igor spoke in a monotone voice. "Russia doesn't tolerate traitors. Campbell and several of our Moscow FSB agents sold US intelligence information to Germany. The Kremlin is denying any involvement with Germany. We will trade you, Campbell, for our agents that you have in custody."

Maxwell shook his head no. "You already have our information. Why would we exchange prisoners? What use is Campbell to us now? Would you be willing to let our tech teams sweep your computers clean and you turn any paper trail over to us?"

Igor stood. Slapped his hand down on the table. "No! We paid for the information. He also sold the same information to Germany."

Maxwell's tone was calm and collected. "It seems to me Campbell is of no use to either one of us."

Igor still standing, waved his hand towards the door like he was conducting an orchestra. "What about my agents?"

Maxwell had backed him against the wall. "What about them? They were caught trying to kill my men and you confirmed your men were working with Campbell. You need to make a decision."

Igor sat down. The look on his face showed he was used to getting his way. "I offered you, Campbell."

Maxwell stretched his legs out under the table, folded his hands behind his head, leaned back in his leather chair, and shook his head in frustration. "Campbell is not the issue here. The military secret information you have is what we are discussing. You could cause a world war if you misuse the information you have. Igor, don't press me to call Interpol. You have broken treaty laws and if I have to, I will get the European Justice Court involved. I know you don't want that.

We can prove everything that has been done and EJC can put pressure on your cabinet members to remove you from office. As head of the FSB, why would you jeopardize everything you have accomplished over the years? You have one of the highest positions in your government. Agree to my conditions or your next meeting will be with the EJC. Play by the rules and the laws and this will be over."

Igor sat quietly for about five minutes, then stood. "I'll meet with you next week." He clicked his heels and retreated out the door.

Maxwell crossed the room and gazed out over the courtyard. "I didn't want to have to use that threat but he dug himself into a hole and wasn't going to budge."

Adam stood and pointed to the door. "Igor won't give up his position but what he doesn't know is that after I found out Campbell was selling our information to the highest bidder. I changed the satellite launch codes so they couldn't track them, and scrambled the latest secret intelligent information that other countries were sending us."

I shifted in my chair. "Do they know they have the wrong information now? What are we going to do about Wesley?"

Maxwell smiled. "They probably will find out over time but one of two things will happen. Campbell will be delivered to us either alive or dead or we'll imprison him with a life sentence without parole."

Maxwell started towards the door. "Okay everyone it was a long night and day. You're free to go."

Brett left. Adam and I were the only ones in the room. I moved next to Adam. "Can we talk?"

Adam reached for my hand. I pulled it away and smiled. "Follow me back to my hotel. I don't want our conversation to be disturbed."

Adam smiled and jumped to his feet.

When Adam knocked on my door. I handed him a beer. He smiled and raised his bottle to my wine glass. "Julia, I've been waiting for this moment."

I backed away and sat in the small chair across from the sofa, trying to control my anger. "Adam, you have a lot of explaining to do. We didn't have time earlier today to go into it. I suggest you start after the week we spent together."

Adam sat still not moving a muscle. His eyes drooped, he was as tired as I was. "I'm sorry that I never tried to find you. I didn't know your married name and that you had moved to Jacksonville. I knew I couldn't let my identity be known and had to disappear to find out who was behind the assassinations. Julia, I don't have to tell you this, you know my world is a dangerous place. I'm constantly chasing thieves, assassins, criminals, AWOL soldiers, and anyone else who has broken our federal laws. I couldn't put anyone in danger—especially you—my mission was to prove Campbell was behind the killings."

I interrupted him. "You were going to France. I didn't see a future for us. What don't I understand is why you left me your estate. You have a family, and I had only known you for a week. How could you let me accept your Impressionist Award of the Year?"

His entire face turned into a frown. "For one thing, I didn't know about the award at the time, thank you for accepting it for me, and second, I couldn't blow my cover."

"It was a big deal. It was your honor, not mine." I stood and stared out the window. I wasn't going to let him see my tears.

"I have no regrets for not being there. I'm glad you agreed to accept it for me. There is no one else that loves my paintings as much as you do. I knew you would take care of them." I turned back towards him and forced a smile. "Julia, I still love you. You are as beautiful today as you were then. You never left my mind. Your smile and your laughter have always been with me. Sometimes things happen that we don't understand, like falling in love in a week. You have to accept things as they are whether you understand them or not."

He reached into his pocket and handed me a wrinkled worn envelope.

My stomach pinched as if I were hungry when I saw the envelope with my name on it.

Dear Julia,

I looked out at the bright blue-green water this afternoon wondering where you are and what you are doing. I regret not being more persistent to have you with me. To make you take a risk for us to share a life together. I still hope to hear from you one day.
Love you Forever.
Adam

My voice was loud. "Adam! Don't! Not now! I can't go there!" My heart and brain were confused and I didn't want to deal with possible love emotions at this moment.

He stood and reached for my hand. I folded my arms around myself.

He sat down and leaned back against the sofa. "I have great memories of us and that got me through a lot of tough situations, but I couldn't allow myself to be with you until I knew I was safe and that you would be too. I still love you more than you know. I want to be with you at Folly Beach."

I walked towards the door. "Adam, I can't. Not now but who knows what the future holds."

Adam walked over to me, leaned over, and lightly kissed my cheek. "Enjoy the rest of your day."

It was five o'clock and all kinds of thoughts were still racing through my mind. I went to the hotel bar and ordered a glass of Resiling. The bartender offered me a tray of snacks but I declined. I needed to put my life in order and I knew now that I couldn't give my heart to Adam after he let me think he was dead. I know he said he was protecting me, but his actions told me he couldn't trust me. How could I ever trust him now? He had turned away from his family and me. He said it was for our protection. I don't think now that Adam and I could ever have a future together. The thing for me now was to do my job and make sure I keep my emotions guarded where Adam was concerned.

"Hi, beautiful."

I looked around and saw Brett. "You surprised me." Laughing, I padded the bar stool next to me. "Have a seat."

He held my hand in his. "Are you all right? I know you and Adam talked."

"Yes." I knew I couldn't keep my conversation with Adam hidden from him. "Would you like a drink? I've always heard, a woman should never drink alone."

"Sure." He motioned for the bartender. "Gin and tonic, please."

"I hadn't left the FBI parking lot when I saw Adam leave. I followed you to the hotel. I hate to have to admit this but I was jealous."

I explained Adam's connection with me. "It's over. I don't have the same feelings as I did years ago and after the other night with you, I had to make sure that Adam wasn't going to be in my life, and he's not."

Brett laughed, then chuckled.

"You're remembering something. Tell me what's so funny?"

He smiled. "No, not remembering, had a thought. Do you think he wants to handle a woman that looks like Jaclyn Smith on "Charlie's Angels" and with a voice that can turn from angelic into a sergeant's in the same sentence, can shoot an MP5 and a Beretta 9MM?"

She frowned. "Is that how you and other men perceive me—a tough woman?"

"No! No! That's not what I'm saying. You are everything. Beautiful, smart, loving, and someone who can take care of herself all rolled into one." He touched my chin and gently moved his face toward mine. Our eyes met and time seemed to stand still. "It makes me want you even more."

She answered in her sergeant's voice. "Want and need have two different meanings."

His smile didn't alter. "Yes, but not at the same time. There are times when I need sweet and loving, and there are times when I worry about you. But I know that you can take care of yourself. Let's go to your room."

I nodded to the bartender to close out the tab and put it on my room.

We entered my suite and Brett instantly held me gently in his arms but his strong arms made me aware of his taut muscles. I saw the emotion in his eyes along with his desire. The more time we spent together, the more complicated my feelings became but I had an overwhelming urge to be with him. His strength, energy, and warmth destroyed my willpower. I wasn't ready to admit how much I loved him. I stood and led him to the bedroom watching his caramel-brown eyes dance.

I unbuttoned his shirt and gently pushed him back onto the bed. "Turn over on your stomach." I closed my eyes and enjoyed the luxury of touching his sensuous body. Hearing his soft moans that he was enjoying my hands kneading his biceps. I moved my hands from his arms across his back and traced the indents with my finger. I opened my eyes and gasped and removed my hands from his body as if an electric shock when through me.

He said, "What's wrong? I was enjoying your touch."

I couldn't keep the tears from welling up in my eyes. "Your back is full of scars."

He gave a soft groan then turned over and stared out the window. "Over the years, I've had seven bullets extracted. Nothing too serious. I was lucky that my spine wasn't hit or otherwise I would be in a wheelchair. The ones that hit me to the left and right of the spine were the worst and took the longest to heal. I was out of commission for a year. Sometimes I feel pain points but most of the time I don't think about it anymore. I laid down beside him and pulled his head gently to my shoulder, holding him as tight as I could. We lay in silence for over an hour.

The setting sun's light dimmed the room. I ran my hand over his trim waist and nestled tightly against him. My awareness of wanting him grew stronger. I let my tongue trace his ear. I placed my left hand over his heart to find it was beating as fast as mine. He moved and before I knew it, he was on top of me. His kisses were soft and heated and made my inner body tremble. At that moment, in the heat of passion, I felt free, drifting into a dream-like state. With one hand he cupped my hips, holding me against him he rolled over on his back. I had never experienced so much heat concentrated in one place. He touched my thighs and let out a soft low moan. I leaned over him letting my tongue trace his core from his center button up to his lips. I felt his body temperature grow from warm to warmer to hot.

I opened my eyes and saw the dawn's light. Brett was still asleep in the same position that I had last remembered. I moved to the edge of the bed but before I could swing my feet to the floor, he lightly pulled me next to him. I gave him a gentle kiss on his cheek and smiled. "I could wake up every morning like this."

He pulled me closer. "So could I."

We snuggled. An hour later I opened my eyes again. He smiled. "I love watching you sleep. You look so peaceful."

I gently kissed his lips. "I am when I'm with you."

I opened the living room drapes and let the warm sunbeams through then turned and saw the room service tray from last night. "Brett, dinner is here." I laughed. "We forgot to eat last night."

Brett stood up. Yawned and stretched before he answered his phone. "Julia, I have to go. We don't have one-night stands." He tucked the phone into his pocket and headed out the door.

My phone rang and Adam's name and number appeared. "Julia, we found Campbell. Meet me at 4605 Tverskaya Street now. It's in Red Square."

"I'll be there in thirty minutes."

I tossed the phone on the bed and ran to shower.

Chapter 38

Earlier today I never thought the beautiful sunny day would have turned into one of gray charcoal snow clouds but it was January not July. Snowflakes doused my windshield. My heater had not warmed my car when I parked next to the curb where Adam was standing.

Brett pulled in behind me. He gave Adam a half-smile and said, "You look like a gangster, all dressed in black from head to toe and your black and green camouflage baseball cap. Where is the rest of the team?"

Adam responded in a low voice. "We're it. We don't need a battle to take place in this neighborhood. We're going to take Wesley as quietly and quickly as we can. Julia, you're going with me. Brett, you're on lookout."

Both sides of the street were lined with gray Victorian concrete brick villas. The black staggered chimney stacks across the roofs looked like big, bundled-up men against the snowy skyline. It looked like a good cover for an ambush.

I pulled my coat hood over my head and buried my face in my scarf. I headed south across the street and down the sidewalk rechecking the numbers on the apartment building. Adam called out. "You look like a floating shadow. Where are you going? You look like a shadow moving around in the dark."

I turned towards Adam but kept walking backward. "We can't barge in the front door. Wesley could be watching." I turned left in the alley behind the building. A short stocky man with a tattoo on the right side of his face passed me. Adam picked up his pace now walking beside me.

I glanced back at Brett. He was standing next to an iced-draped lamp post studying the surroundings.

Adam entered the back stairwell of the apartment building. He turned to me, raised a finger across his lips then continued up the steps. He quietly inched his way to the door with the 4 on it. I tiptoed behind him with my beretta cocked. Adam stood at the door and counted to ten. He lined his foot up under the lock and kicked it with all his might. The force was strong enough to shatter the door frame. The doorknob slammed against the wall knocking in a big hole. I went to the kitchen and Adam headed to the bedroom. "Julia." Adam's yell hurt my ears. I ran to the bedroom door. I peeked around his waist to see Wesley's feet dangling and his neck in a noose. He had tied the rope around the showerhead in the bathroom, secured the rope to the ceiling fan in the bedroom, and kicked the chair from under his feet.

Adam pushed the chair back under his feet, hopped up on the chair, and loosened the hangman's knot. Wesley opened his eyes and coughed. His words barely escaped his mouth. "Leave me alone, Adam."

I said, "Wesley, we understand. You backed yourself into a corner and became desperate."

Adam's voice was cold. "You're not dead yet but it doesn't mean I saved your life. You're going back to Quantico. That will keep you from being tortured to death by the Russians or the Germans and I have called off the CIA's team." Adam gently shoved him against the bed, making him sit. "What do you know about the London Mafia? Why were they at the monastery? Did you sell intelligent information to them too?"

Coughing, he asked for a drink of water. I took a glass from the kitchen cabinet, filled it with tap water, and handed it to him. "I don't know how the London Mafia got involved. I sold information only to the Russians. The Russians sold part of the information to the Germans and they sold it for more money than I got from them."

Adam shook his head, cuffed Wesley's hands, and shoved him toward the door. "I like London. It's too bad you sold the information to Russia. I would rather be working in London than here."

I gave a muffled laugh. I didn't know if Adam was serious or not.

Wesley continued to talk. "I connected with a Russian through a rogue CIA officer who had been assigned to the NSA. The Russians went through all our computer files and made a list of our weapons, all emails that pertained to the US's newest developments, and all the technology instructions that went with it, along with atomic weapons. He offered me money to stay quiet. I countered with more money and said I would help them throughout the western world. The money was more than I was ever going to make if I worked to be a hundred." I sat at the kitchen table, pushed the speaker tab on my phone, and recorded everything Campbell said.

Adam pointed to me and the door. I was the first one to reach the ground floor. Everything seemed to be quiet. Wesley and Adam trailed behind me. I stopped at the street curb listening for any kind of disturbance but heard nothing. I waved to Brett who was still standing by the lamppost. His coat collar was tightly gripped around his neck and his hat was pulled low over his eyes. The light snow earlier was now a storm.

Adam turned to me looking at the ground to keep the snow out of his face. "Julia, you can go back to the hotel. Get out of this snowstorm. Brett and I will take care of Wesley.

The next morning, watching the news was interrupted with Maxwell's phone call. "Good morning, Julia. Your job is done in Moscow. You'll fly out at noon today by private plane from Sheremetyevo International Airport to Ramstein Air Base in Germany and then on to Quantico. I'll have someone pick up the car at the airport. Text me your parking number. Your next orders will be waiting for you at Quantico.

I checked out of my hotel at 10:30 a.m. A mile after I left the hotel, I saw a black Jaguar recklessly weaving in and out of traffic racing toward me. It was a block behind me but at his rate of speed it would catch up to me quickly. A gap opened up in the right lane I floored the gas pedal and took a quick left turn. My tires squealed when I made the turn and the cobblestone street shook all the fillings in my teeth. I hadn't paid attention that I was on a one-way street until a wall of oncoming vehicles started honking and running into the snowbanks on the sidewalk. At the next street, I turned right again and slammed on my brakes to drop in behind the snail trail of cars that were behind a horse-drawn carriage full of tourists. My rearview mirror and my side mirrors showed no sign of the black Jaguar. At the next cross street, I turned left. Every car I passed looked like a drug dealer or that it had been hot-wired stolen. The next right that I made put me back on the main highway. I didn't know what happened to the black Jaguar but it wasn't in sight for the time being. After a couple of miles, the airport directional signs came into view. I pulled into the airport parking garage and punched the button for a parking ticket. The black Jaguar pulled in behind me. Climbing and turning up each level, my tires squealed. I heard a crash and looked down at the level below. A car backing out of a parking space rammed the right front quarter panel of the Jaguar. I texted Maxwell level 4 space number 24. I ran to the terminal shuttle and requested the private plane terminal.

I was ready to be out of Moscow and back home. After the short flight to the air force base in Germany, I could put my mind and body on cruise control for the next eight and half hours.

I arrived at Quantico at 5:30 a.m. Dick had his car waiting to take me to the hotel. The cat nap had given me enough sleep not to be sleepy but tired. I read and sent emails until 6:30 a.m. Then showered and dressed.

"Julia." Dick's voice was light and airy. "My car will pick you up at 8:00 a.m."

I was taken by surprise to see Brett seated at Dick's conference table. My smile didn't fade but I tried to hide my delight. "When did you get here? I thought you weren't coming in until today."

He answered with a smile. "A few minutes ago, and you?"

"Early this morning."

Brett's bags under his eyes told me he had been up all night but he was still handsome as ever. Dick entered the room looking like he was the only one who had enjoyed a full night's sleep. The room came to life with the officers, agents, and employees from the CIA, FBI, and NSA.

Dick announced. "I have some disturbing news. Campbell was abducted last night on the way to his plane by four FSB agents. During the skirmish, two FBI agents and one CIA agent were killed. This morning the Grand Cayman Bank notified the CIA and the FBI that yesterday two million dollars was electronically withdrawn from two of Wesley's accounts. This morning two million was deposited in the St. Kitts-Nevis-Anguilla National Bank (SKNA) in Nevis in a numbered bank account only. Ms. Haspel, head of the CIA, has assembled her team over at the Pentagon, and Bryan Wilson, head of the FBI, has called a team together over at Langley. They have appointed Brett Jones to be the liaison between the CIA and the FBI. He has worked for the president's Foreign Intelligence Agency before." Dick took a sip of water and continued. "SKNA has refused to give out any information on the account. Ms. Haspel met with the Vice-President and secured his alliance. He warned the prime minister that if he didn't cooperate, he would ban US travel to St. Kitts and Nevis. That would be a shock to the island's economy. The prime minister made sure the bank gave us everything we requested. The numbered account was traced to Wesley Campbell and Igor Turgeuer, the head of the FSB."

I shook my head and said, "That wasn't smart. Why didn't they split the money up and use several banks and several countries? Igor was stupid. His job should be worth more than how much Wesley was going to give him. I assume Wesley was splitting the money since his name was on the account with Igor's."

Brett poked me in the ribs. "You're incorrigible. Whose side are you on?" Then he laughed.

"I'm saying they were stupid."

Bryan entered the room like a bull. "Early this morning word was sent that the Russians had executed Wesley Campbell. An all-out gun battle commenced at the FBI building in Moscow. Maxwell had been tipped off and was on top of the situation. There were no casualties on our side. We still have the two FSB agents in custody from the raid at the monastery. The worse news: Adam is missing. Our assessment of the situation is this, we think Adam may have been kidnapped as bargaining power for the FSB agents."

Silence filled the room. There wasn't even a whisper. I wanted to scream, I looked at Brett and our eyes locked. Dick continued. "The US ambassador and our President will speak in a few minutes."

I looked at the two black monitors in the room—one in DC and one in Moscow. Both monitors flickered.

"Good morning, Maxwell. Any new developments?"

"Good morning, Mr. President. We have a code name - Sycamore. We have not involved the President of the Russian Federation yet. The head of the FSB was supposed to meet with us last week but we haven't heard from him as of this morning. We have two of their agents in custody that we're using as bargaining power to get our intelligence information returned. This morning the CIA in London reported that undercover FSB agents executed Wesley Campbell, he was the head of the NSA. I don't see any reason to bargain with them now. They attacked the FBI headquarters here early this morning. A couple of my men were shot but there were no fatalities. I think they have one of our best CIA officers, Adam Robinson. I haven't been able to verify that yet. The President of Russia is now asking for you to call him."

The President looked away from the monitor and talked to his Chief of Staff then replied. "Okay, I'll call Russia and the Chief of Staff will call Langley. I don't want to start a war over this. Our NSA director started this mess when he sold confidential security information to Russia. We have lost good American CIA and FBI people over this including other CIA and FBI agents from other countries.

Maxwell cleared his throat. "Mr. President, I don't know what the Kremlin knows. I've only dealt with Igor Turqeuer, the head of the FSB."

"Well, don't do anything until you hear from me but keep yourselves protected."

The call ended and both monitors turned black.

Brett jumped up and in a loud rough tone yelled. "I'll get Adam back."

On impulse, I jumped up and yelled. "No!"

Instantly, all the eyes in the room were focused on me.

Dick turned to the CIA officer in charge. "You need to determine what our exposure will be and make the call to operations." Dick looked at me. "Julia, you'll sit this one out."

I opened my mouth to protest but decided to sit quietly. I nodded my head in agreement and left the room.

My bags were packed to head back to Charleston, when I heard a knock on my hotel room door. It was Brett.

Chapter 39

"I'm surprised you're here. Come in. I thought you'd be on a plane back to Russia by now."

Brett walked in and gazed around as if he was looking for something. "Julia, I've never had a problem working with anyone but it has become one with you. I've always kept my work and personal life separate. I need to put our relationship into perspective. I have allowed myself to become emotionally involved. I tried to keep us in an agent and partner relationship and keep everything simple and light but you are different and special. You're beautiful, strong, independent, intelligent, and sweet. I feel closer to you than I've ever felt to anyone. I guess what I'm trying to say is I need to know if you are still involved with Adam or not. I saw your expression when Maxwell said Adam could have been kidnapped. Then I saw another expression when you yelled no." Brett's tone had changed. "We're all on the same team but maybe not on the same social plane. Do you have feelings for both of us?"

I was known for being a quick thinker on my feet but I had no words. This completely caught me off guard. Before Brett said anything else I raised on my tiptoes and kissed him. My answer was in my kiss. His eyes widened and I saw the shock on his face. I backed away knowing at that moment I knew what I wanted.

His strong arm reached out and pulled me down to the sofa as he traced my lips with his tongue. His mouth was soft and warm. He pressed his weight against my body. The way he looked at me made me weak. I put my hand on his chest and gently pushed him away.

"Brett, you asked me about my feelings for Adam. He let his Uncle Jack and his sister April, think he was deceased. My head has raced through thoughts of what-ifs. He could get into another situation and turn his back on me. How much he loves me I don't know, but I won't allow myself to have a future with him."

I let out a sigh and laid my head on Brett's chest. His heartbeat sent warmth through me making my desire for him grow stronger. I moved my mouth to his. He let out a quiet moan. In a whisper, I said, "I want you."

He took my hands and pulled me to my feet giving me another passionate kiss. "I want you too but you have to be sure that I'm the one you want."

At that moment, I knew I was in love with him.

We moved to the bedroom and a trail of fire ran throughout my body. With my head lying on his chest, I listened to the rhythm of his heartbeat. My passion continued to swell as I concentrated on him.

He traced my lower lip with his index finger. "Your lips are soft, warm, tender, and giving. You have a spell on me that makes my entire body shudder. I want more." He whispered.

I moved on top of him. We made love all afternoon until the shared feelings of satisfaction and exhaustion overtook both of us.

My heart wouldn't let Brett go back to Russia without me. At 4:30 p.m. I was in Dick's office pleading my case to return to Russia. "I know the FSB, how they think, plot and attack, and I know the territory. Brett needs a backup agent that he can trust."

Dick cleared his throat. "Julia, I saw your face this morning when I said Adam's name and when you came to defend Brett for wanting to return to Russia. Are you involved with Adam and Brett?"

I arched my shoulders back, sat straight up, and stared at Dick with the strongest glare I could muster. "No. I have worked with both of them. This is a job and I do my job well."

Dick started to protest and then raised both of his hands as if I'd pointed a gun at him. He laughed. "I can't argue with that. Both Adam and Brett speak highly of you and you've proven you can do any job that has been given to you. From now on you and Brett will be a team. Brett is ready to take off but I don't want the two of you on the same flight."

He picked up the phone and called communications. He looked up at me. "You'll fly out at 6:00 p.m."

I repacked and doubled checked my list. I was finding it hard to concentrate, concerned that I might be walking into a situation where I would have to choose between Brett or Adam. My stomach clenched and I knew I had to keep my emotions at bay. I turned my attention back to the present. There was no need to worry about what might not ever happen.

I landed in Moscow four hours after Brett. There were a couple of military men on the flight with me from Langley. When we landed a light rain was falling, a captain took off his coat and reached to place it around my shoulders. I declined and pointed to the car that was parked at the bottom of the stairs.

When I stepped on the tarmac in Moscow at 10:20 a.m., Brett opened the car door. I laughed. "I didn't expect you to be my welcoming committee."

He smiled. "I met with Maxwell at seven this morning and told him I would brief you on the way to his office."

My body was completely out of normal rhythm due to the flights back and forth and adjusting to all the time zone changes. I was starving. "Can we stop for a quick sandwich?"

"Good idea. I haven't eaten either." He laughed. "McDonald's?"

I walked into Maxwell's office surprised to see Igor, the head of the FSB.

Igor greeted Brett and me with a handshake. Maxwell motioned us to the two chairs at the end of the conference table.

Maxwell said. "Our President has talked to the Russian Federation and a compromise has been made for the two FSB agents. The US State Department has hired Moscow's security company. The head of the Elite Security Holding Company is a former FSB counter-espionage agent, an American CIA alumnus, and an ex-MI-6. They provide security protection at four of our American facilities here in Russia. The two FSB agents will be turned over to them to be under the custody of the ESHC but they will be held in our jail. That's the best compromise we can do. It takes the US out of the hostage situation."

I leaned forward in my chair. "What about Adam?" I looked at Igor. "Where is he? It's been over a week."

Maxwell frowned. "Julia, they're going to find Adam. Let's sit quietly for a couple of days and see what happens now that the security company is involved."

Igor spoke. "I've worked with Adam before. We're all going to work together to find him."

I draped my arms over my shoulders and leaned closer to Brett hoping he would say something to back me up. Brett didn't say a word. He sat still looking at me with his stubble-covered face, wavy black hair, crooked nose, from being broken so many times, and his curled-up smile. He stood and left the room.

Maxwell knew by my actions that I wasn't happy with the decision.

There had been no word from the White House, and with the time difference, it was now after seven p.m. I walked to the door, turned, and said to Maxwell. "I'm beat. I'm going to the hotel, taking a hot bath, and going to bed. Call me if anything develops before morning.

Brett was waiting for me in the lobby. He placed his hand on the lobby door but before he pushed it open gunfire echoed throughout the FBI compound. Two explosions destroyed the office building next to us. Windows shattered and glass flew in all directions. I saw a couple of American military men positioning themselves on the roof of the building across from us. Brett pulled his gun and I detached my gun from my shoulder holster.

Brett reached for my hand. "On three let's make a run to the car. 1, 2, 3."

We ran out the back door. There was a small fire still burning from a Molotov cocktail along the sidewalk in the courtyard in front of us. Another explosion went off behind the cafeteria which sent a couple of garbage barrels into the air and bounced around in front of us. The agent on the roof across from us was scoping the other building roofs. One man in an army uniform ran across the compound to the left of us as a deafening sound blasted. The black mushroom cloud rose and the ground shook throwing dirt ten feet in the air along with the man. A drone flew over and Brett and I knew it was Russian.

Brett pulled me around to the basement door. It was locked. We continued to the front door and ran back inside. All the windows were blown out and glass was lying everywhere.

Brett said, "The problem with mortars is you don't hear them until they hit. Spetsnaz, the Russian OPS team doesn't know the two FSB agents in custody have been removed from the compound."

We entered Maxwell's office. He was on the phone with the Elite Security Company. He silently motioned to the two chairs in front of his desk. "You need to send us some air cover to get the Russians off our property." He yelled into the handset.

After Maxwell finished his call to ESC, he called Langley. The three of us went to the lobby. The compound fire department had called for additional units. A couple more Molotov cocktails were tossed over the FBI wall sending a fireball into the air.

Shortly, two F-16s were flying over the compound. Then seconds later two more fighter jets flew over from a different direction. In the dark, none of us could pinpoint how many aircraft there were or which way they were flying. After their third pass, the gunfire ceased.

Chapter 40

The next morning, when I entered Maxwell's office he raised his eyebrows when he saw Brett nod to me and smile. "This is what we know." Maxwell slowly paced back and forth in front of the conference table. "Elite Security has assured me there won't be another incident with the Russians here at the compound. They have also given me what they think is Adam's location. That's all I know at this point. I have a meeting in Washington with Mrs. Haspel, Bryan, and MI-6. We don't want another confrontation with another country but we do want to get Adam back. In the meantime, the two of you will work my cases here."

After the meeting, I took a short break, then entered my temporary office to find Brett sitting at a desk across from me. His back and shoulders were ruler-straight. He looked like a model dressed in a navy blue suit, a white laundered shirt, and a red, yellow, and navy striped tie.

His big smile showed how happy he was. "Looks like we'll be working together on the same case."

My heart raced as if I had been doing an Irish jig. "Sounds good. The key word is working." My smile turned into a frown when I looked at my desk. "There's a lot of folders here."

He cracked a crooked upper lip, which seemed to be like a trademark, then he shuffled some files from one stack to another. "Yes, there is. They're already translated from Russian to English."

I put my hand on one of the files. "That's good. It makes my work a lot easier."

From his desk, I could feel his eyes on me all day. At 5:00 p.m. he asked. "What about dinner tonight at the Dublin Pub?"

I laughed. "We're in Moscow and you want Irish food?"

He smiled and grabbed his coat. "Sure."

We were finishing our bread pudding when a man with the build of a linebacker walked over to our table. His face was scared. He leaned over and whispered into Brett's ear then handed him an envelope marked 'urgent.' Brett motioned for the waiter and gave him his credit card. He looked at me. "Julia, please go wait by the door."

Brett gave me a quick kiss on my cheek. "Sneads will take you back to your hotel. I have an assignment tonight on a case I worked on several years ago. I'll call you when I can."

Maxwell sent me a text. 'Be in my office at nine Wednesday morning.'

After a week in Washington, I was anxious to hear what news had come from the higher-ups. I walked into Maxwell's office to see Brett already there. I know my smile ran from ear to ear.

Maxwell's face was drawn and he had dark circles under his eyes. "Brett and Julia, the Iceland embassy in Moscow has confirmed that Adam is in a small village named Vik, but the Russian embassy in Reykjavik will not confirm Iceland's information. Iceland believes in human rights and democracy and they are on board for us to rescue Adam. They provided us with their investigative report. It's sketchy and doesn't give us many details. There have been more FSB agents in the area in the past few weeks than in a whole year. Iceland knew the Russians were there but they weren't aware of our purpose until I talked to them yesterday. We are on our own. Our military pulled out of Iceland in 2006. Iceland is a founding member of NATO but they have no military. Their Coast Guard fills their military mission out of Keflavik Air Base. They will allow our aircraft to use their facilities occasionally but not for this mission. They take a neutral stand and don't get involved in other countries' affairs. Iceland will not allow us to fly into Reykjavik or Keflavik. We will have to enter Vik by water. Vik is on the southern coast with a population of around 400 residents. This will be a night mission. We have to slip in and out silently. That means no gunfire. There is no port. SEAL TEAM TWO commands all the European teams. The Captain of SEAL TEAM TWO is Commander John Toms he will lead the mission."

I interrupted Maxwell. "Does that mean we are going in by submarine? Will Brett and I be allowed to go or will it be only the SEAL team?"

"Yes. Everyone in the State Department, the Pentagon, and the White House has permitted the two of you to be on this mission. The submarine you will be on is the USS South Dakota. It's the latest stealth in the Virginia-class and equipped with state-of-the-art electronics, satellites, intelligence gathering, and weapons systems technology, and it's heavily armored with laser-based missiles. You will board the sub in Holy Loch, Scotland. The captain will make the decision when you will leave for Vik. The two of you will fly to Glasgow, Scotland Friday morning. Do the two of you have any questions? Julia are you up to this assignment? No emotions, lead with your knowledge."

I nodded. "Yes. Adam's safety is the priority."

At six o'clock Friday morning, Brett and I boarded Lufthansa Airlines for a three-hour flight to Glasgow. We rented a car at the airport for the hour's drive to Holy Loch. If all went well, we would be at the shipyard before noon.

We entered the town of Paisley. I had no idea that buildings would still be standing that were built in the 1500s. I started laughing. "Brett, I never knew the paisley print fabric got its name from this town. There are paisley prints on signs everywhere. They are also boasting they are the largest town in the Lowlands of Scotland."

Brett smiled. "See what you learn when you travel."

I gave him a smirk.

We had passed through one small town after another and each town had white sheep everywhere. We turned a bend in the road and joined the M8 motorway that led to Greenoch, the largest port and shipbuilding company in the UK. Green craggy mountains surrounded the valley town. The sides of the mountains were dotted with white sheep. We turned at Greenoch to catch the Argyll Ferry at Gourock. The gray waves were hurling into the shoreline with fury. The ferry captain was fighting the choppy water and the wind. After his third attempt, the dock hands were able to tie the ferry to the cleats. The angry sky turned black, thunder rolled, and the clouds looked puffed to the max as if the sky was going to unleash all its anger at once.

I turned towards Brett. "Is this your way of preparing me for the submarine?"

He laughed. "Maybe."

We stood on the bank and watched a team of FBI agents and CIA officers swarm the dock and board the boat. Each person was doing their job, and no one was talking. They covered all areas of the ferry like one big black storm cloud from the bilge to the captain's wheelhouse. More agents arrived and appeared to be searching g for something along the dock. Brett cranked the car and put it in reverse but before he could back up an agent knocked on his window.

He was short, stocky, and had a long scar that ran from his ear to his nose. "Do you have permission to be here?"

Without answering Brett pulled out his ID. "We were going to take the ferry to Dunoon Terminal. We are on a mission. What are you guys looking for?"

Before he answered a CIA agent called out. "Let's go!"

He stepped away from the car. "You can board now."

"Brett, what were they looking for?"

"I don't know. It could have been a routine check."

We exited the tunnel at the Dunoon Terminal two hours after we left Glasgow. Brett parked the car at the end of the parking lot. We stood as close as we could to the water's edge watching the ferry come across the water. I snapped a couple of pictures but the fierce wind blowing from the north was making it hard for me to keep my balance and it was giving the ferry captain a challenge. The ferry was zig-zagging from one channel marker to another. The incoming tide wasn't helping matters either with the water splashing over the bow. The seagulls overhead looked to be working as hard as the ferry captain to stay airborne and on course. We drove onto the ferry and fifteen minutes later we were in Holy Loch.

Captain Horne welcomed us aboard the submarine. He introduced us to the Officer of the Deck, 1st Lieutenant George Myers. "Lt. Myers will be your go-to person when you are on the sub. If you need anything at all see him. We will be at sea for three days before we reach Vik. I understand your mission and know you're walking into an unknown situation, so enjoy the cruise." He gave us a slight smile.

After dinner, Brett and I went to the rec room. Brett picked up a ping-pong paddle. "Let's play."

I laughed. "You're going to get beat. Are you sure you're ready for that outcome?"

Brett laughed. "Bring it on Miss Confidence."

We both laughed.

"How many Russians do you think are guarding Adam?"

"I don't know. Shouldn't be many since Adam is the only prisoner."

I lay in my bunk that night wondering what danger awaited me tomorrow, whether was Adam still alive and would the Russians be expecting us.

The second day at sea was sunny. After breakfast, I walked around the deck. Everything around us looked magnificent. The cobalt water, the clear blue sky, and the holes in the ice caps captured the sky inside the ice. I passed by the bridge where Captain Horne and Lt. Myers were bent over the chart table discussing the treacherous approach to Vik. Lt. Myers traced a waxed pen over the chart. Captain Horne pointed to the radar. "The weather today will be good. Let's hope it stays that way through tomorrow night." Then he checked the sonar screen.

After breakfast, John Toms, the Navy SEALS Commander, entered the bridge. "I'm calling a meeting in the wardroom now." Toms introduced the SEAL team.

The conference table was almost as long as the room and there had to be at least twenty chairs around it. Commander Toms said. "On the Robinson mission my name is TANGO, then he introduced all the other mission seals and their code name. After the assignments were given TANGO said, "Everyone has to know their job. There can't be any mistakes. A man's life is at risk here. If anyone has any questions or is in doubt about anything, no matter how minuscule you think it may be, ask." He waited a few minutes. "Okay, none. You are free for the rest of the day."

The quieted engines woke me. At first, I was disorientated thinking we had arrived at our location. My watch showed 4:00 a.m. but I hadn't changed it through any of the time zones. I wasn't sure what day the watch was displaying. I lay still looking up at the bunk over me, thinking about the day ahead and what situations we were going to encounter. I dressed and headed to the bridge. In the predawn hours, the night crew was still on duty.

I glanced at the map seeing we were off the coast of Iceland near Vik. Lt. Myers was sitting at the tactical station. He shifted his attention to the right screen and pushed the icon showing our geographical display. He silenced the sonar beep. Captain Horne rechecked his charts and took over the submarine's movements. He called the engine room. "Ahead one-third. Make your depth a hundred feet."

TANGO looked at his coordinates. Thirty minutes later, Captain Horne announced for all stations to prepare to periscope depth. The sonar radioman confirmed we were close to an iceberg. TANGO gave the order for Captain Horne to surface. Lt. Myers made sure we surfaced behind the iceberg, giving us cover. The sub vibrated as the water rushed over the sub's surface rising above the water. I walked to the starboard side to see a row of pointed basalt sea stacks. Mother Nature's artwork was breathtaking with all her rock formations.

Captain Horne gave a quick history lesson. "That's Reynisdranga. It's our navigational point coming into Vik."

I blurted out. "Captain Horne, everything is green. I thought everything would be snow-covered. Every town must have green craggy mountains dotted with white sheep. I saw them in the car on the way to Holy Loch. I've never seen a black beach before. The sand looks like tar."

Captain Horne laughed. "You sound like a child."

A SEAL codenamed ALPHA looked through his binoculars and pointed to land. "There's the cottage, but there's also a fishing shack behind it. How do we know which one Robinson is in? There are lots of people walking down the beach."

TANGO replied, "Don't worry about the people on the beach they are walking away from the cottage. If we see any movement at the cottage or the shack. That may tell us where Adam is."

Thirty minutes after we surfaced, Captain Horne picked up his binoculars. We all watched a speedboat pull up onto the black beach. A man in a bright red oilskin coat climbed out of the boat. He was tall, broad-shouldered, and had long brown hair. He knocked on the cottage door opened it and entered. Shortly, he and two other men all dressed in black, exited the building carrying a large trunk and hoisted it over the side of the boat. The driver climbed back in the speedboat and the guards pushed the boat out into the water. When the boat had drifted far enough, the man started the engine and roared around to the other side of the island.

As the extraction neared, the water's horizon had covered three-quarters of the setting sun. The town's lanterns had been lit and the smell of dinner foods filled the air. Moods were somber and subdued. TANGO emphasized a few points. Thirty minutes later when the darkness settled. TANGO asked. "Is everyone ready? You all know what to do. Let's go."

I was wet with perspiration. I don't ever remember sweating this much in my whole life. My clothes were sticking to me like glue.

A SEAL codenamed VICTOR stepped into the Rigid Hull Inflatable. I was second and the rest followed. TANGO, Brett, and I slipped up behind the guard on top of the hill. TANGO placed a knife on the guard's throat from behind and whispered. "Don't move or I'll cut your throat."

I stooped, reached up, and took his gun. In Brett's Russian accent he said. "Give me the code." TANGO pressed his knife a little harder against the guard's throat.

The guard whispered in Russian. "Black Beach."

Brett nodded. "We'll know in a few minutes if he gave us the right one."

I touched Brett's arm and pointed to several red and black wires running down the hill toward the house. Brett touched TANGO on his shoulder and pointed to the wires. TANGO nodded.

Brett traced the wires down the hillside to a canister lying against the house. I watched him continue to follow the wires to a timing device that was hidden under what looked like a bedroom window. Brett carefully cut the wires disarming the bomb.

TANGO kept the pressure of his knife at the base of the guard's neck as we headed down the hill. At the corner of the house, Commander Toms pressed the knife a little harder. "Give the code." The guard moaned and said, "Black Beach."

The door opened from inside the cabin. Brett stepped out from the side of the house with his gun pointed at the Russian's head. All five of us entered the cottage.

The smell of beets, cabbage, and onions almost overwhelmed us. I held my gun on the guard as Brett launched himself toward the man inside the cottage. At the same time, the SEALS DELTA and ZULU barged through the back door. I hadn't paid attention to how large they were until they filled the entire door frame.

I ran into the bedroom looking for Adam. The room was dark. I tripped over something lying on the floor and when I flipped on the light switch the small bulb gave very little light. In the dimly lit room, I saw four bunk beds, a guard lying on the floor, and Adam tied in a spread-eagle position on one of the bottom bunks. He was motionless. I shook him but he didn't move. I leaned over him and gasped, then went to find Commander Toms.

I whispered to TANGO. "Adam isn't here. Come outside with me."

As they started to the front door, a Russian started to speak. "Adam…." A comrade of his gave him a killer stare. He lowered his head in silence.

Outside Julia said, "There's a dead guard lying on the floor that isn't Adam. My mouth dropped open when I saw a rubber curl behind his ear. Someone had made a rubber mask of Adam's face and put it on someone else." TANGO lowered his chin. I watched his expressions change as I spoke.

TANGO charged back through the front door and into the bedroom again. He yanked the mask off the dead man's face, then he barked orders to ZULU and VICTOR. "Tie them up and separate them." Then he motioned the team to go outside.

"I'm sure Adam was in the trunk we saw loaded into the speedboat this afternoon." He pointed to DELTA. "Go into town and see what you can find out."

TANGO ordered ZULU AND VICTOR to stay with the Russians. ALPHA, TANGO, Brett, and, I boarded the inflatable and headed back to the sub. It was freezing cold, pitch-black, and windy.

Chapter 41

Onboard the sub, Commander Toms called his commanding officer, and I called Maxwell giving him the update on Adam.
"Julia, I will try to research the situation from here but follow Commander Toms's orders. He has the advantage of being on the scene and I'm sure they'll be on top of Adam's situation immediately. In the meantime, any updates will be given to Washington."

We stayed on the sub the rest of the night but none of us slept. I heard Commander Toms send ALPHA to the cottage at midnight to replace ZULU and VICTOR. My bunk was next to the wardroom. I heard Commander Toms on the phone until the wee hours of the morning. My mind raced back to when I first met Adam remembering the day at the art show as if it were last week. I never thought I would be back with the FBI trying to save his life.

The next morning at breakfast, I pushed the eggs and sausage around on my plate. My stomach was in knots, food didn't look appealing or maybe it was nerves and I wasn't hungry. Commander Toms ate as though this was going to be his last meal. Our breakfast was interrupted when Captain Horne announced his morning debriefing meeting was over and the wardroom was available.

Commander Toms sat and stretched his palms down on the conference table. "I'd like to stress that we have to handle Adam's situation delicately. We have to keep a low profile. We don't want Russia, Iceland, and the US to get into a confrontation.

Captain Horne knocked on the door and handed Commander Toms a satellite phone.

"Yes, Mr. President." Commander Toms pressed the speaker button.

"Commander Toms don't do anything until you hear otherwise. I'll call a meeting with our Jean Conners, she's our national security advisor, and William Deans, the Secretary of Defense. We need to look at all our options. Lay low until you hear from me or one of my cabinet members. You need to find out who the dead man is that was wearing the mask and get him to the morgue. His face is smashed. Order a DNA test if you have to. Vik police will jail the Russians you have in custody. I'll be back in touch."

I moved forward in my seat. "Commander Toms, what happens if we find Adam before we hear back from the President? Can we rescue Adam, and if so, can we get underway?"

He smiled. "Yes, if we get Adam without any confrontations, we are free to proceed with our mission."

VICTOR and ALPHA had orders to go take care of the body. Commander Toms, Brett, and I went with the Vik police to jail the captured Russians. As we drove away from the cottage, a small dark cloud drifted overhead dropping a few sprinkles. I watched from the back window the body bag being dragged out the front door, thinking this could have been Adam.

The policeman said. "This is Route 1 also known as the Round Ring Road because it runs around the entire island and through the middle of town. You can't get lost on the Ring Road."

I pointed to the white church with the red roof. The policeman's face beamed as he spoke. "Myrdal Church is our landmark. It can be seen from any place in Vik. It was built in 1932. Its concrete walls have withstood many storms."

"It looks so regal sitting on top of the hill overlooking the town."

When we turned onto the main street in town, Brett yelled. "Stop" He jumped from the van and ran up the sidewalk and darted into Lava Café.

I turned to TANGO. "Where's he going? Did he see something we didn't?"

TANGO retorted. "I don't know. Let's drive around back."

I left the cab and ducked into the cafe, cased it quickly, but didn't see Brett. A woman who looked to be in her fifties came from the kitchen wiping her hands on her torn red and white checkered apron. She was short and overweight, and her blond sprinkled gray hair looked like she had been a true blond in her younger years. "Choose a seat. In a few minutes, you won't be able to find one." Some of the locals that were there were already engaged in multiple conversations. They acted like nothing out of the ordinary was happening in their town with us running around in and out of their places of business.

TANGO stood in front of the woman. She nodded toward a side door. He ran and yelled back to her. "Thank you."

I was on TANGO'S heels. He ran into a bar and heard a door slam in the back of the room. He didn't slow down and I kept my pace with him.

In the alley behind the bar, a policeman yelled halt. "Turn around slowly with your hands in the air."

Slowly the man turned. I yelled. "Adam!"

TANGO stared the policeman down. "This is my man. Let him go."

The policeman still had his gun pointed at Adam. "He's going to the station with me. If everything checks out he'll be released to you."

DELTA charged into the alley and came to an abrupt stop when he saw us. The four of us rode in the back seat of the caged van to the station. The difference was we weren't handcuffed and Adam was.

TANGO asked to speak to the police chief. Brett was sitting in a straight-back chair. I rushed over to him. "What are you doing here?"

He smiled. "Waiting for you."

I took in a long sigh. "I'm glad you're all right. You disappeared down the hill. Why did you jump out of the car? Where did you go?"

"I thought I saw Adam but I lost him after he ran into another restaurant. I didn't know where everyone was." Brett laughed. "I figured eventually one of you would come here to the police station."

TANGO motioned for us to follow him. We entered the chief of police's office. "I have four sworn statements from witnesses that Adam Robinson killed one of our citizens. I'm waiting for Interpol to take over."

TANGO's voice was stern. "Who were your witnesses? The Russians?"

The police chief pulled a document from the file. "The coroner reports that the body that was brought in was beaten until it was unrecognizable."

TANGO stood. "The body wasn't beaten when we left the house. Since the Russians and we were the only ones there, I would bet my life on it that the Russians beat the body. You have nothing that proves Adam was the killer. Who are you going to believe Russian spies or a CIA officer?" His voice was adamant.

The police chief motioned to a guard. "Bring Adam in here."

After hearing Adam's kidnapping story, the police chief dismissed all charges.

We left the police station in the middle of a rainstorm with thunder and lightning jumping all around us from the sky to the ground. The patrol van was weaving and sliding on the road. The driver frowned and acted annoyed. He barked. "You should've stayed at the station until the storm passed. We haven't had any rain in weeks and our roads are slick. The run-off from the hills makes it more dangerous than on a dry day."

TANGO gave a half-wit smile. "Would you like for me to drive?"

The commander's question added to the policeman's frustration. "No, I'll get you back to your boat. For several weeks now we have had more Russians here than we've had in years. Now you are here running through our streets and an unknown beaten body in the morgue. This week our island has been in chaos because of you people."

At that time, a herd of sheep crossed the road. The policeman slammed on the brakes and the car started sliding. I reached for Brett's hand. Adam looked at me and raised his eyebrows.

We slid down a concrete embankment and came to a stop under a bridge at the river's edge. The driver's side of the car was in a foot of water. We were wedged between two I-beams under the bridge. The good thing was the van wasn't submerged. Everyone tried to open their doors but they were jammed. I was in the back seat sandwiched between Brett and Adam.

Brett asked. "Julia, are you all right?"

Before I could answer, Adam looked at Brett and in a sarcastic tone said, "It looks

like she's okay."

I answered. "I'm fine."

I didn't feel uncomfortable, but I didn't like Adam's attitude that he was developing toward Brett.

I climbed over Adam to the door on the high side of the van. An I-beam was halfway across TANGOs and Adam's window down the side of the van. I was able to get the window lowered enough to climb out between the van and the beam, then grabbed a low cross I-beam and swung myself onto a girder close to the front of the car. I kept winding my way through the maze of iron. Several gusts of wind held me against the van and the girder. When the wind subsided, I inched forward toward the front of the van, holding on to an edge of a cold girder hurling myself to the hood.

TANGO reached for my arm. "Julia put your foot on top of the tire."

I laughed. "I'm practicing my acrobatic skills."

Everyone laughed except the policeman. He yelled. "Now see what you caused."

TANGO answered. "I didn't cause anything you were driving."

I looked around at where I had been and what my next move was going to be." I yelled. "TANGO there's a body in the water!"

The tow truck driver had arrived and hooked the back bumper of the van to his wench. He reached for my hand and pulled me to him. He took another wench and pulled the van from under the I-beam. When we were on land, Tango, Brett, and I walked under the bridge and down the concrete incline to the water's edge. Brett reached down and turned the face-down body over.

Tango shook his head. "I don't know how long he's been dead. Decay starts the minute a person dies. The process is quick if the body is exposed to the air. But if the body is submerged for a while where the oxygen levels are low, the decaying process is slower. If he drowned he would float to the surface immediately. I think he has been underwater and not too long ago surfaced. He's not one of ours."

Brett answered. "Not with that swastika tattoo on the back of his neck."

Tango motioned for the policeman to join us. The policeman called in the death and started writing his report. Before long Vik's entire police department arrived. The tow truck driver took the five of us to the cottage. He pulled onto Ring Road and around a curve, the cottage came into view.

I smiled. "If we'd known we were this close to the cottage we could have walked."

TANGO walked around to the tow truck driver's door and held out his hand. "Thank you."

The driver refused his tip and smiled. "It was my pleasure to make that crotchety old coot wait. He's like that all the time."

TANGO had called ALPHA to bring The High Ridge Inflatable to the cottage before we left the police station. Back on the sub, Commander Toms herded the three of us into the wardroom. "Adam, you've had quite an adventure. Bring us up to date after you were kidnapped."

Adam looked to be in automatic mode. He propped right leg over his left knee like it was a trademark whenever a CIA officer was being questioned. "After the FSB killed Wesley, I paid a corrupt Russian agent to let me use his computer. I doctored our intelligence information that he had sold to the Russians."

Commander Toms smiled. "Adam our country owes you a lot. Thank you. What about the rubber mask?"

Adam laughed. "Oh, that. Years ago when I worked undercover in Paris, I had a lot of people hunting me. I knew if I was going to survive all the manhunts, I needed another person to look like me so I had the mask made. One night, the FSB raided a safe house. I killed one of their men and put the mask on him. After they left, I went back and retrieved my mask. It threw them off my trail for months. Here, I needed them to think that I was dead. They always check for a pulse but never anything else. I killed the Russian put my mask on him and slipped into town. They thought the Russian I killed had deserted. Rogue agents will do anything for money, that's how I got them to take me away in the trunk."

For the next two days, I deliberately tried to stay away from Brett and Adam. There was no need to have a conflict between the three of us while we were still considered on assignment. I followed the bright warm sun from one side of the deck to the other finding places to stay out of the cold. We had accomplished our mission, therefore, there was no need to run silent and deep returning to Holy Loch.

Once back in the States, Adam had a debriefing with the CIA, Brett reported to headquarters at the FBI, and I headed home to Charleston.

Chapter 42

I was excited to be home. I was singing at the top of my lungs when I pulled into my garage, disarmed the security system, and gave a big sigh when I walked into the kitchen. I jogged next door to Hector's. There were many times in Moscow and Berlin that I wished I had never re-enlisted in the FBI. The accomplishment I felt in finding Adam had offset my sadness of being away from home. Adam was safe and I had done my job.

I knocked on the front door and called Hector's name at the same time. Dexter heard my voice and came charging from the back of the house. His nails clawing , scratching, and sliding on the polished floors. Hector opened the door and Dexter tackled me at full speed, knocking me backward against the porch rail.

Hector gave me a quick hug. "Julia, glad you're back and obviously Dexter is too. He has been fine, but on our walks, he always pulled the leash towards your house."

I rubbed Dexter's ears and head. "Good boy. You did miss me." Dexter woofed.

Hector continued. "I hope you will like my news. I'm your new neighbor. The house came on the market six months ago and since I've been here more than any other place in the last three years and loved it. I decided to become a homeowner."

I gave Hector a big smile. "This is a pleasant surprise. I'm glad you are permanently next door." I laughed. "Now Dexter has two homes."

I was at Hector's gate when a blue BMW sedan parked in front of his house. Rebecca got out and waved.

Laughing, I said. "We didn't expect to see you grace our doorsteps."

She smiled. "With Adam accounted for, my files are closed. Bryan doesn't need my services any longer."

I shook her hand. "Thank you for all you did. With Hector next door, I'm sure we'll still see one another. Have a good day."

The following week, Dexter followed every step I took to make sure I wasn't out of his sight. Hector had taken great care of him but Dexter was making sure I wasn't going to leave again.

Monday around mid-morning I left word on Bryan's voicemail to return my call.

I looked at my watch. It was 6:00 p.m. when my phone showed Bryan's number. In a happy-go-lucky voice, I answered. "Hello."

Bryan chuckled. "Julia, you sound great."

I laughed. "I am. It's good to be home."

I heard his chair squeak. I could imagine his smile and knew he had leaned as far back in his chair as it would go. He always did that when he was happy or had closed a case. "Maxwell kept me informed on your assignments in Berlin, Moscow, and Iceland. I'm glad all went well and that you are home safe."

I let out a sigh. "It was a long three years. As you know, Adam is alive, Wesley was killed by rouge FSB agents, and Maxwell is dealing with the FSB on the intelligence information"

I changed my tone to a business voice. I want to resign. I've done what I set out to do and that was to find Adam or to prove he was dead or alive. I'm forty-three years old. I want my quiet life back."

Bryan gave a faint sigh. "Julia, I'm not surprised. You stayed in the FBI longer than I expected. You did your job well and you went way beyond what you should have been asked to do. When you left for Moscow none of us expected that the situations you encountered would have been that dangerous. I understand your decision and I can't fault you for wanting your life back. We will miss you. Do you have a resignation date in mind?"

"Yes, I have accumulated paid leave. I want my end date to be at the end of my leave. Can you start the paperwork?"

Bryan's voice was solemn. "Yes. I hate to lose you. I want you to know that you have my sincere gratitude and best wishes."

It didn't take long for word to circulate that I was on leave and resigning.

Rebecca was the first to call. "Julia, I hear you're exiting the FBI. Would you consider coming to work for my company?"

My voice was strong. "No! When I went back to the FBI it was for one reason and that was to find Adam's killer. I never expected it would have taken almost five years. You know Adam is back at the

CIA. It was good to be back in the trenches but I'm ready for a simple life again."

"I don't suppose there is anything I could say to get you to change your mind."

I laughed. "No way! But if you need to bounce cases around with me, I will be glad to do that over a glass of wine."

I heard the disappointment in her voice. "Okay. Deal."

Hector rang my doorbell. I opened the door and Dexter jumped and brushed his tongue across his face."

We both laughed. "Here Julia, I brought you dinner. Ziti."

"Thank you. Would you like to join me?"

His smile covered his entire face from his mouth to his eyes. "I was hoping you would ask."

At dinner, Hector and I hashed over our friendship and how he had protected me over the last few years.

It was June and I had been home for two months, Adam surprised me when he knocked on my door. His blue eyes were bright and clear and his wavy blond hair was long and touching the top of his plaid black and tan collared shirt. Adam grabbed my hand and pulled me out the front door and planted a passionate kiss on my lips.

I backed away and gave him a slight smile. "Come in."

Dexter ran sniffed his pants leg and retreated to his favorite spot at the window watching the squirrels.

Adam cracked a half-smile. "Dexter doesn't want anything to do with me. I hope that's different with you."

Adam followed me into the kitchen. "Would you like something to drink?"

"No. I want to talk." His eyes were more like a steel bluish-gray now. "Julia, the day at the art show and the week that followed you knew I had fallen in love with you. I saw Charleston and my paintings in a whole different light because of you." I sat in my comfy chair across from him. He padded the cushion next to him on the sofa and in a soft voice whispered. "Come sit next to me." He stretched his hand out and pulled me against him. I pulled away and left a cushion between us. "Julia, I love you. I know you love me or you wouldn't have done the things you did to find me. If I lived a thousand years, I could never repay you. Will you marry me?"

I didn't answer his question only replied. "I'm still against you leaving your estate to me. I want to sign it back over to you."

"No, I gave it to you and I'm not changing my mind."

"Adam, our lives are different now than they were years ago. I didn't make the wrong decision in marrying Robert. I married Robert because I thought he was more stable than you. You were on your way to France and who knew where after that? I didn't know you were a CIA officer. My vision then was seeing myself chase you around from art show to art show. I tried to find you after Robert's death which eventually led me back to working with the FBI to find you. There has been a lot of water under the bridge over the last five years. I wanted to find you and let you know how much I loved you, but chasing you around the world changed my perspective on marrying an FBI agent or a CIA officer. I couldn't stand losing another husband and we both know what is involved with your job. On all our missions together, I saw your face and heard the excitement in your voice. You love what you do. I would never ask you to give that up. You treat your job like a game and you love playing that game."

He moved to the front of the cushion, then stood shifting his weight from his right to his left foot, and walked over to the bay window. The wind was blowing fifteen miles per hour, the Atlantic was choppy and the waves were breaking over The Battery wall before the next one started to ebb. "Are you in love with Brett? I've seen the way the two of you look at one another. He's more protective of you than he was of the other female agents. The connection between the two of you unites electricity. I don't see that or feel that when you look at me."

Dexter had moved from his favorite spot and lay next to my feet. I rubbed Dexter's ears. "When I went back into the FBI my one goal was to find you. There were times when I thought you were dead, then on other missions, I thought you were alive. I was on an emotional roller coaster that kept my mind in turmoil. The job in Moscow changed me and gave me a different perspective on life. Brett saved my life several times while I was searching for you. You were always one step ahead of me. On some missions you were like a ghost, you were there then gone. I'm not going to lie to you, but being the same age, single, and on the same missions did bring Brett and me close together. We have covered each other's backs more than once. We haven't talked about marriage if that's going to be your next question."

Adam turned away from the Atlantic and looked at me. "In time, do you think you could love me again? I will wait forever if I thought I had a chance for you to be my wife."

I went over to the kitchen in silence and poured us a glass of wine. With this conversation, it had to be five o'clock somewhere and I needed a drink. I retraced the last few years, it was like living two lives that raced through my mind in rapid-fire—moving back to Charleston, finding Adam, reinstating into the FBI, and falling in love with Brett, which I wasn't willing to admit to Adam at this point. My heart began to pound. I didn't know until this moment that I was really in love with Brett.

I handed Adam a glass of wine. My doorbell rang.

"Brett, what a surprise, come in."

He entered and greeted me with an I haven't seen you in a while big kiss. Pulling me tight against him.

Brett's eyes widened when he saw Adam.

I had to think quickly. "I just poured us a glass of wine. Your choice, wine, or gin and tonic?

Adam gave a smirk smile. "Don't be the odd man out. Have a glass of wine."

Brett gazed back at the front door, then looked back at me. "No, I should've called first."

He headed for the door. I reached out and tugged on his arm. "Brett, wait. Have a glass of wine with us."

"Brett, you don't have to leave. Stay."

I poured Brett a glass of wine and motioned him to sit on the sofa where I had been. I sat in my comfy chair across from them. I was more emotionally shaken with the two of them together that I was uncomfortable. With them sitting there, it was as if I was supposed to choose one. I set my glass down and started talking about the missions we had been on and all the close calls of how we were able to survive.

Adam told us about some of his assignments that we didn't know about and some funny stories. We laughed.

The tension in the room lightened.

Brett cleared his throat.

Adam looked at me when his phone buzzed. He set his wine glass on the kitchen counter and walked to the front porch. I followed him. He frowned. "I have to go, but we're not done talking. We'll pick up this conversation later."

I stood next to him. "Honestly, Adam. I don't think at this point there is anything more to say."

Dexter ran to my side. We both watched Adam drive away.

Chapter 43

Dexter ran back into the house, jumped on the sofa, and put his head on Brett's lap. I sat close to Brett but didn't touch him.

"Julia, I'm sorry for charging in unannounced. I wanted to surprise you. I had no idea Adam was here. His expression showed that he wasn't happy to see me."

"It's fine. He showed up just like you. He wanted to continue our relationship where he left off before he went to his uncle's cabin. He understands now that it's not going to happen. He's used to adventure and traveling the world. He would never be happy in one place. He knows there is no us, and he'll have to accept that. Now tell me why you're here?"

I wanted to know, when was the last time you actually saw Washington, DC?"

I gave him a puzzled look. "I guess it was my high school senior trip. Ever since then it's been work-related not sightseeing."

"You can't say no to what we are going to do." His big smile lit up his entire face.

With squinted eyes, I asked. "What are you up to?"

He lightly brushed my cheek with his lips. "We're going to play tourist in DC. I have everything lined up and pulled in some owed favors. Go pack. And pack a special dress for dinner tonight and tomorrow night. You go to Washington, and you work. We haven't done anything fun or leisurely together. Tonight and tomorrow are going to be about us."

Brett took Dexter over to Hector's while I packed.

At the Charleston International Airport, Brett had arranged for a private plane to take us to Ronald Reagan National. After we landed in DC, a limo took us to The Willard Intercontinental Hotel which overlooked the White House and the National Mall.

Twenty minutes after we had checked in to the hotel, there was a knock on our door.

I turned toward Brett. "Who could that be?"

With a big smile, he said, "Open it and find out."

I opened the door, and the concierge stepped in with a vase full of every flower that bloomed in June.

I motion for him to set the arrangement on the coffee table.

Brett smiled and tipped him. "Thank you."

I was giddy. "Brett, they're beautiful. But you shouldn't have."

He took me in his arms, held me tight, and kissed me like never before. "Why not. It's your special day."

My heart was full, I hadn't felt this much love from any man in a long time. His kisses were passionate, and his arms caressed me gently. I was safe, protected, and loved. At this moment in time, we were not FBI agents, we were two ordinary people in love.

We need to get dressed for dinner.

Brett took one step back. His eyes sparkled. "I'm breathless and have no words. "You could walk down the red carpet and accept your Oscar. I don't want to touch you for fear of breaking you."

I laughed. "It's a crimson satin dinner dress. You can touch me all you want. I'm the same person that runs around with AKs and Kevlar vests on."

He grinned from ear to ear. "Not tonight. You don't have crystal dangling earrings and a necklace that matches your AK. "

We stepped out of the elevator and the entire lobby stood still as if they were awestruck. Brett beamed from ear to ear and whispered. "They think we're important."

I smiled. "You are."

Brett gave the driver directions to the Old Ebbitt Grill.

I pointed to the bumper-to-bumper traffic. "We aren't the only black limo in DC. I'm surprised the cars are getting out of our way."

Brett laughed. "They can't see through the black glass. They think we're important and you are."

We arrived at 6:00 p.m. when dusk was settling over the skyline. The Maitre D' pulled out my chair and placed a black napkin over my lap. I gave him a smile and a nod.

Brett asked. "Can I order for you?"

I smiled. "You know you're spoiling me. Sure."

The waiter approached our table in a black-tailed suit, with a white napkin draped over his left arm. Brett ordered two glasses of Dom Perignon. For dinner, he ordered the pan-seared Atlantic Salmon with sugar snap peas and mint jelly for me, and for himself, he asked for the swordfish and cannellini beans. After dinner, the waiter set an Old Fashioned in front of me and gave Brett a gin and tonic.

We were finishing our lemon chiffon dessert when a man with the build of a linebacker walked over to our table. His face was pitted and scarred. He leaned over and whispered into Brett's ear then handed him an envelope marked 'urgent.' Brett motioned for the waiter and gave him his credit card. He smiled. "Julia, please wait by the door."

As Brett read the note, his facial expression changed. His forehead wrinkled and the smile that he had earlier was now erased.

On the way back to the hotel, I asked. "What was in the envelope? You had a worried look."

He cracked a slight smile. "Work. But we aren't talking about our jobs tonight."

He changed the subject by pointing out the city lights and buildings of interest. "Tomorrow in the daylight it won't look like this."

Our limo driver arrived back at our hotel at 10:00 p.m.

Brett backed me against our door before he unlocked it. Kissing me like this would be our last kiss. He smiled, took my hand in his, and led me toward the bedroom. We were kissing all the way to the bedroom leaving a trail of clothes behind. Our bodies met with heat and friction. His hands caressed every inch of my skin. He pressed his lips against mine again and ran his hand down my thigh. With a low groan, I feel his pleasure with mine. The fireworks that exploded within me were something that I hadn't experienced in a long time. I was swept away by his passion. I had missed all the years of young twenties sex but all the needs, cravings, and wants were prominent. For the first time in my life at age forty-three, I understood how intense true lovemaking could be.

The next morning, the limo driver dropped us off under the north portico of the West Wing Capitol building. Brett told the driver. "Be back in two hours."

Brett flashed his badge and handed the tickets to the two marine guards dressed in their formal blues.

After our Capitol private tour, we walked behind the building to the reflecting pool. As we started towards the World War II Memorial, Brett said. "You seem to be enjoying our day. I haven't heard you laugh this much since I met you."

I kissed him on his right cheek. "Your history lessons are fun. You should've been a teacher. The students would have loved the way you talk about our country's politics, scandals, and wars. I had forgotten a lot about our forefathers and what they did to give us our freedoms. Thank you." I looked out over the vast buildings. "We get busy with work, survival, and life in general and we forget the adventures of having fun."

He laughed and hooked his arm in mine. "You're making me laugh acting like a schoolgirl. Is there something or someplace in particular that you want to see?"

"Yes, before we leave can we go by the Vietnam Wall? My mother lost over half of the boys in her senior class over there. She grew up in Pensacola, and most of the boys in her high school had parents in the navy that followed in their father's footsteps. She talked about the wall and how many names she knew. It's like I owe them a visit."

I stood motionless staring at all the names. I was aware of the emotion that was welling up in me. It was a nostalgic moment, and I could feel my mother's pain. Brett put his hands on my shoulders, turned me toward him, and held me tight. He stroked my hair and kissed me. When we reached the end of the wall, the black town car was waiting for us. "Brett, thank you for a wonderful day."

He squeezed my hand. "It's not over yet."

"It was good to see DC through the eyes of a tourist.

Mid-afternoon Brett frowned. "Julia, I hate to spoil our day, but I need to go see Bryan. The driver will take you to the airport. There's a plane waiting. You'll be home before dark. If you don't mind, please put my things in the suitcase and leave it at the front desk."

"Brett, I can't thank you enough for dinner last night and tours today."

The plane landed in Charleston at 6:05. Hector brought Dexter home. It was good to be home enjoying the peace and quiet, but I was missing Brett.

Chapter 44

At 6:00 p.m. the next day, Dexter beat me to the door with his tail wagging a hundred miles an hour. With my arms wide open and a big smile, I said, "Good evening, Agent Jones."

He stepped back and eyed me from head to toe. Then moved forward and gave me a bear hug. We held on to one another like it was the last time we were going to see one another.

"Why didn't you call? Have you had dinner? Do you want a drink?"

He laughed and took a breath. "I don't think you have the correct order there. It should drink then dinner."

He sat down on the sofa. "I wanted to surprise you and sweep you off your feet as you did me."

I fixed him a gin and tonic and poured myself a glass of wine. "Well, if you wanted an element of surprise, you accomplished it."

He put his hand on the back of my neck and gave me a slight squeeze, then moved his hand through my hair and gently pulled my head to his shoulder. "I had to see you. DC was wonderful seeing you being a tourist. Sorry, I had to leave you last night, but as you know nothing is predictable workwise." He repositioned his body but didn't let go of my hand. "After being together yesterday, I know now I can't be without you. You said I surprised you, you can't imagine how surprised I was this afternoon to find out that you had resigned from the FBI. Why didn't you say anything about quitting yesterday?"

I squeezed his hand. "I enjoyed the day with you and us being us. I didn't want to talk about work. You said we were going to have a fun day and I didn't want anything to interfere with that."

He smiled. "You know, Rebecca is going to miss you."

I looked at him and lightly bit my bottom lip. "Maybe, but I had never planned on going back in the field, but after Adam's death or as it turned out to be his disappearance, I felt compelled to help Adam and his family."

With his drink in hand, Brett moved to the other end of the sofa. My eyes narrowed with my frown. "Your tone has changed. You look serious."

He gave me a slight smile. "I hope I'm not taking too much for granted, and you don't ask me to leave but I've been thinking about us for the past year. The missions we were on had forbidden me from talking to you about us. Now that you have resigned from the FBI, do you think we can have a romantic relationship that could lead to the rest of our lives? I'm ready to retire too and you know I love you. I think you have the same feelings for me. Stop me if I'm way off base here."

I moved next to him and reached for his hand. "You have it right. I never thought about marrying again after I couldn't find Adam. Something happened inside me when I found out that he was alive and he didn't relinquish that fact to me. I felt betrayed and the love I thought once existed disappeared. I never wanted to have a conversation with him as to why he didn't confide in me. Now he's off on another Timbuktu assignment and I don't know if he will return. No matter what was there those feelings are gone forever. I'm in love with you, not because you saved my life several times, but because you are you."

He gently pulled the back of my head toward him. Our lips touched giving one other several soft kisses. "That's the answer I was waiting to hear. I'm ready to resign and then we can plan our future. No more agents for either of us." I squeezed his hand and he continued. "I liked you from the first time I saw you in the garden in Miami. Then after our conversation on the gurneys in the hospital, I knew if we could spend some time together maybe a relationship would develop. I asked for the job at the chalet in Crested Butte and after that, I kept tabs on you. Whenever I could swing an assignment with you, I did. I didn't know how long it was going to take for us to be together but I was willing to wait no matter how long it took."

I laughed. "And you were that sure?"

He stood and turned towards me, kneeled in front of the sofa, and reached for my hand. "Will you marry me? I don't want to be pushy but we aren't getting any younger. You can have the biggest wedding and invite all of Charleston. It will be the social event of the year"

I smiled and gave him a passionate kiss.

His smile ran from ear to ear. He said. "Would you like to set a wedding date?"

I squeezed his hand and answered. "Right now?" I laid my head on his chest. "I want a small quiet simple wedding in White Gardens Park. I'm making a commitment to you, not to the whole town of Charleston but I'll do whatever you want. Brett, if you want a big wedding that will be too.

His kiss this time melted my heart. "I want what you want. Small it will be. I'll wait for that YES for however long it takes."

His phone rang and I heard Bryan's voice.

Brett left on the red-eye flight back to Langley.

Chapter 45

The doorbell rang. I snuggled deeper under the covers thinking how I didn't want to get up. Opening the door in my robe, the surprise was Rebecca. "Good morning. You're out early."

She laughed. "Came by to stop my curiosity. What's going on with you, Adam, and Brett? I've seen the way they look at you and the way you gaze at them when you think no one is watching. Sometimes I see a confused look on your face."

I walked to the kitchen. Have you had breakfast?"

She took a seat at the counter. "I didn't come for breakfast but I'll have a cup of black coffee."

"Here take a scone. It will complement your coffee."

She smiled. "Okay, if you insist."

"Rebecca, I haven't talked to anyone about my feelings. My emotions have been on a roller-coaster. Adam had plenty of opportunities to let me know he wasn't deceased. He let me think he was dead, also he never told me he was a CIA officer, he led me to believe his job was being an artist. Brett was assigned to me to be my protector in two safe houses, one in Miami and the other in Crested Butte. Six months later, after the Colorado house, the FBI assigned us to the same cases. I was hurt, mad, and betrayed by Adam and I didn't know if I could ever trust him again with any emotional feelings. Over time, Brett became attracted to me. Last week he asked me to marry him, but I haven't given him an answer."

"Julia, I'm impressed. You never showed any feelings about either one of them in your work. I did see a glance or smile now and then toward Brett. I had no idea you were battling with relationship emotions. Kudos to you. I don't think I could've dealt with that."

I poured myself another cup of coffee. "I had a job to do. I kept my brain in work mode."

She smiled. "I will say if I were in your shoes, I would feel the same way about Adam. You work impressively well under pressure. You're one of the FBI's best agents."

"Honestly, Rebecca, I don't know if I want to get married again. My first marriage ended in a divorce and my second husband was killed in an airplane crash. I have given a lot of thought about Brett and us working together, we know how we respond to all kinds of situations. I think most people don't know that about one another before they get married. We have a head start in that aspect but I can't go through losing another love of my life. Time will tell if Brett and I are supposed to be together."

Rebecca stood and walked towards the door. "Whatever you decide you have my blessings. I'm on my way to China on another assignment. I don't suppose I could talk you into going with me."

I laughed. "Not on your life. I'm done."

Late the next afternoon, Brett's number appeared on my phone. "Julia, I'm sorry I haven't been able to talk to you today. I've been trapped at the FBI headquarters since six this morning. I'm on my way to Hong Kong. I don't know for how long. I'll call you when I can."

"Brett, why are they sending you to China? Adam is already there."

There was a long silence before he answered. "The CIA is not sure where Adam is. All intelligent agencies are looking for him. The last we knew he had an apartment on the 35th floor in the Wan Chai district, but he hasn't been there in weeks."

I tried to keep my voice calm. "Has something happened to Adam that you're not telling me?"

"Julia, I don't know. Maxwell has agents already there and he's sending Rebecca over too."

"Brett, I haven't officially resigned from the FBI. I can go."

"Julia, No! China isn't the place for FBI women. You know Adam disappears all the time. I'm sure he's okay. I'll call every chance I get."

"I've been in dangerous situations before. I can handle myself."

Brett's tone was harsh. "Haven't you had enough thrills running around the world?"

I pressed the disconnect button and went to my rocker on the front porch thinking Adam was captured or dead.

The next morning, I called Bryan. "I'm ready to go to Hong Kong. Adam is my responsibility. I found him once before, and I can find him again. Officially, I'm not retired only on vacation status."

Bryan laughed. "Maxwell asked for you but I told him you were getting ready to retire. Are you sure you want this assignment? If you keep going from assignment to assignment you'll never retire."

I laughed. "Yes, I will. I'll take my vacation pay when I get back. That will fully retire me. Are you going to tell Brett that I'll be under his command?"

"I'll call Maxwell. He will inform him. You'll have to take a commercial flight. The military doesn't fly into China. Make your arrangements and let me know."

Later that afternoon, I called Bryan. "My flight leaves the day after tomorrow. I'm flying from Charleston to Los Angeles on Jet Blue, then from LAX to Hong Kong on Cathay Pacific. It's a two-day flight with time zone changes. Will you approve these flights?"

"Yes. But I'm sorry you have to fly commercial. Flying back, I'll see what I can do to get all of you on a military flight. Check in with Brett when you arrive. I'm sending you an email with your hotel reservations. Have a good flight."

My phone awakened me. In a groggy sleep, I looked at the clock. 2:00 a.m.

"Hello." My words came out about a whisper.

Brett yelled. "What do you think you're doing? I don't want you in Hong Kong. It's too dangerous!"

"Calm down. Hold on a minute." I rushed to the bathroom and splashed cold water on my face to make myself alert enough to contradict anything Brett was going to throw at me. "Have you heard anything about Adam?"

Brett's tone was still abrupt but lower and calmer. "I don't know where Adam is. We have agents from all over the western hemisphere here. All our hotel rooms have been bugged. Our phones ping constantly from the satellite beams as they're being traced. We're trying not to have any body counts. I want to know one thing. Are you coming because you're still in love with Adam?"

I struggled with Brett's rudeness. "No. I've told you I love you. I thought you knew that. You do know that I love you, don't you? I don't understand why you don't want me to help you?"

"Julia, I don't want to have to worry about doing my job and about you. Call Bryan back and tell him you've changed your mind."

"No, I can't stand being here and not knowing what's happening over there. You know I'm a good agent and I can help. You just try and keep your emotions intact, remember I'm an agent. I have a twenty-five-hour flight. I'll see you in a day and a half."

The phone went dead. My mind raced to what Adam might be involved in and what Brett and I were going to find. Then the phone immediately rang. I laughed. "Did you change your mind?"

Bryan asked. "What are you talking about? No, I didn't change my mind but changed the place. Adam is in Shanghai. Everyone in Hong Kong is being transferred to Shanghai. You need to change your flights."

"I just finished talking to Brett. He didn't say anything about Shanghai."

Bryan's voice sounded tired. "Maxwell is telling Brett and his men now. I'll let him know you'll meet him in Shanghai."

I disconnected my call with Bryan and called the airlines.

Chapter 46

On the descent into Shanghai, the flight attendant pointed out The Bund, telling us it is what the waterfront area is called and she told us about all the skyline views we could see from the Huangpu River. When we touched down on the tarmac, I saw tractors moving artillery tubes to a KC-130. I was a little bewildered wondering how the Chinese had acquired the US plane since our military wasn't allowed to fly there. Why were they loading ammo? These planes were used in Vietnam, Desert Storm, and Iraq. Did the US know this plane was here? I wondered if there were more somewhere else.

I took a private transfer from the Pudong International Airport to my hotel. For some reason, I thought being on the East China Sea the terrain was flat. I didn't expect to see all the mountainous steep slopes. Except for the warm weather, the topography reminded me of Vik without the goats. We rounded a bend, and my driver came to a halt. He talked to the two uniformed men standing by their motorcycles on the side of the road. I didn't know if they were military or policemen, but they were holding AKs. There was a woman squatted on the ground next to a car. She was dressed in a Qipao with a conical hat. A man in handcuffs was standing beside her. After talking to the men in uniforms, my driver took the woman by the arm and pulled her into the car. I looked out the back window to see if one of them would follow us.

In front of the hotel, the driver took my bags from the trunk. The doorman tried to shelter me under his umbrella but the wind was blowing the rain at a slant. The fact that he looked like an overstuffed penguin and took up most of the umbrella didn't help. The driver tipped the attendant, bowed to me then drove away with the woman in the front seat next to him. I was checking in at the Shanghai Marriott Marquis City Center front desk when a familiar voice whispered in my right ear. "It's about time you got here."

I turned around, leaned into Brett slowly, and gave him a slight hug and a light kiss on the cheek. The elevator rose to the fifteenth floor in ten seconds then eased to a smooth stop. Brett opened my door all I could see was the city's magnificent skyline. He smiled and gestured. "You're overlooking the southern estuary of the Yangtze River, and the Huangpu River flows through it. Hong Kong is known for its shopping but this hotel is in the middle of the best shopping here—People's Square, New World City Plaza, and Bailian shanno International Plaza."

"It's a beautiful view. Too bad I won't be here much to enjoy it." I laughed. "I don't think I will be doing any shopping on this trip."

Brett walked across the room and sat down in a high-back leather-armed chair. "Julia, let me bring you up to date. While we were trying to chase the intelligent information that Wesley Campbell sold to Russia, and Russia sold to Germany, we let the Italian Moffia slide. They paid more for our intelligence than Russia and Germany did, but they sold it for an even higher amount to China. Adam was sent to Hong Kong to find out who sold the information and what did China actually buy. He found that Campbell had also sold Geographic Information data which tells the geolocation of people, weapons, and where our satellites are in space. China is trying to build a network of undercover agents to infiltrate all foreign countries. It's not a government network now the information is being sold to criminals and crime organizations. The FBI and CIA investigations found that Campbell had an operation here. The Port of Shanghai is the world's busiest container port. They have equipped some cargo containers with satellites, which gives them access from any coordinates throughout the world. A good cover to know when the satellites change positions. The CIA has found that the Director of National Intelligence, Carter Daniels was involved with Campbell. More like a silent partner but his involvement makes him eligible to be charged with committing espionage. He has a data transmission trail across the universe. We have to prove he's done this and was paid for the information. Right now he can say it was his job to keep our military informed. At this time we don't know if he did this on his own or if he worked with Campbell. That's why our phones keep pinging. Someone in his organization knows our every move and they know where Adam is. Nothing was ever said about the geolocation when we were chasing Campbell."

I pulled a bottle of water from the minibar. "Bring me up to date on Adam?"

Brett stared at me not blinking an eye. "I don't know. We haven't found him. We know Daniels's men are in a warehouse on the Yangtze River. There are thousands of warehouses in the port, but we haven't located the exact building. Satellites are operating out of there. Adam could be there. For now, the CIA and FBI agents are working with informers. We have to make sure there are no moles. There's no room for error or we may put Adam in even more danger. The Russian and German ambassadors contacted the United States embassy in Beijing about Daniels That's how we found out."

I stared at Brett. "What do the embassies have to do with intelligence? They help replace lost and stolen passports, help lost travelers, and with medical care. You know people will do anything for money including ambassadors if they think they won't be caught."

Brett's eyes were bright and his voice strong and adamant. "The FBI took a lot of people into custody yesterday. Maxwell is trying to find out what organization they belong to. Igor Turgeuer, head of the FSB, is talking to the Russians that were captured, and the Inspector of the German Army, Konrad Denhart, is interrogating the Germans. We may find out where Daniels is staying or hiding."

Brett's phone rang. "It's Maxwell." He hit the speaker button.

Brett and I could hear the power in Maxwell's voice. "Years ago the CIA bought a decommissioned ship from the Navy's mothball fleet. They have rebuilt it to look like a container carrier and have used it when they needed a camouflage vessel. We can put a satellite on that ship and maybe with the proximity, it will pick up the signal on the ship in port. Daniels has no idea we have a ship in there that belongs to the CIA"

"I'm curious, Maxwell. Are we moving the ship or leaving it in the port?"

I could hear the smile in Maxwell's voice. "Julia, I can read you like a book. I knew you would ask that. British Defense Singapore Support Unit in Sembawang, Singapore. If the signals change we can move it again."

For the last three weeks, everything seemed to have been quiet among all the intelligence agencies. CIA, FBI, and Interpol, knew the information was still being transmitted but for some reason, we weren't picking it up. Right now we couldn't prove any violations, and there was nothing in concrete to show that Daniels was involved.

On the fourth week, I was in the hotel coffee shop around nine a.m. Two men came in and sat in the booth behind me. After they had ordered hot tea, one of the men started speaking in English. "A CIA agent by the name of Robinson is being held in custody in an old water tourist town thirty miles from here."

My ears perked up on high alert. I reached into my purse for a book. I sat frozen with my head down, looking like I was reading. The other man asked. "How do you know that?"

"Ming, a senior Chinese justice minister, was in prison with 300 other prisoners. They were going to execute him for covering up his brother's criminal acts but a friend of his, higher up in the government, had him moved to what the Chinese call a "black jail" which is a house. A lot of high-powered government people and ex-lawyers are taken to houses like this all over China. A German FSB agent headed a raid on the prison to get their agents released. They managed to free one hundred prisoners before their FSB agents were killed. Two Chinese officers moved Ming and Robinson to the water town."

I gathered my belongings and quickly scooted out of the booth and went straight to my room. When Brett answered, I blurted out the conversation that I had overheard in one breath.

"Julia, are you sure you heard this correctly? Why would they take people to a tourist town and hide them there?"

I was annoyed with Brett but I didn't want the inflection in my voice to portray my impatience. "Brett, why would anyone suspect people to be held there? The town is surrounded on three sides by water. It takes fewer guards to watch them and who would suspect a jail to be in the middle of a tourist town."

Brett called Maxwell.

Chapter 47

Maxwell answered on the first ring. I heard him say. "Is Julia there? Put me on speaker. Hello, Julia. How are you doing?"

"I'm fine, sir." I didn't want to chit-chat. "What are our orders to get Adam?"

"Hold on a second, Julia. A lot is going on at the moment. I was sent a list of Italian Mafia names that we captured yesterday in a raid close to the Shanghai docks. This is the closest we've come to getting the names of everyone involved."

I interrupted Maxwell. "What about Adam?"

"You and Brett are to rendezvous with one FBI agent and three CIA agents at midnight at the end of Street S222. They will take you to the water town where Adam is being held. If all goes well, you'll find Adam."

I sat quietly and listened to Maxwell lay out the rest of our instructions.

At midnight, Brett and I met Austin, the FBI agent, and Rick, Jonas, and Russ, the CIA agents at the workboat. Captain Dave piloted the boat at top speed for an hour. His GPS buzzed when the coordinates reached the setting. "You have thirty minutes. If you're not back, you'll be on your own. I can't risk getting caught."

My mood improved thinking we were going to find Adam. The four of them scouted the buildings but all the doors were locked and silence filled the air. A lone building surrounded by hibiscus bushes was five hundred feet to the left of the other building. We crept up the steps and Austin gently pushed on the door. It squeaked open. Brett turned his flashlight to low beam. I ran to Adam. His ankles were strapped to the square legs and his wrists were tied to the arms of the chair. Some of his fingers were skinless and all of them had been broken. In a panic, I untied him and he fell to the floor. My breath caught in my chest, I started shaking and screaming. "Adam! Wake up! Wake up,

Adam!" He moved slightly and groaned. His face was covered in dried blood. "Adam, it's Julia. Wake up."

Adam stirred but was having difficulty breathing. I pushed back his open shirt. His chest was black and blue as if he had been beaten by a sledgehammer. I knew his lungs were damaged.

A cough came from across the room. Brett turned his flashlight and saw Ming's chalky face. Brett ran his hand over his body. He didn't find any broken bones but he was badly bruised. Ming tried to talk but his sentences weren't coherent. Brett yelled. "Ming!" His pupils were dilated. I moved towards the minister. "Ming. Is that your name?" Through the mist of his drugged mind, he smiled.

I turned to Brett. "What do we do with him? When they find Adam gone, they'll kill him."

Austin, Rick, and Jonas were trying to get Adam to his feet.

Brett looked at the agents. Austin shrugged his shoulders and said, "She's right. We have to take him with us."

Brett looked at Rick. "What do you want to do?"

"We can't take him. We have our hands full with Adam."

Rick, Jonas, and Russ looked at Rick. "Okay, we have to take him."

Ming could walk on his own but was unsteady. Brett and I held on to Ming while the others carried Adam. We were almost to the boat when a man wearing a thong charged toward us. His enormous belly shook like pudding and his legs were the size of elephants. I'm sure it would've taken four people holding hands to encompass his body. Brett yelled. "Samurai wrestler!"

Jonas took the first Kung Fu kick, which knocked him cold. Brett let go of Ming, pulled his Smith and Wesson Model 10 revolver, and fired five successions shots. The man kept coming toward Brett. Austin rapidly fired his M16 and didn't stop until the Samurai fell to the ground with a thump.

I knelt over Adam. He was unconscious but still breathing.

We pushed through the trees and bushes until we reached the sandy beach. Captain Dave had the boat running. He yelled. "Hurry! Searchlight beams are flashing around the bend. We need to leave now."

We were slowly backing away from the dock when a man surfaced next to the boat. I grabbed an oar and swung as hard as I could hitting him in his chest. He yelped as his lungs expelled the air. I hit him again in his rib cage pushing him underwater. He resurfaced and raised his right arm to ward off my next blow. He grabbed for the oar and missed. I hit him with a crushing blow on his head. The oar broke and he sank into the dark water. Captain Dave pushed the throttle as far forward as it would go. The boat was on a plane and we were in deep water in seconds.

Adam was still unconscious when we reached the dock at S222. I checked Adam's pulse but couldn't find one.

Adam wasn't breathing.

Brett talked to Maxwell around four a.m. giving him an account of Adam's attempted rescue and death. I could hear Maxwell's disappointment in his low voice. "The United States doesn't have any military planes in China. To get Adam's body out of China his death falls under the Foreign Relations Authorization Act. You need to list Adam's death as undetermined and unknown and report it to the Department of State as such. You and Julia then need to get a flight to London with Adam on board. I know it's a twelve-hour flight but it's the quickest way to get all of you on a military flight back to Langley. Your total flight time will be about thirty hours."

I called SAS airlines. Before I finished my call with the airline, Maxwell called Brett back. "Do you have your flight to London?"

"Yes, Julia booked it a few minutes ago. We leave tonight at eleven and get to London tomorrow afternoon at two. I don't have the flight numbers. Do you need them?"

Maxwell cleared his throat. "No, I know what airline you are on and your flight time. I'll contact you when you arrive in London. Have a good flight."

When we were settled in our seats, tears slowly trickled down my cheeks. "I can't believe we didn't get Daniels, and Adam is in a coffin in the cargo bay."

Brett reached for my hand. "We didn't get Daniels but we gave them enough action for them to know we were on to them. They shut down for a month. You know we had a successful mission. We found Adam."

Walking through the Gatwick Airport in London, we heard our names called over the PA system. "Brett and Julia, please report to the security office."

I looked at Brett. "They didn't say our last names. I wonder what this is about?"

He laughed. "We'll get to security and there will be four other people there with Brett and Julia names. Don't you love working for the government?"

When we walked into the security office an officer handed each of us a ticket to Milan, Italy. "A man by the name of Maxwell Alexander made all the arrangements. You didn't have time between flights to make the reservations yourselves. Your luggage is being transported to the plane now. Our security tram will take you to the gate. Have a good flight."

Brett and I walked out of the office and stared at one another. I spoke first. "I never thought about us going to Milan."

The three-hour flight put us in Milan at 6:20 p.m. CIA Agent Thompson met us at the gate. Brett shook his hand. "Stephen, I'm surprised to see you."

He smiled. "I asked for the assignment. I felt like I needed to finish what we started in Shanghai."

Brett pull our luggage off the carousel "Have you heard anything about Daniels?"

Stephen shook his head. "A confidential agent embedded in the Italian Mafia is willing to help us. We're to meet him tonight at nine."

At seven, a driver and Stephen picked us up at the hotel. The wind was blowing hard across the mountains and the air had turned colder. I was shivering while waiting for the car heater to warm. A mile from town the gravel road's incline went almost straight up before it started snaking through the rocky mountainside. The full moon showed its reflection in the river below and I saw rocks tumbling below us into the river. We twisted through the tight bends in the narrow road and it gave me a feeling like we were doubling back from where we had come.

At the next S curve, we heard a sound like a train falling off its tracks. The driver stomped the brake pedal to the floor. We skidded a little sideways but stayed on the pavement. I screamed as the gigantic boulder toppled from the top of the mountain above us. It hit a small level place on the mountainside and bounced over us, crossed the road in front of the car that was coming toward us, then continued down the mountain. Gravel and stones were flying everywhere following the boulder. The sound of the stones bouncing off the car was like bullets.

Our driver inched forward. Five miles farther up the mountain, the driver pulled up to a wrought iron gate. The surveillance camera's red light flickered and the camera moved in a semi-circle before the gates opened. The driver drove at a snail's pace up the hill, then turned into the driveway. The headlights brought three people into view holding AK-100s. We all exited the car except for the driver. One guard opened the front door and another guard followed us into the foyer.

A man dressed in black jeans and a black polo shirt greeted us. "I'm Armando. I understand we have someone you want."

Stephen took one step forward. "We want Daniels."

Armando chuckled. "How much are you willing to pay?"

Brett smiled. "It's not about how much we are willing to pay but what you want in exchange for him?"

Armando walked into the great room and motioned for us to sit. The black leather sofa was plush and screamed expensive. He walked over to the wall of glass windows and peered out over the swimming pool. "He has supplied us with tracking coordinates. I'm carrying on my father's legacy. I'm the head of my family's business. I supply what people need." They keep me informed of the smallest details of happenings in Italy. That's how I knew you were after Daniels. It looks like under the circumstances we are back to money if I give you Daniels."

Brett stood up and walked towards Armando. "You can have Daniels. He can't give you anything anymore. His entire operation has been shut down all coordinates have been changed. He has no access to anything anymore. At this point, he is of no use to you and if you kill him, it makes our job easier. You'll be saving us money because we won't have to prosecute him and keep him in a federal prison for the rest of his life."

Armando gave a half-smile. "Looks like we are at a stalemate." He motioned for one of his bodyguards to leave the room. He pointed to Brett and me. "You two follow him." He motioned for Jonas to sit. "You are staying here with me."

We entered a small gray room with high ceilings. The room reminded me of an old castle dungeon with damp walls. A gagging sound came from across the room. The bodyguard turned on a dim light and pulled Daniels's blindfold off and removed the rag from his mouth. Daniels was hanging on the wall spread eagle with his hands and feet in iron shackles. His wrists and ankles were bloody. Daniels took in a deep breath and let it out slowly. His eyes were half-open. He whispered. "Get me out of here." He had a bruise on the right side of his temple the size of a navel orange.

A door opened from a recessed wall on the other side of the room. A small-statured man with a limp entered the room with a syringe in his hand.

The bodyguard who was now standing by the door motioned for me to exit the room then he pushed Brett into my back and closed the door. We followed the guard upstairs.

When we were back in the great room, Armando said. "How much are you willing to pay?

Brett answered. "Our conversation is over. We've already agreed that Daniels is no use to either one of us. He has no more information to give to you and we don't need him."

Armando walked to the front door, opened it and the bodyguards walked Brett, Jonas, and me out.

Chapter 48

It was 5:00 a.m. and we were on the way back to CIA headquarters to drop off Jonas. He assured us we had done the right thing leaving Daniels with Armando. I knew he was right, but my insides were fighting my brain.

Jonas opened the car door. "I know that was a hard thing to do but who knows where Armando would have stopped asking for extortion money."

I couldn't rationalize my conscience anymore. A wave of despair swept over me. "Jonas, Daniels is a US citizen. He expects his country to help him. Yes, he broke the law, but we are the ones who save our citizens in a foreign country. We can't leave him behind."

"Julia, you saw the syringe. Daniels could already be dead."

"Jonas, we don't know if it was a sedative or poison. How can you be certain he's dead?"

Brett and I walked into our hotel room I headed straight to the shower. "Brett, call Maxwell and find out what he wants us to do about Daniels and if he says nothing, see how fast he can get us home."

Brett had ordered room service. I eyed the tray but waited for him to get out of the shower. "I didn't know I was this hungry until I started eating. I love Italian desserts."

Brett walked over and gave me a light kiss on my forehead. "You're going to miss Italy. This time tomorrow we'll be at Langley. Maxwell is going to send in another team to get Daniels home if he's still alive."

"I like Italy but not under these circumstances."

He folded his arms across his chest and smiled. "I'm going to request a vacation chit. I know what you're going to do. You're going to cash in your vacation time and retire from the FBI."

I moved next to Brett on the sofa. "You're right and this time it will be a full retirement." Laughing, I said, "I'm going to make sure Bryan watches me clean out my desk and have him escort me off the property. I'm looking forward to going back to my quiet and boring life in Charleston. No more Marriott Hotels."

Brett reached for my hand. "We have some unfinished business."

I kissed him on his cheek. "Are you telling me you're going to do the exact same thing that I'm doing?"

He kissed me with passion making me want more. "Maybe. Sometimes the things we think we want and look for end up being something entirely different."

The phone rang. Brett put Maxwell on speaker. "I have your and Julia's flight information. Are you ready to go home?" Then he chuckled. He knew the answer.

"Maxwell, I have a pen and paper. Give us our flight numbers."

"Julia, You and Brett will fly out of Caserma Santa Barbara military base. It's about ten blocks from your hotel. You have a nine-hour flight. You'll land in DC at seven a.m. I'll let Bryan know. Have a safe trip. Both of you did excellent jobs. Thank you."

Julia's voice was light and airy. "Maxwell, it was great working for you. I'm going to retire but if you are ever in the US please let me know."

He laughed. "You can count on that."

Our flight had been delayed two hours due to inclement weather. The air conditioning system was broken in the base terminal. My clothes were damp, and my hair was dripping wet by the time we boarded the plane. The flight was full of military dischargees, deployments, and a few military brasses. An enlisted man with thick black hair and eyes as blue as the ocean was kind enough to give up his seat for Brett and me to sit together. The captain announced we were waiting for one more passenger. A general was the last to board.

The captain opened the cockpit door and walked straight toward Brett and me. I couldn't hear what he whispered in Brett's ear. Brett stood up and took our overhead luggage down. When we were back in the terminal Brett said. "We need to call Maxwell."

"Brett and Julia, Haspel wants Daniels. I've called for Special Operations. These men are not military. They're all handpicked volunteer civilians. They do dangerous and difficult jobs and they are specialized in hostage situations. I'm sending them in to get him. I want you to wait in Milan until they rescue him or until we know for sure that he's dead."

I wasn't expecting to hear this news from Maxwell. I tried to keep my voice calm. "When will we hear from Special Ops?"

"You won't. You'll hear from me. Sit tight until I get you the information on where and when you can pick up Daniels."

After the call, I asked. "Brett, what do you want to do? We don't know how long it's going to be before we hear back from him."

Brett laughed. "Well, in Rome do what Romans do. We're in Italy let's go sightseeing for the day."

I nudged his arm. "First, I think we need to see if we can get our hotel room back."

After we checked back into the Marriott and talked to the concierge, we did a walking tour around Milan. We spent three hours along with other tourists looking at Leonardo da Vinci's The Last Supper.

"Brett, I'm exhausted, and I know you are too. What do you think about ordering room service?"

He laughed and took my face in his hands and kissed me. "That sounds good to me that way I get all of your attention."

When we started to bed, I said, "I wish we knew what was going on with Daniels."

Brett reached for my hand. "We'll know soon enough. Right now, it's our time. I'm going to hold you until you fall asleep."

I smiled and gave him a gentle kiss.

"My phone's alarm sounded at 6:15 a.m. I showered and looked through the tourist magazine lying on the coffee table. At 7:30 a.m., I ordered scrambled eggs, bacon, sausage, and of course an assortment of wonderful Italian pastries.

Brett woke when the concierge arrived with breakfast. He stumbled into the living area as if he was half asleep. He leaned over and gave me a morning kiss. "What would you like to do today? I know you aren't going to stay in the hotel and wait for Maxwell's call. We can play tourist again."

I checked with the concierge around nine. She suggested a boat trip around Lake Como. The lake was pristine in all the shades of turquoise, azure, tiffany blue, baby blues, cobalt, and cornflower. We exited the boat in the beautiful lakeside town of Lombardy. We had lunch in an 1800s café. After lunch, we took a ferry across the lake to Lugano, Switzerland. The shoreline was lined with glamorous villas. As we stepped off the ferry, Brett's phone showed Maxwell's number.

Chapter 49

Maxwell sounded stressed and tired. "Julia and Brett, we lost a Black Hawk and two men but considering the firepower Armando had, we were lucky the rescue was a success. The two of you have a flight in an hour from the base. Daniels will be arriving there shortly."

The aircraft lifted off the runway, I looked below and watched all the lights glittering throughout the city. For the next hour, my mind wandered over all the cities I had been in, the close-to-death calls, and how Brett had protected me. I gazed out over the darkness to see the full moon. After my anxiety settled, I slept most of the flight.

The rain and wind prolonged our flight back to Langley. For part of the flight, we were tossed as if we were a boat in rough seas. We touched down on the runway at Langley close to noon due to the turbulent weather and the pilot trying to fly around the thunderstorms. Bryan greeted us when we landed. "It's good to have both of you home."

Brett waited until the last passenger was off the plane before he handcuffed Daniels. At the bottom of the steps, the military police swarmed around Daniels from all directions. I stood in a comatose state watching him being escorted to the brig.

Maxwell touched my shoulder. "Julia, are you all right? You're very pale."

"I'm fine. Rough flight. How can money become such an object that a person would be willing to give up his country? Now he'll spend the rest of his life in prison if his inmates don't kill him first."

Bryan guided me to his car with his hand on my elbow. "Let's have lunch. I know you must be hungry. Julia, I have a flight for you at three this afternoon to Charleston."

After the waitress had taken our plates away, Bryan said. I'm hearing rumors around The White House. Something big is going on over there. Julia, are you interested?"

I laughed. "Good try, Bryan. No. I'm going back to a quiet life in Charleston."

He smiled. "I knew you would say no, but I had to try."

At Langley Airfield, I said my goodbyes to Bryan and Brett.

Brett turned to Bryan. "I'm going to apply for vacation time. Do you think you can rush the paperwork through for me?"

Bryan answered. "Sure, after all the two of you have been through, I'll do anything for you. When do you want it to start?"

Brett grabbed my hand and smiled. "Now. I want to go to Charleston with Julia."

Bryan laughed. "That doesn't surprise me either. I'll take care of the paperwork. Goodbye, you two."

Brett paid the taxi driver and I ran over to Hector's house. The first knock on the door brought Dexter barking and wagging his tail. I sat down on the porch and let him lick me all over. "I promise I'm not going to leave you again." I laughed hearing his familiar woof.

"Thanks again, Hector. Brett and I will have you over for dinner in a couple of days."

Hector smiled and waved.

After two days, I had my house back in order and all the laundry was done. "Brett, I need to go check on the cottage. How would you like to go spend a couple of days at Folly Beach?

"Are you sure that's what you want to do.? Are you ready to face Adam's memories?"

"I have no memories of Adam there. Eli is the memory and I didn't have any emotional ties to him. The beach will be fun."

We loaded our suitcases and Dexter in the car. We arrived at the beach around noon. I drove by the cottage to find everything on the outside looking in tack. "Let's go to the Lost Dog Café for lunch and then come back to the house."

The waitress seated us on the deck. I clipped Dexter's leash and secured it under my chair leg. Brett pointed to the painted wall across the street and laughed. "That looks like you."

I stared at the painting for a few minutes. It had been sandblasted, small concrete chunks were missing, and the colors were faded. "Adam painted it." I cracked a half-smile. "That is me. While we're here I will go see Suzie at the Atrium Art Gallery. Maybe she knows someone who can restore it."

After lunch, I did a little grocery shopping before we headed to the cottage. I opened the back door for Dexter, he took off running to the water. Brett started after him. I yelled. "He'll be fine. He loves playing in the waves."

Late that afternoon, I tossed a towel out over the sand, pulled a beer from the small cooler, and handed it to Brett. I twisted off the cap of my wine cooler. Dexter made his way back to us and shook the water and sand off him onto us. I ducked my head into my arm. "Dexter stop!"

Dexter inched himself between Brett and me and slept. Brett and I watched the warm yellow sun sink behind the clouds. The orange, purple, green, and red hues from the setting sun reflected off the blue water as the white waves lapped at the shoreline. The seagulls darted in and out at the edge of the water trying to catch small minnows. Dexter took off running down the beach darting in and out of the water. He stopped to paw at the sand crabs as they burrowed themselves into the soft wet sand.

Brett leaned next to my shoulder and gave me a passionate kiss. "This is beautiful and you are too. Why wouldn't you want to live here full time and keep your Charleston house as a refuge during the hurricane season?"

"The spring is full of college kids and the summers are too crowded with tourists. You can't get into any restaurant and the noise never ends. Some residents have tried to get a quiet ordinance after midnight but so far, the city council hasn't approved it. I come in the offseasons. It's like a mini vacation."

I left Brett and Dexter on the beach and went in to wash the sand from my body. I stepped out of the shower to find Brett waiting for me in the bedroom. I placed my left hand on his bare chest. His warmth made my mind and body want more. I slid my hand down to his waist. He smiled. "I haven't showered."

I laughed. "You should have showered with me. We could've saved water." I stepped aside and let him enter the bathroom.

Shortly, he was back in the bedroom. I smiled. "That was quick."

He ran his hands over my shoulders. "I didn't want you to have to wait too long."

I saw his emotions run across his face when he drew me against him. His kiss was gentle and full of passion. He buried his head in my neck and my right cheek was pressed against his chest. Time stood still. Our breathing became synchronized and our heartbeats were in unison. I placed both my hands on the small of his back and pulled him tightly to me letting our warmth ignite and flow through both of us. He moved his lips to mine and let his tongue part my lips. His gentleness made me want more and I saw the want in his eyes. The heat welded within me and it was a heat that I'd never experienced before. A ravishing body hunger was growing inside me. I wanted him more than I had ever wanted any man. We had found a rhythm together and I knew his fire and needs were as strong as mine.

He whispered. "Julia." My pleasure exploded along with his. He held me tight until our breathing became normal.

The morning light woke me to a perfect sunrise. I moved slowly out of bed trying not to wake Brett. I threw on a kimono, knotted the sash, and pushed open the oceanside door. I had enough energy to race with Dexter down the beach. When we returned Brett was sitting on the porch bench holding two cups of coffee.

"Good morning, my love. I think after last night I can say that."

"I can agree."

He put his arm around my shoulders and drew me next to him. His kiss was light and soft. "We have some unfinished business."

I looked out over the ocean. "And what might that be?"

"You never answered my question about being Mrs. Jones."

I smiled and continued to look out over the Atlantic.

Mid-morning Brett and I entered the Atrium Art Gallery at Folly Beach. Suzie yelled. "It's about time you got back to the beach." She gave me a sister hug. "I've missed you."

"I've missed you too." I took Brett's hand in mine. "This is Brett. We have worked all over the world together. I wanted him to see Folly Beach. We had lunch yesterday at The Lost Dog. Adam's mural is in disarray. Do you know anyone who could bring it back to its original state?"

"I saw it after Hurricane Sharon and it didn't look too bad but to be honest with you, I haven't been over there recently. I do have a local artist who paints murals. I'll call him and get you an estimate"

"Suzie, do you trust him?"

"Yes, of course."

"Then I don't need an estimate. Have him fix it and let me know how much."

Suzie smiled. "Okay, I'll send you the bill."

I dropped Brett's hand. "No. I don't want him to have to wait for his money. Could you pay him and I'll pay you?"

"Yes, I can do that."

On the way back to Charleston, Brett pulled my right hand from the steering wheel. "Julia, you still haven't answered my proposal. It's been two years since we met. Do you or don't you want to marry me?"

I pulled into my driveway and turned the ignition off and faced Brett. "Yes, I want to marry you, but I want our timing to be right. I need to settle into a retirement routine and you need to be sure retirement is what you want. In three months, I don't want you bored and wishing you were working somewhere out of the country on a case."

"Julia, I thought you knew how much I love you. You said yes but you haven't made any progress toward setting a date. I promise my FBI days are over, all I want is for us to be together."

I opened the back car door and Dexter bolted up the front steps. He paced back and forth as if to say open the door. I went to the mailbox. Brett took the house keys from my hand and unlocked the front door.

Chapter 50

I was going through my mail when the phone rang showing Adam and Eli's uncle's number. "Hi, Jack. How are you?"

"Julia, I was waiting until you were back in town. I'm calling to let you know we are having a 'Celebration of Life' ceremony for Adam next Tuesday. Can you come to Greenville?"

"Yes, Jack. I'll be there. Can I bring one of Adam's fellow agents?"

"Of course, and anyone else you would like to bring will be fine. It would be nice if your brother could come."

"I'll call him and let you know. See you next week."

With Kevin and Katherine coming to Adam's wake, Brett stayed one more day before making his flight arrangements back to DC.

Monday afternoon, I picked up Kevin and Katherine at the airport. On the way home, I said, "I wish you and Katherine could stay longer than two days."

"I know Sis, but my corporate clients want me at their fingertips twenty-four-seven."

"Kevin, it sounds like to me you're working too hard."

He laughed. "Who's calling the kettle black now?"

Katherine spoke up. "You tell him, Julia. I haven't gotten through to him. He's become a workaholic."

I smiled. "It's your lives and your decisions. I'm staying out of it."

Tuesday morning around ten, I picked Brett up at the Greenville Spartanburg airport. The four of us pulled into Jack's yard. Jack greeted me with a quick peck on the cheek. I introduced Brett and Katherine to Jack.

Jack clapped his hands. "Everyone, please make your way to the chairs on the lawn."

The bright sunny afternoon helped everyone's mood. The majestic southern oaks sang softly as the gentle June breeze rustled their leaves. Jack's eyes were dry and his voice was strong. "Thank you, everyone, for taking the time today to remember Adam. The way he lived his life, we never knew when he was going to pop in. Don't be surprised if he walks in today." Jack's big smile made everyone laugh and shake their head in agreement. He continued. "I'm saddened that it won't happen this time." He shifted his feet and his voice became stronger. "Adam's work carried him all over the world. When he came on between assignments by the third day, he was ready to be on the move again. Adam lived an incredible life and loved the CIA. It wasn't work, or a job to him, it was a game. His art was exceptional but to him that was work. After a week or month of painting, he would say. "I need to go play." And that's how he worked through his assignments. Now he has left his footprints in our hearts. Our world changes yearly and our lives change daily but the memory of Adam will be in our hearts forever."

My thoughts wandered thinking about what all Adam and I had been through. How many times I thought he had been killed and now the words today finalized his death.

After Jack's eulogy, the handshakes, hugs, and laughter keep everyone's mood light and airy. I walked past several groups of gatherings and listened to them tell Adam's stories. I waited until a large group of people walked away from Jack then gave him a slight hug. "That was a great tribute to Adam and his work." I reached for Jack's hand and led him to the closest chair. "I want you to hear the news from me. Brett and are going to be married. We haven't set a date yet. If you want to change any of Adam's estate, I'm fine with that."

Jack squeezed my hand. "Julia, everything is as it's supposed to be. I carried out Adam's wishes and they still stand. Nothing is going to change. Congratulations to you and Brett. I would like to come to the wedding."

"You're invited. It's going to be family only but we would love for you to be there. We're getting married in White Gardens Park. I know that may seem strange since that's where Adam and I met but I know he would have given me his blessing."

Jack started to walk away, turned, and grinned. "Thank you. I'll be there."

I found Kevin, Katherine, and Brett at the dessert table. "Brett, can we take a walk?" I turned to Kevin. "We'll be right back."

"Brett, I know this going to seem odd, but my family is here and I'm ready to set our wedding date."

Brett gazed at me with a puzzled look. "Julia, are you sure you want to do that now? I know this was a hard day for you."

"Actually, it wasn't. Adam was a closed book long ago. This may seem weird but I'm at peace with my surroundings and my life and you've been patiently waiting for an answer. It may be weird to tell you today but I love you, I want to marry you and now I'm ready, and while Kevin and Katherine are here maybe they will stay a few days and we could get married next week. I told Jack a few minutes ago about us and he wants to come to the wedding. He will be the only non-family member there but I don't consider him an outsider."

Brett picked me up and twirled me around. "You don't know how long I've waited to hear those words." He laughed. "The quicker the better. I knew the first day I met you that we were going to be together. Now we're retired and going to live a long boring life as Mr. and Mrs. Jones. His kiss was long and passionate and his lips were firm as they molded against mine. Then he parted them with his tongue invading my mouth with intensity. I was lost in his kiss. My body tingled. The kiss intoxicated me and awakened all my senses. He deepened his kiss making my heart pound and my breathing shallow. My toes curled in my shoes. I wrapped my arms around his neck. He held me tightly as if he would never let me go. His presence next to me brought my senses to an all-time high. My body went limp as his kisses slowed. I could feel his hunger and knew it was as strong as mine. With his lips next to my ear, he whispered. "I want you more than I have ever wanted anyone."

I answered softly. "I want you more."

On the way back to Charleston, I said to Kevin and Katherine, "Brett has proposed to me and I said yes. Can you stay a few more days and be Brett's best man and Katherine will you be my matron of honor? If I can get White Point Gardens Park for an hour on the weekend we'll get married there. You and Katherine can stay at Folly Beach. It will be a vacation for the two of you and that way you won't have to make a turnaround to come back to the wedding. I won't get married if you aren't here."

Kevin looked at Katherine and smiled. "Let me make a few phone calls but yes we'll stay."

My phone rang. "Hi, Jack." I hit the speaker button.

"Julia, as a notary in South Carolina I can perform weddings. If you would like I'd be glad to officiate your ceremony."

Brett and I looked at one another and before I could answer Brett answered. "Yes, we would like for you to do that."

The next morning, I called White Point Gardens. After finalizing everything with the parks department, I ran to find Brett. "White Point Gardens has a wedding scheduled for Saturday afternoon but Saturday morning is open. I booked our wedding for 11:00 a.m. Is that okay with you?"

Brett's big smile answered my question. "Can you pull a wedding together in four days?"

"Yes, it's our wedding, not the whole town's."

I called Jack and gave him the time and place. I made arrangements for Katherine to meet me at Condon's Bridal Boutique on Ashley River Road at 10:00 a.m. I wanted a simple light pink linen suit and a small headband of white and pink miniature roses across my hair. I entered the fitting room with the shop owner, Frances, close behind. "I have another client in the next dressing room. I have chosen these four suits based on what you said you wanted. Nothing white or lacy. I'm starting you with these suits, if you don't like any of them let me know, I have more. I'll be back in a few minutes to check on you."

The suit I liked the most had short sleeves and the fabric was taffeta and silk woven together but I didn't like the way the skirt fit. Frances entered the room. I smiled. "Everything is perfect."

Frances gave me a slight turn at the waist. "Oh, no!" She screamed. I looked down to see red on my hip. Frances had a horrified expression on her face. "I must have cut my finger on a tag. Here, get out of the skirt as quickly as you can. I'll be right back."

I walked over to a rack and slid each dress to the opposite end. The last dress I touched, I knew it was the one. A fitted light pink dress with cap sleeves. I went back into the dressing room, unzipped the dress, and slipped it over my head. I walked out on the floor to the pedestal that was surrounded by three mirrors.

Frances took in a long breath. "You look beautiful. It looks like it was tailored for you." She circled around me three times eyeing me from all directions. "Brett is going to be in even more awe when you stand next to him."

Frances helped me choose my shoes and the rest of my accessories. Her shop had everything I needed.

Chapter 51

I called Brett. "Katherine and I are through shopping. Can you get Kevin and meet us for lunch at Queen 82 on The Battery."

We were on our second glass of wine when the love of our lives joined us. Brett was giddy. I asked. "What have you been drinking?"

He laughed. "Nothing. What makes you think I've been drinking?"

Because you have a catbird smile, like a child that had done something he wasn't supposed to do. I laughed. "What are you up to?"

"How do you know I'm up to something?"

"When we worked a case, you had a deadpan expression but when we were off the clock that grin meant you were up to no good."

Brett stood, then got down on one knee next to my chair. He reached for my left hand and kissed each finger before placing the ring on my fourth finger. The people around us clapped.

I held up my manicured fingers over my head and waved my hand in the air showing off the impressive diamond. I stood and kissed Brett. "I love you with all my heart and soul Mr. Jones."

Saturday morning when we arrived at White Point Gardens Park, the florist had the gazebo covered in pink and white carnations and chrysanthemums. The floor was covered with a white cloth with a few pink and white flowers sprinkled here and there. From the gate to the gazebo pink carnations covered my walk space.

Kevin walked with me and placed my hand in Brett's. Jack smiled and nodded to me.

"Brett, I love you. I take you to be my husband. You have become my best friend and protector. I will always be by your side. My love will always make our life easy and simple."

Jack nodded to Brett.

"Julia, I take you to be my wife. We have shared good times and hard times side by side. I give you my heart and my love for the rest of my life."

We exchanged rings. Jack did what we asked and kept the ceremony short.

Kevin and Katherine had a plane to catch and Jack said he had business to attend to back in Greenville. We did a champagne toast back at the house before everyone went their separate ways.

Brett picked me up and held me tight. "We need to plan our honeymoon."

I lightly kissed his cheek. "I've been thinking about that. We've traveled all over the world and I promised Dexter, I wouldn't leave him again. What do you think about spending a week at the beach cottage or however long we want to stay?"

He brushed my hair away from my face. "I would like that. The main thing is, I want to do what you want."

We arrived at the beach late that afternoon. The ocean breeze was crisp. As a matter of fact, it was too cool to be June. We laughed watching Dexter run up and down the beach barking at the sand crabs.

Brett pulled me in front of him with my back to him and wrapped his arms around my shoulders, then placed his chin on the top of my head. We looked out over the horizon watching the clouds cast gray hues on the Atlantic. When the sun looked like it reached the water the sky turned to a pale blue. He ran his fingers through my hair and pointed west. He laughed. "Look, we have the whole ocean in front of us."

He pulled me closer against his chest and took a deep sigh. "I don't want to think about the past and what we missed. The important thing is we have one another now. We're two middle-aged lovers walking on the beach and I'm thankful for a second chance at love with you."

I laughed and looked up at him. "I'm in a magical world. The sky is clear and sunny. I'm warm in your arms, and life is simple."

Dexter heard our laughter and ran towards us. I patted Dexter's head and rubbed his ears. He wagged his tail. The night had drifted over the water and the vast diamond-studded sky portrayed infinity. We strolled back to the cottage in the moonlight arm in arm.

I stepped out of the shower, put on a sheer negligee, opened the door to the bedroom, and moved toward the window. Brett gasped.

"What's wrong?"

He flexed his chest muscles. "Nothing, I've never seen you in this light before."

He exuded sexuality in the way he moved toward me. "Close your eyes."

His kiss was soft on my lips. I leaned into him kissing him in return. He moved his mouth to my neck, then to my ears. His breath was hot and he left a trail of moisture wherever his lips touched my skin. He backed me against the bed and slowly removed my peignoir. He had me mesmerized with his eyes. He laid me across the bed and gently touched my breasts. I reacted with a soft moan and struggled to find my breath. We were moving in unison, both of us giving and taking. My body trembled underneath him. We were embraced together, both of us hungry for love. I'd never made love to anyone like this. My body shivered and his vibrated as his hands moved over my skin. My mind shut down allowing my body to respond to every sensation that flowed through me. It was an intimacy that was unknown to me. When one vibration ended another one took its place. The more my body responded the longer the sensations lasted until exhaustion set in with both of us.

I whispered. "I didn't want you to stop. I've never had sequences in succession one after another like that."

He gently kissed my lips and before I knew it his tongue was playing with mine again. He pulled away and gave me a private smile. "You look radiant."

"I could get used to this." I snuggled closer to him if that was possible. I remembered how I had pictured him and our lovemaking in my mind over and over again after the first time we made love. I had hidden my emotions for years about how much I wanted him and I had carried him in my heart all this time waiting for tonight.

We went to sleep in each other's arms but the sleep was short. I woke to his kisses and his knees next to my hips. My breathing was labored as I pulled him down on top of me. He pulled away and kissed my body from head to toe. He looked at me and smiled and listened to my soft whimpering. Then our lovemaking started over again. His body glistened with droplets of moisture. He had given me all of himself and I had accepted everything he had to give.

We woke at sunrise and the day started as if the night hadn't ended.

Chapter 52

At 11:30 a.m. a noise woke me. It took me a few minutes before I became functional. In a daze, I reached for the phone. "Hi, Suzie."

"I saw your car at the cottage yesterday. How about lunch tomorrow? Tell me where you want me to meet you."

"That'll be great. Did you know Brett and I got married? We're spending our honeymoon here at the beach."

Suzie gasped. "No, I didn't know. Congratulations and no to lunch. You two have fun. We can have lunch some other time."

"No, all is good. Tomorrow at noon, The Lost Dog Café. See you there."

I looked over at my husband, who was still asleep. As I brushed my body across his back, he let out a soft moan but kept his back to me. I giggled and pulled the blanket off him. He flipped over. "What's so funny?"

"You. I didn't ever think you would turn your back on me."

He gave me a smirk and pulled me next to him along with the blanket. "I love you, Mrs. Jones."

I felt a peaceful silence between us. After an hour, I raised my head, kissed him, and smiled. "What's your preference for breakfast? Or would you rather have lunch? I can cook anything you want, even brunch."

He laughed and made a grab for me as I was moving off the bed. "You. Breakfast, lunch, and dinner." I backed away and he moved to the edge. "This is our honeymoon you aren't going to cook. Let's go to The Lost Dog.

After we had ordered breakfast, I turned my head and pointed my finger at the painted wall. "Brett, look at the mural it's as if a storm never pounded the wall and destroyed the colors. Suzie didn't tell me her painter had restored it."

I picked up my phone and dialed Suzie. "Brett and I are at The Lost Dog for breakfast. You have to come and join us. I won't take no for an answer."

She hesitated and then replied. "Okay, if you insist. I'll be there in fifteen minutes."

Suzie pulled into the parking space in front of the verandah. She gave a slight wave before she stepped out of the car. Suzie and I hugged and she shook Brett's hand. I gestured toward the wall. "How much do I owe you for the painter fixing the mural?"

"Nothing. I've sent a lot of work to him. He wouldn't let me pay him."

After breakfast, she reached for my hand. "You look happy. I have to run. It was good seeing you. Stay in touch." She turned toward Brett. "Take good care of her. She's one of a kind."

Brett and I stood. He reached for my hand and smiled. "I know."

At 6:00 p.m. after Brett and I had finished dinner, Brett's phone rang. "Hi, Bryan. This is a surprise."

Bryan screamed. "Brett, have you heard Daniels is getting a pardon."

Brett hit the speaker button. "Bryan, what are you talking about? How could Daniels get a pardon?"

"The President in his last hours in the White House is pardoning embezzlers, people who obstructed justice, perjurers, murders, people dealing in stolen firearms, and even people who committed treason."

I blurted out. "Why would he give pardons to a bunch of crooks? He got in office by the skin of his teeth and most of his four years have been a disaster."

Haspel chimed in. "I've been the director of the CIA for fourteen years and never has a president before given so many pardons and certainly not to anyone of this lot. The press is going to have a heyday with this group. He's stumbling out of office, and throwing his pardons back in Washington's face."

Brett's voice was flustered. "Is there nothing we can do? Daniels has only served six months. Bryan, are you thinking about putting a tail on him the minute he walks out of prison?"

Haspel answered. "I am. I can have the prison infirmary put a chip under his skin. When he walks out the last gate, I'll put a Black Ops unit on him. His first wrong move, he'll be back in prison and I'll push for the death penalty."

I laughed. "We can always make a call to Armando."

Bryan laughed. "Everyone, sit tight. We'll get him sooner or later."

One month after the inauguration of the new president. I received a call from Bryan. "Julia, this is an update. I have guards in the prison giving me reports on Daniels. He's in a cell in the maximum security block with a twelve by twelve inches window. The glass pane is shatterproof and has triple steel bars over it. The temperature in his cell has been lowered fifteen degrees. He's being given half rations and his food is served cold. The guards are playing loud music throughout the night. He's not feeling well and has been taken to sickbay where they will install his tracking device."

Two days later, I watched the local late-night news and saw Daniels being taken by limo from the penitentiary to his home in DC. He stepped out of the limo and surveyed his surroundings.

"Brett, look at the way he's casing the area. I bet he knows or thinks he's being watched or followed."

"He won't see the Black Ops men."

I continued to stare at the TV. "Did they give him any restrictions? Is he allowed to leave the country?"

He reached for my hand. "He's not our problem anymore. Don't worry about him. I don't know what his instructions were or if Haspel gave any."

CNN news hadn't given up on him. For the next three nights, Daniels's home was flashed on the screen and a short blurb was given about his pardon.

A year had gone by. It was one of the fastest years of my life. Brett, Dexter, and I headed to Folly Beach. This time we stayed a month playing in the Atlantic's surf, eating at our favorite restaurants, and basically, being tourists.

At midnight Brett pulled me next to him. "Julia, are you happy?"

"I couldn't be happier." I stretched my arm across his chest and put my head against his shoulder. "This last year has been one of the best years of my life. We've worked, played, and laughed together. I love you more than I have ever loved anyone but what I love the most is your returned love. There's not another you."

He laughed and pushed me over on my back. "You're sparkling, radiant, beautiful, clever, and fearless." He laughed. "Should I go on?"

I kissed him. "Oh, please do. I'm enjoying this."

His laugh made me laugh. "You're confident and loveable all rolled into one. You want me to keep on going?"

Now I was laughing harder. "No, that's enough. You'll give me a big head."

He traced my lips with his fingers and looked into my eyes. "I have the same feelings. I never thought I would find anyone like you. You touched my soul and my heart."

I gave him a gentle hug and entwined my fingers with his. "At my age, I didn't think I would find love as deep as this. After Robert died, I didn't think about marriage again. I had a connection with Adam but something wasn't quite right. I knew I could never love Adam after he wasn't honest with me. Then when you were assigned to be my protector and we were thrust into work together, I began to see you in a different light. The more we were together the more I wanted to be with you."

He leaned over and lightly kissed my lips. "You made me step back and take a good look at myself. Every assignment that we were on together made our distance closer."

"I had the same feelings."

At 3:10 a.m. Brett's phone rang. I rubbed my eyes. "This is not good."

"Hi, Maxwell. This is a surprise at this time of the morning." He pushed the speaker button.

"Brett, I'm in a bind. I have a situation that my new agents are too inexperienced to handle. The FBI is designating a backup team. There will be a primary team in front. I would have assigned Bill Carter but he had a heart attack. Tom Wilson could do the job but he had to take Bill's place. If you and Julia take the backup team position, you'll be based out of my here in Moscow."

"Would you and Julia consider taking the job?"

"Do you have an approximate timeline?"

He cleared his throat. "I don't know. It depends. If all our information has been correct and the accuracy has been validated, it should be an in-and-out assignment."

Brett looked at me. I shrugged my shoulders. "Let us think about it. I'll call you tonight with an answer."

Maxwell laughed. "I hope it's the answer I want."

Brett hit the end button and looked at me. "Lady's' Choice."

We lay staring at one another without saying a word. He winked and then we both burst into laughter.

About the Author

Cheryl J. Corriveau is a native Floridian and an international author. She has always been an entrepreneur. After her day of teaching high school students, she taught evening real estate licensing classes. Twenty years later, she retired from the classroom and started a real estate corporation which led her into several other businesses—an aerial photography business, and a commercial interior design business. Her love for boats led her to become the sole proprietor of a boat dealership on the St. Johns River in Central Florida. Her novels are The Demanding River and The Tangled Web. In her spare time, she became an avid golfer.